Authors Note:

This book was inspired by a chance visit to the Glasshouse Mountains in Queensland, Australia. I had a morning to kill before boarding an airplane to Los Angeles, and I took a side trip off the main highway from Noosa to Brisbane to look at the local scenery. I found Tibrogargan and his family, and was intrigued by the story the aboriginal natives had constructed around these mountains formed by volcanic activity around seventeen million years ago. The story the locals told was of a great battle between the father, Tibrogargan, and his son, Coonowrin after the cowardly son had run away rather than help his pregnant mother when a flash flood had threatened her. Coonowrin had his neck broken in the fight, and his parents had disowned him. Over time, the giants had turned to solid rock, and it was the majestic Tibrogargan that I met that morning, before the heat of the day made climbing any mountain impossible. Being a Scot, I am fond of my beer, and I found the opportunity to climb Mt. Beerwah impossible to pass up. I was not to be disappointed. From my vantage point at the end of a strenuous climb, I had an amazing view over the gum tree covered plains to the Glasshouse peaks. The morning mists were slowly clearing and I could see Coonowrin, with his broken neck, and Beerburrum, the pregnant mother and largest and bulkiest local mountain peak as the sky cleared. It was not difficult on the plane trip home to spend some time sketching an outline of what might occur if these sleeping giants came to life, perhaps in a part of the world that more people would recognize. I invented the island of Sandeagh Mhor ("Big Sandy") and borrowed the legend of the Irish giant Finn McCool to anchor the story in Scotland. The rest, as they say, is history. I have always had a dream to cleanse the world of its current corruption, and to repopulate it with a revitalized population of people with an improved ethic. This is the story of that rebirth. The names of the mountains have been changed to protect the innocent. I hope you enjoy the story as much as I enjoyed creating it!

Slainte Mhath

Tibran's Revenge!

A Novel of World Destruction

Max Dahlstrom

authorHOUSE®

AuthorHouse®
1663 Liberty Drive
Bloomington, IN 47403
www.authorhouse.com
Phone: 1-800-839-8640

First published by AuthorHouse 5/10/2011

ISBN: 978-1-4567-3611-8 (e)
ISBN: 978-1-4567-2999-8 (hc)
ISBN: 978-1-4567-3000-0 (sc)

Library of Congress Control Number: 2011901217

Printed in the United States of America

Prolog

Eastern Australia, circa 17 million Years BC

THE TWO BEHEMOTHS BATTLED ENDLESSLY IN the hot tropical sun, or so it seemed to those who had been watching them for the past three days. The summer's day was glaringly bright with the sun directly overhead in a clear blue sky. The distant mountains shimmered in a heat haze generated by the unusually hot temperature the giant beasts had generated on the plain. The giants were not fighting over territory, nor were they fighting for a mate. It was a battle of supremacy between father and son. The giant apes pounded each other's bodies mercilessly using their massive fists. As they grappled with each other, their huge feet churned up billowing earthen clouds from the dusty plain. They twisted and turned as both sought to achieve a critical competitive advantage in their fight. Two separate tribes observed the struggle. A small gathering of tiny shrew-like mammals cowering in the underbrush of the lush swampy marshland bordering the plain witnessed the powerful blows each giant slammed into the other. The primitive creature's eyes were wide with fear and collectively they shivered as earth tremors generated by the battle of the huge creatures penetrated deep into the primeval forest. Much later in the history of the world, the place where the giants fought would be called Queensland on the east coast of Australia. But for now it had no name, and no human beings were present to witness the event.

The diminutive creatures hidden in the greenery observed the giants warily, and prepared themselves for flight should the gargantuan beasts come too close.

These seemingly innocuous creatures would, in time, evolve to dominate the planet, but for now they were prey for the many carnivores that inhabited the jungle. In many millions of years, their progeny would travel over the land bridges between Australia and Asia, eventually settling in Africa on the Serengeti savannah plains. They would evolve considerably in the process as they faced many difficult challenges in their migration. Those that survived, through some physical or mental advantage, would mate and create a radical evolution of their species. The plains had copious food for the tiny creatures in the form of nuts and fruit in the treetop canopy, and it was essential that they could reach that food. The trees also provide safety from the numerous predators they faced. The dominant advantage they possessed was simple, but very effective. They had developed a hand with an opposing thumb. What might appear at first glance to be minor advance for their species would turn out to be critical for their survival. With the ability to grasp objects, and to climb high into the forest canopy of trees indigenous to the area, they could escape the evil carnivores patrolling the plains. The progenitors of mankind would flourish above the ground. When danger threatened below, they would scramble into the treetop canopy and yell threats of their own and rotting fruit at their adversaries. Their hands would also allow them to use tools, and their enlarging brains would find uses for their versatile fingers. For now though, the creatures huddled together, terrified, awaiting the end of the battle, and the chance to get back to the important task of hunting for food.

Aside from the mammalian audience, the kin of the two fighters circled the battlefield. The remaining tribe members had placed themselves in strategic positions around the circular arena and would be witnesses to the outcome of the struggle. They called themselves the Fire Tribe, an apt name for beasts born in the earth's mantle, lords of lava and creators of volcanoes.

For days now, the two monstrous creatures had been sparring together. Howling with rage and pain, they thumped each other without mercy. Great tongues of fire exploded from their gargantuan hands as each creature landed colossal punches on the body of his adversary. As their fists connected with glowing skin, they produced an explosion of flame and showers of red hot sparks. They were both impervious to the flames they generated but the local vegetation was not. As a consequence, knots of forest close to the action caught alight and were consumed by flame. As they dueled, the titanic pair roared horrible curses at each other. Time after time, their massive feet slammed into the sand and rocks littering the plain. Boulders lying on the ground where the battle was being fought were thrown into the air like pebbles. The supreme one, known as Tibran, mercilessly pounded his son, Cowrin, but Cowrin fiercely returned the blows.

As he and his son sparred, Tibran recalled the events leading to the battle with smoldering anger. His son had dared to challenge his strength and his wisdom. Above all though, Cowrin's greatest crime had been his failure to help his heavily pregnant mother in her greatest time of need. Beerwah, his wife, had been fishing by the side of the Yarra River with Tibran and her son, and they had caught many good sized fish. Unbeknownst to the family, there had been a major thunderstorm in the mountains that had dropped several inches of rain over a thirty minute period, creating an enormous wall of water, coursing down the normally tranquil Yarra River as a flash flood. The results of the deluge had threatened them all. This action was unforgiveable. Cowrin had the height strength and agility to help them all get to high ground. But he had run away in fear from the deluge, leaving his mother to drown for no apparent reason, other than to save his skin. Tibran had also come very close to succumbing to the flooding river, but unlike his treacherous son, he had held on tenaciously to a tree limb and had reached out his other giant hand to rescue his wife. Totally exhausted, Tibran and Beerwah had clambered together to safety above the roaring flood waters of the river. They were covered with mud, and together they collapsed on the ground, breathing heavily, trying to regain their strength. It took Tibran several minutes to recover. Feeling his enormous strength returning to him, Tibran had leapt to his feet. He was furious with his wayward son. Cowrin had disgraced the Fire Tribe by turning his back on his mother in her time of greatest need. Tibran turned toward Cowrin, his mind filled with hate. Cowrin knew that he was in serious trouble, perhaps his life was in danger. He could see the deep anger written in his father's smoldering expression. But then

Cowrin started to think. His father was getting old, and Cowrin was in his prime. His father had just escaped from a strength sapping fight with a flooded river, and Cowrin had not. Tibran had always dominated Cowrin, but now the son was not so sure that his father would be able to fight and win. Cowrin could finally rid himself of the father he feared and loathed. It could be done. He could kill his father, and rid himself of all his troubles. Was Cowrin not as powerful now as his father? He had the strength, the training, the power. He could do it! Cowrin mentally steeled himself for a fight, and belligerently faced his father. Beerwah, the pregnant mother of the family, was there with her children. She looked at her offspring with pride. Tibuccum, her second child, was approaching manhood, but she was concerned to see that he was cheering for his brother. The youngsters, Ngungun and the twins, Tunbudle and Coochin in contrast yelled out their support for their father. It was clear to both giants and to their family observing them anxiously from a distance that there would be no reconciliation that day between the two. Now, on the smoking dusty plain, the father and son sparred intently. It was indeed a match of equals. Both were cast from the same mold, arrogant titans with fierce pride and immense power. Battles had been fought through the ages on this sacred ground between members of the Fire Tribe. Eons ago, the forefathers of the tribe had placed a circle of giant boulders to act as a ring for any fights between the tribe. The stones were placed to create a giant arena over three miles wide. This would be the boundary for the conflict. To step outside the ring, meant defeat and banishment. However, inside the ring, there were no holds barred. The two lumbering beasts continued their contest in the ferocious heat. But only one would win. It seemed to the family that Tibran, the leader of their tribe, their father, had at last met his match. But the intensity of the fight had taken its toll. The beasts may have had superhuman strength and resilience, but now both fighters were flagging, the repeated tumultuous blows sapping their vitality and strength. Then suddenly, without warning, it was over. While turning to avoid yet another powerful blow, Cowrin slipped on the sandy soil, and as he did so, he stretched out his arms to soften his fall, Tibran seized his opportunity. Raising his clasped fists high above his head, Tibran landed a hammer blow directly on the neck of his unfortunate son. There was a loud and sickening snap, echoing across the plain, painfully audible to the Fire Tribe and to the small creatures in the forest. Cowrin's head hung at an odd angle as he slumped to the ground. Tibran turned to face his entire family who now rushed towards him to congratulate him on his epic victory. He beat his powerful chest with his fists and roared a great victory cry.

"I am the lord of this world! I am the rightful ruler of the Fire Tribe! There can only be one leader and I am your master!"

Settling his feet in the sand, he turned his back on his disabled, defeated and disowned son, and stared triumphantly over the coastal plain towards the sea.

One last time, he turned to his family and bellow out a final command.

"My son Cowrin no longer exists. He is hereby banished from the Fire Tribe. Forever!"

Cowrin was paralyzed and unable to move. He cowered immobile in the dust. His mother, Beerwah, whose stomach was hugely swollen with her soon-to-be-born child, glared at her broken and erstwhile rebellious son. Then, with a disdainful toss of her head, she joined her husband Tibran, turning her back on her son, staring towards the sea. The battle over, Tibran and his Tribe ceased to glow, and cooled into immobile rock statues.

Seventeen million years were to pass. Tibran and the Fire Tribe and their battles were now legend. The Ka'bi Ka'bi aboriginal tribe now lived on the coastal plain in Australia. As they sat by flickering golden firelight in the gum trees of the Australian Bush, they told the story of Tibran and Cowrin, of Beerwah and Beerburrum, and made sure that they would never be forgotten. Each morning, the tribal elders stared upwards at the frozen faces of Tibran, Beerwah and Cowrin, now unmoving giant rock outcroppings soaring above the tree and scrub covered plains. Cowrin's neck still hung at an odd angle, as he cowered behind his parents. Tibran still stared seawards, but for now he was frozen in place.

It took a visit from the explorer Captain James Cook to Australia in the 17th century to diffuse the power of the legend of the Fire Tribe. He too looked at the frozen stone giants. He was not privy to any of the tribal stories, and he dismissed the monsters as mere rocky outcroppings. In typical explorer fashion, he chose to give the landmark rocks his own nomenclature. He recalled a visit to north England and the lime kilns where glass was manufactured. The rocks looked from a distance so much like the kilns that he called them the benign title of the Glasshouse Mountains. However, the aboriginal tribe continued to pass on the stories of the ancient feud. They knew the real story of the mountains, and their genesis from those glowing warriors, the Fire Tribe.

1
Benign Beginnings
June 15, 2012

Robert Fisher

IT CAME AS A PLEASANT SURPRISE to Robert Fisher when Julia Metcalf, his most recent girlfriend, agreed to travel with him for a vacation on the remote island of Sandeagh Mhor off the west coast of Scotland. He had only met her four days ago at a party, and although they had hit it off in a big way that night, he knew there was still a lot they had to discover about each other. While hiking around a remote and rough paradise was Robert's ultimate idea of a good time, he wasn't so sure about Julia. She had seemed to him to be too refined to take on such an arduous challenge. He tried, without success, to visualize her hiking through the mud and gorse bushes on the mountainous and bird-bedecked island. But she had said yes. Julia was a very attractive brunette, with a very pleasing personality, and she would be an excellent companion for him for a short stay on the rugged island. As a result of her agreeing to go with him, he was now really looking forward to the trip. He sincerely hoped she felt the same way about being with him. He had high hopes that their journey together would turn out well for the two of them.

Robert and Julia lived two blocks apart in the upper class Morningside suburb of Edinburgh. They had met each other at a typical Friday evening party held by a mutual friend in a fourth floor sandstone tenement apartment.

Robert had had several girlfriends, who had generally tended to drift away from him after a short period of time. He was, initially, a delight to be with by any woman's standards, given his pleasing and pleasant personality. But having been alerted after a few dates to his introverted tendencies, and his frequent quirky ways, most savvy women moved on to greener pastures. After all, who wanted to be discussing the merits of Star Trek versus Star Wars when world peace could be the intriguing topic of conversation? Most of the shallow women he had met until now had been more prepared to discuss the advantages of the Spanish island of Ibiza versus the Portuguese Island of Madeira as a honeymoon destination, rather than the latest Intel I9 sixteen core computer processor versus the MMX turbo charged 32GHz gamers delight. But Robert didn't mind in the slightest that he was an introvert. He was equally happy reading a good book or a taking a long walk alone in the Trossach Mountains in Perthshire. However, he had learned pretty quickly that having an introverted persona is anathema to achieving his desires in life. His longing for privacy had led to him on multiple occasions to being labeled as a social outcast. There were three key staples in life, and only two were in harmony with his psyche. A roof over his head worked out just fine. He had a pleasant single bedroom apartment in Edinburgh. He would eat in his kitchen, or dine alone in one of the many fine restaurants in his neighborhood. However with regards to having sex, while he could pleasure himself, doing so just didn't satisfy him anymore. If he wanted such pleasant distractions, he needed to communicate at least intermittently with the opposite sex. With time and with practice, his social skills had improved, and intimate communication with girls became much less of a hurdle for him.

It was not that he was unattractive to women. Women were drawn to him at the many student parties he attended, like moths to a flame. When he entered the room, their heads would turn. The bolder and more adventurous ladies would leave their circle of friends and flirt with him. Others would just flutter their eyes at him as he passed, hoping to draw his attention. He had glossy, dark, vaguely unkempt hair, designer day old stubble, and a soccer player physique. These physical characteristics gave him a raffish air. He couldn't see it himself when he looked in a mirror, but somehow women saw him as being a great genetic catch. No doubt, he thought, their real interest in him was to be a father for their children. And he was smart too, with a doctorate in psychology from Edinburgh University. In order to remain inconspicuous, he dressed very conservatively, and tried hard not to stick out in a crowd. He opted for tidy shirts, checked or striped for the most part, with faded jeans and logo sneakers. Although he would not describe himself as a wimp, the cool and damp climate of

Edinburgh necessitated that he wear a warm jacket for nine months of the year. Typically he wore a navy blue blazer with brass buttons, but on occasions he would wear a tweed jacket with leather patches on the sleeves and try to pass himself off as landed gentry. There was certainly a value in having a neat appearance, good manners, a solid body and a good line in chat. Most social occasions when he was in the mood for fun, he would have no difficulty finding a new companion.

So when he had been introduced by a well meaning colleague to Julia, he had smiled at her, and looked her deeply in the eyes. He had found himself drawn to her at once. It was something about her dark auburn hair, her full mouth and her delightful proportions coupled with her subtle expensive perfume and her pleasing smile. She had been wearing a low cut blouse revealing a tantalizing cleavage, and she wore stylish jeans that were molded to her shapely hips and legs. She sported minimalist makeup that accentuated her deep brown eyes, and her full lips. Robert was smitten. To break the ice, Julia had asked Robert if he'd like something to drink, and he had initially found himself tongue-tied. Then he thought, what the hell, and asked her if she'd like to dance. When she agreed, he steered her over to the area in the lounge of the apartment that had been cleared to act as a dance floor. As the evening progressed and the beverages flowed, she had moved in closer to him, and they had slow danced in a very intimate way for the final dances of the evening. They had left the party together shortly after midnight. Once they had reached the privacy of Robert's car, they squeezed into the back seat together and had kissed with an intensity that had taken both Robert and Julia's breath away. After surfacing for air, her lips numbed by the intensity of his kisses, Julia had whispered to him.

"Do you want to come back to my place? I make a really decent cup of coffee. What d'you think?"

"Julia, you darling, that's just my cup of tea!" he had replied, with a crude attempt at humor.

Julia groaned.

"Get in the car and drive." she had instructed him.

Feeling mellow after the wonderful evening he had had, Robert was not in the mood to argue, and with his typical gallantry, opened the passenger door for Julia before settling into the driver's seat. He had quickly driven them the short distance to her apartment. The coffee invitation had of course been a subtle ploy to allow Julia to carry on her seduction of Robert in a place where they wouldn't be disturbed. Robert would have been happy to accept the opportunity just to have an intimate discussion with Julia. While Robert sat himself down on the very comfortable sofa, Julia boiled some water in a kettle, and brewed some coffee using a black topped cafetiere. She had walked up behind Robert and placed her arms gently around his neck. She pulled him in to a deep and tongue filled kiss. Flinging caution to the winds, they had moved rapidly to her bedroom, arms wrapped around each other and lips locked together. The coffee could wait. Robert knew that he would not be returning home that night. Both helped each other pull of their clothes, and they had made passionate love in her bed. Robert could remember every detail of the occasion. It was idyllic. As they lay together, arms around each other, Robert found himself hoping that this relationship would last. Their love making had been intense, and they had moved in perfect harmony, both satisfying each other's needs in every way. Although it was much too early to tell if things would work out for them, Robert felt that he was ready to settle down with someone, and he had a feeling Julia might be the one for him. As he lay in her bed, feeling a marvelous release from the tensions of the world, he found his mind drifting back in time. Robert had had a lot of fun discovering sex. He recalled the many times that, once he had completed his work assignments for the day, he had walked the steep path from Pollock University Halls of Residence to stand atop Arthur's seat. It was a fabulous scenic view looking out over the expanse of Holyrood Park and the orderly streets of the city of Edinburgh. It had also been his favorite pastime to introduce that refreshing evening ramble to new female acquaintances he had met in his favorite local pub, the Volunteers Arms, also known locally as the Canny Man's. The typical Edinburgh pub in those days was wreathed with cigarette smoke, dimly lit, and always had the tang of stale beer drifting through the air. His ideal evening would start with two pints of his favorite Belhaven beer. The slight buzz the beer produced would give him a relaxed feeling inside. Only then would he feel relaxed enough to talk with other students sitting at the bar. If he was lucky, one of the attractive university girls who frequented the pub would accept his offer of a drink, and they would chat. If he was even luckier, the girl would accept his offer to see the lights of Edinburgh from Holyrood Park. He remembered the soft tongue-tingling kisses, and the smooth curves of the coed students tantalizingly covered by thin and teasing outer garments. Mostly, his romantic encounters ended with a kiss, but occasionally he been astonished by the forwardness of his companion for the evening, as she liberated his manhood in the privacy of the dark parkland, and provided him with an unexpected climax to the evening.

Robert was primarily a thinker, an intellectual, and despite his physique, he did not consider himself as a sporty type. But even intellectuals have a sex drive. His scholarly education had progressed extremely well. He had made top grades in Physics and Chemistry. Initially, given his desire to learn and his shy nature, most of his dates had been with text books. From his early teenage years, given the bragging that his classmates had done, he assumed he was the only one missing out on endless sex. Later on, it had come as a revelation to him that the majority of his peers had not yet experienced much beyond heavy petting, or a lip-synching smooch. He was most grateful to the Belhaven brewery for providing him with such a pleasant social lubricant that also tasted so good.

At college therefore, he had finally obtained a first class degree in geology, and at the same time, he had also received his degree in sex education.

It was a part of his make-up though, that he could never totally disconnect himself from his academic background. As he lay there in Julia's arms that night his mind jumped to the various classes he had attended at Edinburgh University, and the snippets of wisdom he had received from Professors in the geology school. It was fascinating what lay beneath everyone's feet, and how little most people knew about it. On a trip with his parents to the Grand Canyon, he had marveled at the layers of colored rock eroded by the Colorado River. Other trips had taken him to see fossils embedded in sandstone rocks eroded by the massive power of the sea. One lecturer in particular had impressed him the most. The topic of the class that day was the geology of the lowlands of Scotland. Professor Gavin Oldhurst, a diminutive grey-haired man, stooped over the lectern had talked at length about the complex geological history of the fault line that had created the Firths of Forth and Clyde. Professor Oldhurst was a crashing bore on any subject other than geology, but he put pure passion into his teaching, and it excited his students. He explained at length about the volcanic activity that had been the architect of several peaks in the area. The Professor's favorite geological feature, he explained, was the majestic rock where Edinburgh castle was perched. He ignited his student's imaginations with descriptions of explosive and fiery volcanic eruptions. With his hands, he would drag the students downwards into the earth's crust as he imagined them all sinking with the huge tracts of land sliding towards the earth's core. The land sank as a result of faults in the crust of the earth to the north and south of central Scotland. Like an elevator in reverse, large areas of the landscape between where Edinburgh and Glasgow would be built, would sink over the years to be swallowed by the sea.

There was something magical about Edinburgh for Robert. Perhaps it was the history of the city. Perhaps it was the ancient castle dominating the horizon. Perhaps it was the Edinburgh festival and the fringe festival each August. Robert loved living in the city. It was a very cosmopolitan city, with a lively night life, despite the cold and damp conditions prevalent for most of the year. Around the time of the Edinburgh Festival, the city came alive with tourists. Thousands of visiting artists, hoping for fame and a coveted supportive review in the Scotsman newspaper, sang, played music, danced and acted out small plays in local pubs, churches and on street corners. In fact, they performed just about any type of performance anywhere they believed they might attract a few passers-by as an audience.

Robert adored visiting Edinburgh Castle. The stark fortress was a monument to middle ages engineering, and was molded to the dark and damp rock face of the ancient volcanic plug arising from the flat grassy parklands of Princess Street Gardens. The castle had been virtually unassailable during times of war because of its position, perched on the steep black slippery stone cliffs arising from the greenery of the gardens. Castle rock was just one of the volcanoes here that had formed the hilly terrain contrasting the grassy plains of the Lowlands of Scotland. These volcanoes had originally erupted many millions of years ago. The resulting basalt and cinder cones they had created sank with the fault plain ending up in shallow seas, and were buried in silt over time. Over the millennia, the land had risen again and re-exposed the conical peaks. Multiple ice ages, and the resulting sheets of thick glacial ice, had scoured away the softer ash and rock to leave the harder central craggy cores of the volcanoes. These plugs of core volcanic rock had resisted further erosion from harsh weather and winter's ice to form the craggy volcanic rock peaks that provided such stark and striking counterpoints to the flat Lothian landscape.

Julia shifting in her sleep disturbed his train of thought. She snuggled against his chest, and sighed. In return, he gently stroked her soft blond hair. She sighed again, and he felt her relax as once more she drifted into deeper sleep. But Robert was not yet in the mood for sleep. "I've had too much excitement for one night." he said to himself. He got out of bed and took a trip to the bathroom to relieve himself. He trotted through to the kitchen, and poured himself a cup of Julia's excellent Arabica coffee. He sipped the coffee in silence and tried to gather his thoughts. Too late he realized, after three cups of the brew, he felt not unexpectedly more awake than ever. His mind racing, he returned to the bed and settled himself under the duvet cover, trying not to disturb Julia's rest. Too much was going on in his world for him to drift quietly off to sleep right now. He was especially excited about the trip to Sandeagh Mhor. There were two major things pulling him in the direction of the distant and isolated island, and one of them was lying next to him. The other was his passion about all things to do with the science of geology. Sandeagh Mhor had had a particularly fine birth those millions of years ago. It would be fun to explore the island and trace its volcanic past. But he was also ready for a vacation, and that was the real pull of the small and remote Scottish island for him. He had read the web site information on the island. He thought that the language used in the pamphlet was a little flowery and it had not been written by anyone with any knowledge of science, but it remained intriguing. The e-pamphlet had not been enough to satisfy his scientific curiosity. However it was roughly in keeping with what he knew of the history of the development of the Scottish islands.

The brochure described Sandeagh Mhor as a romantic island, surrounded by the Irish Sea off the coast of western Scotland. The island was constructed of a combination of a core of solidified volcanic rock, and surrounding the core, there was a framework of supportive basaltic columns, generated by slow rock crystallization in a cooling pond of lava that had circled the volcano. The island remained uninhabited, but during the brief summer hiatus where living on the island could be described as pleasant, there were several companies that for a fee would take tourists to discover what it was like to live on a remote and virtually deserted rock close to the Atlantic Ocean.

Sandeagh Mhor's distance from the crowds made it very attractive as a getaway. Robert had realized long ago that time out from the milling throngs of people coursing through Edinburgh's arteries on a daily basis was a necessity for him to be able to recharge his batteries. He knew how much, for example, he detested walking along Princess Street, Edinburgh's main shopping thoroughfare, amongst the Saturday afternoon crowds. Some people might get a kick out of dodging slow moving pedestrians as they paraded up and down the sidewalks in their never ending quest for retail shopping satisfaction, but in no way did he count himself amongst them.

Anyway, he had succeeded in persuading Julia to go with him to the island. A trip together might allow them to cement their new relationship. He felt their relationship was pretty hot right now. As he said the words to himself, he felt a curious hot flushing sensation, followed by shivers running up and down his spine. "How strange." he thought to himself. "I hope I'm not sickening for something." The sensation passed. He put any thoughts of illness aside and relaxed, as his post coital torpor, and the lateness of the hour dragged him into a deep and dreamless sleep.

Julia Metcalf

JULIA HAD FALLEN IN LOVE WITH Robert the moment she had clapped eyes on him. This was a totally novel experience for her. In fact the experience had metaphorically knocked her off her feet. Not that she was unused to the modern practices of being introduced to boys. She had survived multiple days of internet dating, fifteen minute speed romances and completing endless online compatibility questionnaires, all to no avail. She found the encounters mindless and in short order most unfulfilling. She gave up using these tools after a while, and resigned herself to try more traditional routes. Despite her obvious attractiveness, she had still ended up without a permanent boyfriend. However, on this occasion here in her friend's apartment, something new and delightfully unexpected had happened. Out of the blue, she had fallen head over heels for a handsome stranger. She thought back to the evening. Robert had approached her as she was standing in the living room of her best friend Sheila. She was in the company of her girlfriends. He had cat-like lithe grace, and was subtly muscular; a soccer player she had thought. He had looked trustingly into her green-brown eyes. And then he had started to treat her as if she was the only girl in the world. Other boys had been kind to her, but generally they were after one thing, and when she wouldn't deliver, they had backed away, seeking more fertile pastures. But Robert had seemed totally sincere. Without any conscious effort, he had her believing that she was the only girl on the planet for him. She had witnessed a special sparkle in Robert's eyes. His aftershave had been subtle, and blended perfectly with his masculine aroma. Her stomach had been filled with a fluttering cloud, as if a thousand tethered butterflies were floating there, dragging her onwards. She was feeling exactly the same sensation now, as she engaged in small talk with

Robert on the phone. They had been discussing a romantic getaway to an uninhabited island, dotted, in Robert's words, with darling fluffy white lambs frolicking in the warm sunshine. At least that was what she thought he had said. She hadn't really been listening to what he had been saying, but his voice was hypnotic. Perhaps she had embellished his picture of the island somewhat, but the concept resonated well with her. Robert had continued to wax lyrical in his description of Sandeagh Mhor, literally translated from Gaelic as the Big Sandy Island. Despite her concerns about the so-called pleasures of hiking on a rough and remote island off the coast of Scotland in June, Robert had won the day. He had painted her such a vivid picture of a remote yet romantic getaway, untouched by the twenty first century, where they could unwind and enjoy some prime time together, that it was impossible for her to turn him down. His deep brown voice was very soothing. "Come with me, sweetheart." he had breathed in her ear. "You won't regret it." It really hadn't taken too long for her to make up her mind to go with Robert. Besides, a week with him would give her a great chance to get to know him better. Julia was by profession a graphic designer. As such, she had cultivated an intensely vivid imagination. She came from a well off London merchant banking family, and with a trust fund established by her doting parents, had no need to work to sustain her lifestyle. However, she had seen the idle life ruin many of her privileged friends, as they partied the nights away in the nightclubs of Kensington. Julia, in contrast to these social parasites as she saw them, was determined to make a difference in the world. Her career was flourishing, and she had high hopes for her future creating spectacular marketing messages for new items in the healthcare field.

Drifting back into the conversation with Robert, she recalled her first meeting with him at a party at her friend Kate's apartment. The evening had started in a rather dull and predictable way. As people arrived, the congregated in small knots. It was a perfect venue for those who knew each other to talk the latest gossip about their absent friends. That was until the effect of the unending supply of alcoholic beverages, and some lively rock music had loosened the inhibitions of the twenty something crowd. Robert had stood out as a slightly gauche, but very handsome man. Julia was curious. She wanted to find out more about him. He seemed to be alone and unattached, and so she turned on her best feminine charms. She had flashed a broad smile in his direction, and concentrated her gaze on his eyes. Her delicately fluttering eyelids had been known to have a devastating effect on most men, and they worked the same magic with Robert. He had casually walked over to her, and had asked her if she wanted to dance. When she agreed, he had placed his hands on her shoulders, and with a gentle touch had steered her to a cleared area in the living room that served as a dance floor. She felt that he had intruded on her personal space with his touch more than she expected, but he had manipulated her so gently, she had instantly forgiven him. She was intrigued by this handsome young man with his gentle touch, and she went willingly with him for a dance. That evening had ended for them with a slow dance, an embrace, and a long and sensual kiss. He offered to drive her home. In the car, they had kissed passionately, and she made the bold move of inviting Robert back to her apartment for coffee. One thing led rapidly to another, and they had tumbled through her bedroom door, pulling off each other's clothing as they went. She was feeling unbelievably aroused, and they ended up nude, writhing together passionately on the bed. She remembered crying out in ecstasy as Robert took her to heights she had never experienced. She smiled softly as she recalled that occasion, and the other occasions later that week that had taken her breath away.

Dragging herself back into the present, she concentrated on what Robert was saying. He was explaining to her what he thought they should do together on the island. They would of course share a tent together. They would wake up each morning to the sounds of sea birds, and the gentle bleating of the summer seasons new lambs. That had sounded a little lame to Julia, as she was more interested in waking up in his arms to make passionate love. But she thought, bless his heart, that he was trying to be romantic with her.

Living for a week in a tent sounded a bit like being at a boot camp. But Julia could deal with that. She was trying, let's face it, to seduce Robert, and when she weighed up the pleasure of being in Robert's company with the minor hardships of a week in the outback, Robert came out the winner. So what if she would have no hot running water and no electricity to power her ever-present hair drier. A week of rough sleeping bag sex with Robert would put all that into perspective. Besides, she could afford to lose a few pounds in weight.

She was a little put off by the description of the food they would be eating, basically as he described the food, it would be rehydrated space rations. Julia was a vegetarian. Robert loved his meat. Well, let him go hunting the native sheep population if he wanted fresh meat.

Julia was looking forward to her trip with Robert. Although he spent way too much time on the details, she recognized that he was at heart a scientist, and that's what he did best. Scientists liked discussing the details. She did not. She could talk the hind legs off a donkey, but she wanted to see the plans of her world from forty thousand feet. She yawned. Robert wanted to discuss the more mundane details of their trip. Well, good for him. Julia was glad that he took pleasure in making arrangements, but in her advertising practice she had subordinates to do that. Robert rambled on about the costs of travelling by car to Campbeltown, the time it would take them to get there, and what they could do together once they were on the island. Julia found herself tuning out of the conversation.

"Thanks for doing the footwork, Rob. You know how much that's a no-no for me. I abhor the little details. That's why we get on so well together. I'd be in deep trouble without you. Now when do we leave?"

"I'll come to your place around eight tomorrow morning?" said Robert. "I'll be packed by then. Unless..."

"Unless what?"

"Unless I can come round earlier, say nine tonight?"

Julia raised an eyebrow automatically.

"You're impossible, Rob! Is sex all you think about?" she asked, mildly amused by his ardor.

"Well, just this once, but remember that you are doing the driving tomorrow. We need to get some sleep!"

"That is exactly what I was planning to do, after we kiss and make up?"

"Just what are we making up for?"

"Lost time!"

Julia sighed, a mixture of theatrical denial and delicious anticipation.

"Haven't you had enough this week? No, don't answer that. I'll see you around nine. Get your stuff together, though, we need to leave around seven at the latest."

She put the phone down.

Campbeltown. She mulled over the name. Campbeltown intrigued Julia. She had never visited the place. The first mention of Campbeltown she recalled had been on a visit to her grandfather. Her Scottish grandfather had owned an ancient wind up gramophone. The gramophone was a work of art. It had a large wooden box base and a metal crank with a china handle on its side to wind up its motor. A large horn protruded from the top of the box, and served as an amplifier for the sound created by a steel needle vibrating as it traversed the grooves on the disk. The gramophone turntable rotated thick black plastic disks, each covered with fine wavy grooves. As she recalled, most of the disks had a picture of a black and white haired mutt on a red label stuck to the center. Grandpa MacPherson had explained that the disks rotated at exactly seventy eight revolutions per minute, and if she really wanted to know, the dog sitting there with his ear cocked and pointed at the large brass horn of the gramophone was called Nipper. At the time she wasn't really interested, but she feigned attention, knowing that her grandpa would put a record onto the platter for her. After her grandpa had charged the mechanical motor of the machine, he would place the clunky metal arm and brass horn onto the smooth outer surface of the record as it was spinning. The thick metal needle on the tip of the arm picked up the vibrations of the wavy grooves on the black Bakelite surface. As she placed her ear close to the horn, she could hear music and the sound of people singing. To her young ears, the machine produced a scratchy and tinny sound. But it was still magical. Later in life, when she compared the tinny sound to her own versions of the gramophone, she had realized just how primitive the sounds were. It made her all the more appreciative of her CD's and more recently her iPod, when she compared her grandpa's music to her own. She thought back once again to the recordings she had heard all those years ago. One of the records had produced the scratchy sound of a man's voice. Grandpa Macpherson had told her that his name was Harry Lauder, and he was very famous a long time ago. So famous that she had never heard

15

of him until now. But she liked the way he sang, and at that time his songs seemed very funny to her.

"Oh Campbeltown Loch, if ye were made o' whisky, I would drink ye dry!"

The man had probably been under the influence of a dram or two when he had penned that song. When Julia had been a four year old sitting on her Grandpa's knee, hearing the song had made her laugh. She pictured a drunken Scotsman, whisky fumes on his breath, staggering around the edge of the dry lake bed. Sadly, some of the young men she had courted in her earlier years came very close to mimicking the fat Campbeltown tosspot she had imagined in the song.

The only other fact she remembered about the area concerned Sir Paul McCartney. That iconic singer owned a farm on the Mull of Kintyre very close to Campbeltown. As part of his repertoire, he sang a romantic and wistful ballad about the Mull of Kintyre. She had never been to the area but she had a vivid imagination. It was therefore quite easy for her to visualize mists rolling in from the sea to cover the heather covered hillsides of the Mull. It would be fun to visit Scotland, and especially fun to visit somewhere she hadn't been before.

"Robert is worth a serious gamble." she said to herself. "He's smart, handsome, and I swear he likes me a lot. If we can survive a week together in a remote island somewhere near nowhere, perhaps we can make it together. And sex with him is so much fun."

She felt a delicious tingle in her breast.

"I haven't had much luck with men, but I think he might be the right one for me. Now I need to keep him on the hook! If I have anything to do with it, we'll have the best time of our lives out there, and perhaps I'll forget to take my oral contraceptive pill one night?"

She flushed deliciously, and wondered if she would have the nerve. No, perhaps not she reminded herself, it would be too easy to get burnt if their relationship fell apart. As she thought about the concept for a few minutes, she felt a strange sensation as if someone had walked on her grave.

Marcia Greenwood

ARCIA GREENWOOD HAD NOT ENJOYED HER last birthday. To turn thirty, that for her was a disaster. And to be unmarried as well. Well, that wasn't so bad right now. Marcia had been described by her boyfriends and her erstwhile husband as a real catch. Well now she was a thirty year old fish on the hook, and she predicted that it would all be downhill from here. It wouldn't be too long until this prime catch began to turn sour. But here she was, looking in the mirror at her curvaceous body, newly divorced, thirty and childless. Damn, she looked good!

Marcia was a firm believer in the good things in life, but she was to her occasional detriment, an eternal optimist.

"You don't wear rose tinted glasses." she had been told by her ex-husband. "Yours are bright bloody red."

Above all though, Marcia enjoyed her food. Unfortunately the types of food she most enjoyed, especially Brier's Ice Cream, and Godiva chocolate, had contributed insidiously to her gently spreading waistline, and to some appearance of disturbing cellulite on her thighs. Both of these afflictions she fought vigorously in her local fitness club. But despite her birthday, and her self-induced loss of her husband, Marcia generally tended to keep in good spirits. At heart she was a kind and generous soul. Now that she had successfully ditched her husband of seven years, almost to the day to coincide with the legendary seven year itch, she was finally feeling contented. Gavin, her balding and pot bellied former husband had been caught *in flagrante delicto* with his secretary by the head of human resources at the Falcon insurance office where he had been given a vice presidential position. Now she knew where the vice part came from. He was now shacked up with his former secretary in a tiny apartment in the docklands of London's east end. Needless to say, Marcia was not too pleased when he had been kicked out of the firm and even less amused when the reason had been revealed. In fact, for one of the few times in her life, she was bloody furious with him! But as she later recalled, his demise as the boss and his ultimate humiliation when the tape from the surveillance camera had circulated on YouTube had left her feeling secretly pleased. He had finally given her the excuse to be rid of him, and on top of that she had received a nice settlement in lieu of alimony. Her new found wealth allowed her to be a lady of leisure at least for a short time. She mentally counted her assets. Money in the bank, a house of her own, and then there was of course her body. Marcia had been told by many men that she had a very pleasant smile. She wore it frequently, and it was perfectly placed in a peaches and cream baby face. She had perfect white teeth as a result of many hours of dental and orthodontic visits as a child. Her eyes were wide set in her face, and they shone with a deep golden brown glow. To round off her good looks, she visited a tanning salon on occasions to top up her light olive complexion. She dressed well, in what some might call seductive clothing, and she erred on the side of displaying more of her body than was fashionable for her age. But it suited her. She just loved flirting with men. Why else would she wear low cut blouses, highlighted her ample chest, and jeans that emphasized the long smooth curves of her hips and legs.

Although she always felt she could improve her looks, she realized that she had what it took to get the lads fighting over her.

"Yes." she reminded herself. "No matter what I might think about myself, I *am* hot."

She would walk into her local nightclub, alone or with one of her girl friends, and the males in the club would turn and stare at her. Some openly eyed her up, and others reddened as she caught their eyes travelling up and down her body. Her dalliances with the opposite sex had led her to have a number of short romances, both before and after her divorce. Some of these encounters had ended with a romp in the proverbial hay. Others had given her the chance to be the recipient of a free meal and drinks, for which she was indeed grateful. Rarely, if she had a good feeling about the man, she would invite him back to her house. She would then tolerate a quick grope in the dark as a reward to the man for his pandering to her culinary tastes.

If asked, Marcia would describe herself as a lover of the earth and all living things upon it. She was an atheist and could not abide people preaching to her about an afterlife, and the concept of hell. Those were just figments of some clever church dignitaries imaginations, designed to keep their flock in check. Be good and you end up in heaven. Be bad, and you go to hell. Well, who decided what was good and bad? She attended weekly Friends of the Earth meetings where the flavor of discussions was always green. If she had been of a certain age and alive in the sixties she imagined she would have burned her bra, and lived in a hippie commune, but that was so retro today. Her best friend Julie-Ann had told her she was an earth mother in spirit, but that didn't fit her thoughts of herself. She embraced an enduring vision of one day returning to the simplicity of life that had existed many centuries before. She liked the concept of village life, and could easily imagine herself being a milkmaid or a cook or some such in the manor house. But wherever it was, it would have to be prior to the industrial revolution. How complicated life had become after the invention of computers and cell phones, and especially the invention of the motor car. Unfortunately for Marcia, she knew her vision for her future would never happen in Greenford, Middlesex, despite its idyllic name. So given her current comfortable circumstances, and a real desire to escape the tedium of daily life in the city, she decided to look for a place on the planet where she could escape all that stuff, at least for a week. Driven then by her desire to return to the basics of life, she had done some fundamental research on the internet. Her goal was to find a haven of peace in the chaotic world of modern day Great Britain. She was sure that there was some corner of this country that still had no traffic, no cellular reception, and best of all, no internet. Her labors turned up a delightful sounding escape into the Scottish Highlands, more specifically to a remote sandy island off the western coast.

"No roads, no internet cafés, no houses, only clean living in the fresh air!" boasted the headline on the website she had just found. "Come to the unspoilt island of Sandeagh Mhor, and leave your cares behind."

Taking her courage in her hands, she had booked the trip. It was a camping trip to Sandeagh Mhor, or Big Sandy, if you translated the Gaelic into English. It was an uninhabited island eleven miles off the Mull of Kintyre in Western Scotland. The trip, described on the web by the travel company Island Adventures, provided a short boat journey to get her and a few select travelling companions to the island. The company would also provide camping equipment and supply staple needs. There would be plenty food, water and toiletries. But that was as far as it went. There would be no access to the luxuries of life. No bottles of Poison perfume. No hairdryers, phones or television. No showers or Jacuzzi baths. No automobiles. Others might be horrified, but it sounded perfect to Marcia! She could even ditch her iPad and iPhone for the week. There was no cell phone reception on the island. No bars where she could pick up men, and no bars on her cell phone. She would be totally disconnected from modern civilization for the whole week. It sounded fabulous. Marcia was definitely in the mood to get away from it all, and the whole Island Adventure experience sounded the perfect getaway for her. The way she pictured it, she would be in Eden for a week. It would be the perfect back to nature adventure.

Marcia was still looking for true love. Her husband had been a spur of the moment acquisition. In reality, he was a drunken bum. There had to be somebody better to be her soul mate for life. She had heard that Scots were famously good lovers, and asked for little else material in return. Sandeagh Mhor might offer her a chance for a tryst with a rugged Scotsman in a kilt. That would be delightful! Men in kilts had been a perpetual fantasy for her since she had heard that a man's fertility increased if his gonads were unencumbered. At least she might have an opportunity to seduce the guide. If he spent his life rambling around remote mountainous islands, he would be fit, with strong thighs and tight buns. She shivered delightedly in anticipation. What about a kilted guide! Then she could make it her mission to find out what was really worn under the average Scotsman's kilt, and she hoped the rumors were true.

There were a few short days between her making the booking, and the day she was to travel northwards. The evening before, she had taken her best Gucci suitcase from the attic of the small three bedroomed terraced houses she owned in Greenford. As she looked at the case and its intricate fripperies, she decided to put it back in the attic. That case was, in many ways, totally contrary to the spirit of the vacation she had chosen. Worse, although somewhat practical and utilitarian, the overpriced case represented all that was bad about today's society. Such a waste of money. She climbed back into the dusty attic, and swapped the elegant but impractical Gucci case for a rugged black nylon backpack she had previously used to carry her belongings on a trip round Europe on an Inter-rail vacation. It would be totally inappropriate to meet any potential future husband representing herself as a gold-digging socialite, she thought. She wanted to be seen as a down to earth and practical woman, the future mother to solid and dependable kids.

The morning of the trip, Marcia felt the beginnings of a nagging doubt about the island and the camping holiday. Perhaps she had generated impossibly high hopes for herself for what might happen on Sandeagh Mhor. She had been convinced that the trip had supreme significance for her future life. Now she was not so sure.

"Perhaps Mr. Right will be along on this trip with me." she reminded herself, and her mood picked up. "If he is," she told herself, "he won't know what's hit him. I love a good challenge, and seducing men is one of the most fun challenges I have."

The thought of a romance on a distant island refueled her fervor for the trip and she could feel her excitement rising to a fever-pitch. The black nylon, rather scuffed, rucksack had been stuffed full of her best practical outdoor gear, although she had opted to go light on the storm wear, as she believed in her optimistic heart that the Scottish sun would shine daily on the island.

To whet her appetite further, she switched on her laptop. It would do her no harm to reread the information about the island. The travel company had done a good job talking up the island, and had placed all the information on a professional looking website. Her other best friend, Jinty, had travelled with Island Adventures the year before, and had raved about the experience.

She surfed to the Island Adventures website. There was a description of the island under a magnificent photograph of a tranquil rocky island, surrounded by impossibly blue sky, and rolling breakers of the Atlantic Ocean. According to the information provided in the paragraphs below the photo, Sandeagh Mhor had arisen out of a shallow swamp, as a the result of volcanic activity along the major fault chain that had formed most of the west coast of Scotland and

Northern Ireland over sixty two million years ago. The brochure was a little overly dramatic. It encouraged potential travelers to the island to imagine the plumes of fiery volcanic lava spurting skywards, then falling to earth to run as red hot rivers down the volcanic cone until they eventually were quenched by a shallow local sea. The lava ponds that had accumulated around the base of the volcano had formed basaltic columns as they cooled. These columns were several feet wide, and were typically five or six sided. As the rock cooled, the shrinkage that occurred caused these even cracks to develop. Now the rock columns stood tall, pillars of stone to rival the best architecture in the world, and none of them touched by the hand of man. Over the millennia, the softer volcanic tufa had eroded to expose these cliffs of the tree-like rock columns. They were slowly being eroded by powerful waves generated during the gales of winters in the Atlantic. As a side note, the brochure referred to Fingal's Cave on the island of Staffa. Fingal's Cave, although not part of the itinerary, exemplified the stark beauty of a volcanic landscape. Towering ribs of rock arched over the cave and plunged into a stormy grey- blue sea. The cave itself is a deep inlet with access only by boat. The writer chillingly referred to the legend associated with the cave, a haunting story where a piper and his dog disappeared one ghostly night, with the distant wailing of his bagpipes still being heard in the cave over two hundred years later as a ghostly piper continued to hunt for his dog. The e-brochure also referred for comparison to the more romantic Giant's Causeway in Ireland. Marcia was a fan of the Led Zeppelin pop group. She pulled out a CD from her storage rack. It was entitled "Houses of the Holy". In the background of the cover photograph stark heptagonal and hexagonal rocks arose from the sea. So Sandeagh Mhor had cliffs of these spectacular rock columns, and she could see them first hand.

She returned to her brightly lit laptop and continued reading.

"Sandeagh Mhor Island is a volcanic plug, formed when soft ash was eroded from the volcano. What was left was a stark tower resembling a giant gorilla. The second feature to the island was a long and gently sloping tail of rock, left there by glacial activity in the last ice age. The tail had been ripped by waves into steep cliffs next to the peak. The cliffs gradually petered out at the tip of the island. As an aside," the description continued, "Sandeagh Mhor is almost a mirror of a similar structure in the city of Edinburgh called

Arthur's Seat, where the basaltic columns have the wonderful name of Adam's Ribs."

Marcia poured herself another cup of coffee. Sipping it gently, she continued to read.

"Sandeagh Mhor has several bored sheep scrabbling for fodder from the rough grass on the island. The sheep are the legacy of an arguably certifiably insane farmer called Ramsay Macleod, who hailed from Dunragit, a local rural farming village. He ferried them out to the island one evening on a relatively calm day with the idea to build a cottage and make woolen garments in the old- fashioned Arran knit style. Being a dairy farmer, he had little experience with sheep, and even less with the tempestuous island. Rumors had it that he had also ferried out a year's supply of Laphroaig whisky, and by mistake took a cliff path instead of the gentle pathway to the rough jetty that housed his boat. He was never found, but empty tell-tale bottles of Laphroaigh were scattered in a convincing enough way on a path leading to the ocean's edge, with a mere sheer drop of three hundred feet to the boiling ocean surf and broken volcanic rock, to convince the local coroner's inquiry that he had most likely "died through misadventure." His body of course was never found. It was said that on stormy nights, his drunken singing could be heard in the distance, carried eastwards on the prevailing wind.

So there was a ghost on the island! Marcia pictured the farmer's ghost wandering over the island and wailing as it traveled in search of its lost body.

Marcia laughed to herself. Misadventure. Such a wonderfully simple word, but it embraced a whole slew of different ways to die. She had seen the word used to describe victims of many accidental deaths. She had frequently read about such so-called misadventures in the tabloid papers, everything from self induced drug overdose to strangulation or suffocation associated with autoerotic acts. Well, she wasn't going to have a misadventure, she would have an adventure. She read on.

"So the sheep had survived, as sheep are known to do, in their own stoic way over the years. They had faced the icy winds and snows in winter, and the baking summer heat and despite all the hardships had thrived. Somehow the rough, tough, grasses on the gentle slope leading to the volcanic peak contained sufficient nutrition for them, and every year there were many lambs gamboling in the warm spring sun. Their woolen pelts remained uncut, and as far as anyone knows, there have been no Arran sweaters knitted from the wool off their backs."

There was a final paragraph describing the island itself. Marcia read on.

"The island is about four miles long in its long axis, and the volcanic peak stands two thousand, two hundred and twenty seven feet high. From a distance it looks like a long dead beached whale, with the whales ribs exposed in parts. Then imagine the whale, now almost completely decomposed, having patchy green mold across its back."

Although the description sounded a little morbid for a tourist brochure, Marcia had no trouble seeing a picture of the island without too much difficulty.

"There is a landing jetty that was put together rock by rock by Ramsey MacLeod, the crazy drunken farmer. He had to ferry his belongings out to the island, and he needed a place to dock his boat. If you can still picture the whale, the jetty is perched on the tip of the poor creature's tail. Over fifty years ago, a small consortium of land owners made an attempt to open up the island for farming. They took the farmer's jetty, and bolstered it with cement to make a proper breakwater, and a place for boats to moor. Fifty years of winter storms have not dealt kindly with the breakwater. The elements have most certainly taken their toll. There is still a mooring area for a small boat, with a large rusty but solid enough anchoring point, but the breakwater now resembles nothing more than a jumble of boulders and rocks.

The weather on Sandeagh Mhor ranges from insanely awful in winter during the storms, to picture postcard perfect on a calmer summer's day. You will see scudding puffy clouds and experience a gentle breeze."

Of course, as Marcia knew, the tour company had planned the visit to the island to coincide with the brief window of time when the island could be described as a rough and tumble adventure, but not so unpleasant as to make it uninhabitable. Besides roughing it a little would be a real adventure for her! The brochure ended on a positive note describing the whole Sandeagh Mhor experience as out of the ordinary. The writer felt that he or she had provided fair balance to reflect the potential positives and the negatives of the experience. After the usual testimonials from previous visitors, an e-mail address and phone contact number were provided to link the prospective client to the company, and start the booking process.

Marcia supposed that as her trip was starting in mid June, the worst of the spring weather fluctuations would have passed. The snow that capped the mountains of the islands off the coast of Scotland in winter would be gone.

She studied the photograph of the island once more. From the distance, it looked like there were a few clumps of trees dotting the plateau. Nothing much grew on the peak itself. There was a carpet of grasses and low shrubs, and the brochure assured her that many native flowers bloomed in early summer. And that blue sky, she could do with some of that. It had been a grey spring in London, with heavy rain, and flooding, and she was ready for a little sunshine.

As she made ready to set off for the airport that morning, Marcia wondered fleetingly if there were any hazards on the island that could mess up her dream vacation.

"I'd better pack some bug spray." she decided. "I'll bet there are a few blood suckers on that island. And some sun screen. I don't want to get burnt."

For some unknown reason, as she voiced the thought to herself, a strange feeling coursed through her body and she shivered.

Martin and Sadie Hoff

ATE IN THE EVENING THAT SAME day, Martin Hoff and his pretty wife Sadie were also viewing the web based advertising materials for Sandeagh Mhor. The Hoff's were the envy of all their friends. They seemed to be the ideal young married couple. They were deeply in love, with the stars of young love still shining in their eyes. They had met in a village pub on the outskirts of Huddersfield in Yorkshire in the north of England. After a whirlwind six month courtship, they had a fairytale wedding in a small rustic church in their local village. Now, six short and passionate months into their marriage, having christened each of the rooms in their stone cottage on the moors, they were as yet unencumbered with children.

"This is what I dreamt about when I married you. Freedom to do the dishes!" said Martin to Sadie as they washed up the crockery from their supper. "Married life with you is a load of fun, even doing the washing up!"

"Your sweet, Mart, but I would like to have a break. You know it's been tough at work recently." said Sadie, her hands covered with soap suds.

"Sounds like a good idea to me Sadie. Where would you like to go?"

"We can't afford much, sweetheart, even with my promotion. We can take a trip in the UK somewhere."

"That works for me, dear. You want to go to Blackpool?"

Sadie scooped up a handful of suds and threw them at Martin.

"You daft bugger, Martin; you know how much I hate Blackpool!"

Visiting Blackpool was a standing joke between them. There is no way that Sadie would ever go back there, the Las Vegas of northwest England. She had hated the trips her parents took there when she was young. It had always rained, and she got food poisoning from eating junk food.

"I don't think so, sweetheart," she continued sarcastically, "but I know how much you want to go. Perhaps next century?"

Martin ignored the jibe. He enjoyed bantering with his wife.

"What about this Sandeagh Mhor place?" asked Martin. "We could be alone together on a romantic island."

"I'd like that, Mart. You know, somewhere really out of the way. No phones, no computer and no washing up!"

As if to emphasize the point, she pushed a pile of clean plates into the cupboard with a little more force than necessary, causing them to crash together noisily.

"You and I can indulge each other to our heart's content. Our only companions will be the sea gulls and a few scraggy sheep. There'll be nothing to get in the way of us having some fun! And just imagine the whisper of a warm and gentle breeze ruffling our tent as we make love."

Work had been particularly exhausting recently for Sadie, and her boss was a tough nut. Mind, it had to be cheap, given that they were living in a rented property, and they were looking to buy a small house for themselves. A trip to Sandeagh Mhor had sounded like a good compromise, since going on an adventure safari in Africa was a tad too expensive.

Martin was an amateur rugby player. It was his escape from his routine job providing temporary latrines for construction sites. The job paid reasonably well, and once the initial outlay for the planking he erected for paths across muddy fields, and the PortaPotty's themselves were paid off, the rental he received was all profit. He was pure muscle, solidly built, and proudly boasted that he could bench press two hundred pounds. Rugby was his second passion, after Sadie. He sported two crushed and scarred ears (cauliflower ears they called them in Yorkshire) as a result of multiple traumas as he crushed heads, shoulders, arms and legs with his opponents in the civilized war of the game of rugby. Time after time, his head and the delicate ears were crushed against others in head to head encounters in the notorious scrum, that inverse of the tug of war, where each rugby team's largest and physically strongest players attempt to push their opposite numbers in the direction of the goal line. He also had a broken nose, and some facial scars, that he proudly wore as a trophy of his sport.

Sadie on the other hand was a delicate flower, being almost a foot shy of Martin's six foot frame, and had a fine cheek-boned face with delicate lips. Everything else about her was delicate too, with the exception of her tongue. She was well aware of how to use it as a ferocious weapon, and managed to subdue Martin with it on the odd occasions when he stepped out of line. She was an administrative assistant to an obese, sweaty and balding managing director of a restaurant chain scattered all over England. The chain had been doing particularly well in the recent recession given that it provided solid calories in the form of deep fried sugar and fat concoctions at rock bottom prices. Sadie saw very little of her boss for which she was grateful, as he was constantly on the road, but she kept him organized, paid the bills, and made sure the lights stayed on in the small office suite she travelled to daily in the industrial park. Her light relief from the tedium of the office was embroidery, and she hung the finished tapestries and samplers on the walls of their rented apartment.

Sadie enjoyed nights out with Martin. He always made a special effort to dress up for her, and his broad shouldered and slim hipped physique suited a black roll neck sweater, and tight blue jeans. She herself favored a simple embroidered blouse and plain skirt, cut above her knees to show off her legs. She was also pleased with her slim waist and full hips.

Tonight was a special night. They were on their way to celebrate the pregnancy of Alice Thompson. They were making their way on foot to the semi-detached house owned by the Thompsons, a young couple they had met through working at a local charity food bank.

Sadie recalled her conversation with David Thomson, Alice's husband.

"We'll be just having an informal evening together." he had said. "Alice has been a little off her food recently, but she's doing well in the evenings."

The Thompsons had also invited the MacArthurs, a trendy young husband and wife who also lived in the neighborhood. During the dinner, when the wine had been flowing for some time, Martin and Sadie informed their friends of their plans for the summer.

Martin dabbed his lips theatrically with a linen napkin.

"Alice my dear, you are such a good cook. This is better food than any of the local restaurants cook. How is pregnancy treating you?"

Alice blushed. She adored compliments.

"I feel really good most of the time. So I'm getting cravings for bananas, but I'm otherwise fine."

"You look fabulous, Alice." said Martin. I'd like to propose a toast to the Thompsons, all three of you!"

Alice picked up her glass of mineral water, and they all touched glasses together.

"Since we like you all so much," continued Martin, "I thought I'd bounce an idea past you all." He paused, and took another sip of his Chardonnay.

"Sadie and I have found a wonderful stress-buster getaway for this summer. We know how hard you all work, and so we thought we'd see if you wanted to come with us."

Alice and David Thompson were listening carefully, intrigued by the thought of a break before the baby was born. Gail and Malcolm MacArthur seemed a little doubtful.

Martin continued.

"We are going to take a step back in time. We're camping on a remote island off the West Coast of Scotland." he said.

"I know it doesn't sound like much, but there'll be no cell phones, no computers, no fax, no office ..."

"... and no modern conveniences." finished Malcolm. "I'll never be able to persuade Gail to go, but I'd love to."

Gail glared indignantly at her husband, and thrust out her tongue at him. He shrugged, and smiled at her. He knew that she wouldn't hold the dig at her longer term.

"You two lovebirds go and do what you do best." said Alice after a whispered conversation with her husband. "I have a small issue to deal with here in Huddersfield. We have to save up our pennies for the baby."

David smiled at her fondly.

"Besides, you wouldn't want us along to, ah, disturb your rest?

"I have a feeling that I won't be the only one in the club in the near future." added Alice.

"There's no way I can go. I can't live without my hairdryer." Gail MacArthur had protested, and her husband Malcolm laughed.

"It's true!" he said.

"Gail is a creature of modern times. If she doesn't have her daily hot shower, she won't set foot outside the house. The only way you'll get Gail camping is to have one of these American motor home monstrosities. You know the ones that look like a bungalow on wheels? And by the way, it has to be one that you can hook up to the power grid."

"Malcolm, I'm not as bad as all that, am I?" Gail protested.

"All right children, settle down!" said David. "Here, let me propose another toast."

"To young love, to our growing families, and to our successful lives together!"

He raised his glass, and once again they all clinked glasses in unison.

"To us!"

After dinner, Alice had professed that she was feeling exhausted, and they all parted company, hugging each other as they left the house. Martin and Sadie had drunk a little more than was good for them, and they walked home a little erratically, arm in arm.

As they strolled through the darkness, they talked about going to Sandeagh Mhor.

"You know me, Sade. I'll be out jogging every morning. You saw the pictures of the island. There are paths everywhere." Martin loved the thought of running against the wild backdrop of the Atlantic Ocean. He loved hearing the deep crump from the ocean swell as it exploded in foam on the rocky shoreline.

"Well I'm not going jogging with you." said Sadie. "You set off around six in the morning. That's way too early for me. I'm on vacation for God's sake. I'll be catching up with my beauty sleep. And make sure you keep enough energy to look after my needs."

"Don't you worry about that, Sade. I'll have more than enough stamina to light your fire. Besides, you like me better when I'm hot and sweaty, or so you say."

"I like you any way I can get you, you big hunk. But maybe we can do more than practice making babies while we're there?"

"Just wait till I get you home, young lady, I'll show you what it means to practice. Besides, I'm on fire tonight!"

As he uttered the words, a strange spasm of fear gripped him for a few seconds. He shuddered.

"What's wrong dear?" asked Sadie, concerned.

"Oh, it's nothing. I felt a little weird for a few seconds. The feeling's gone now."

When they reached home, Martin was as good as his word. As they lay together in each other's arms, they agreed that they would sign up for the trip the next day. It would have been fun to have their friends along with them, but they were equally content to be going with each other.

Justin Hardwick

USTIN HARDWICK WAS THE TEAM LEADER for the trip to Sandeagh Mhor. He had been personally selected by Stewart Henderson, the owner and only executive who ran a small but flourishing travel agency he had called Island Adventures. Justin came from a small village in rural Cheshire. He had been educated, although not particularly well educated, in a small school in Tarporley. As befitted a school in a rural backwater, the teachers there good, but not outstanding. As a result, Justin, who struggled a bit with all things academic, slowly drifted through his education, and had left school at age sixteen. He had been brought up in a working class home. His parents cared deeply for him, and gave him a good home, but at school he had the uncanny ability to attract a fight with other pupils in the playground. He became very good at fighting back, but on more than one occasion, he would return home with a bleeding nose or blackened eye. Still, despite the battering he suffered at the hands of the bullies in his school, he had won more fist fights than he had lost. He had been taken under the wing of his local school gymnastics teacher, who made sure he enrolled in a local martial arts class. As a result, he had built considerable muscle, and a tough attitude to life. He was now a rugged and handsome young man, and aged twenty three, and an expedition leader. His only real handicap preventing him from making a better name for himself was that he was, as the Cockneys in London would describe him, a little "dolly dimple". He was not too smart. In fact most folks who met him found out very quickly that although he had a great personality, he really was lacking in mental acuity. He was one brick short of a load, or one can short of a six pack, in the words of his friends. His parents often likened him in a kindly way to Robert E. Milne's Pooh Bear.

"Well, maybe you have something between your ears," his parents would say to him, "but not enough to make you Einstein. But we love you anyway, dear."

Psychologists tell us that the average human intelligence quotient is one hundred. Average means average, so for any genius out there with an IQ of one hundred and fifty, there has to be somebody on the other half of the line. Justin's intelligence was on the low side. His IQ, while not in the idiot range, approached very close. Knowing that he had few, if any, prospects in academia, and that he had a great love of the outdoors, his parents gently steered him into outward bound activities at which he excelled. Preparation for a life in the wild would require some skills. His parents arranged for a series of classes to expand his outdoor abilities. There were many different trainers around to educate him in anything from first aid to survival in extreme conditions.

He took and passed all the appropriate first aid skill tests, and knew how to pitch a tent at twice the speed of any competitor. As he had matured over the years, he learned other important skills. He moved from his parent's house at age eighteen, and took a job as barman in a yacht club in Campbeltown in Scotland. He made friends with the club members who spent many hours in the bar after they had been sailing. It wasn't long before he had invitations to act as a crew member on the boats. He had found he had a natural talent for sailing. He could now steer a yacht though storms and treacherous currents with the best of them. To make some additional money, since the bar job didn't pay him much, he would sing in the club in the evenings he was off. He had a good voice, and he accompanied himself with a small hand accordion. His powerful rendition of local folk songs and his skillful playing of the accordion attracted clients at the club to listen. He took his time to teach the members the lyrics of the songs, and they would sing along with him as they gathered around the fireside in the club in the cool evenings.

His mother had given birth to Justin rather late in life, and unfortunately she had died recently as a result of the ravages of disseminated breast cancer. His father, an inveterate smoker, had dropped dead shortly after of a heart attack while out jogging to try and reduce his weight. Justin attended the funerals, and buried his parents, shedding a few tears as he recalled how much they had done to help him in life. So Justin was alone in life, young and single.

Justin found himself to be very attractive to the opposite sex. However, he had a limited conversational ability. He had no trouble getting dates with the girls at the Yacht Club, it was just that he couldn't keep them interested. He had also had his successes with the local girls in the Campbeltown pubs, but despite all his past relationships, he was currently unattached. He had recently joined Island Adventures, a privately held glorified travel agency, after running into the owner, Stewart Henderson, at the yacht club. Stewart had a fondness for single malt Scotch whisky, and single and attractive young men, and he had sidled up to Justin in the bar with the hope of starting a relationship with him. Justin however had made it clear from the offset that he was not that way inclined, and he was certainly not looking for a sexual encounter with what he saw as an ageing homo. However, despite Justin's initial misgivings, the two had chatted together for most of the evening. Stewart started talking about his business, and how much fun it was to shepherd tourists to the remote places in Scotland. He had made good money through making his outward bound type adventures available for all comers. Anyone in fact who had a pound or two to send in his direction.

"Why don't you give it a try, Justin?" Stewart had asked him after his fourth pint of Belhaven ale. "From your background, you'd be an ideal guide. And you would be based here in Campbeltown. We do an excursion to Sandeagh Mhor, a wee island about ten miles offshore in the Irish Sea."

The whole concept sounded really appealing to Justin.

"All right Stewart. I'll give it a shot for a couple of trips. If I like it, and you haven't kicked me out, then we can negotiate a salary. Besides, you're right. It's just the sort of thing that I'll enjoy, and get paid for it!"

"Young lad, you won't regret this." said Stewart, slapping him on the back. "Are you sure you don't want to come home with me for another drink?"

"Get lost, you bastard! I may be a little tipsy, and I'm grateful to you for the job," Justin slurred, "but can't we just be friends?"

Stewart had laughed. "All right lad, you're hired and I won't ask for any sexual favors in return. Just come over to the office on main street tomorrow morning and we'll get all you paperwork sorted out."

And so, slightly hung over the next morning, Justin had signed on to be a team leader for Island Adventures. Stewart had informed him that the coming Saturday, he would be taking a group of tourists out to Sandeagh Mhor island.

"I hope these guys will be well behaved and not cause me any trouble." he had said to Stewart as they discussed the upcoming trip together in the office. "Big Sandy is a fine island, but there are many ways to come unstuck out there."

"You just keep in touch with me by radio, and you'll be fine. Nobody wants to get hurt, and as long as you read them the riot act before you get out there, they'll behave for you."

Like anyone who had not suffered significant adversity in life, other than the odd knock and scrape in his fights at school, Justin felt invincible. He was convinced that he was on top of his game, and he had enormous confidence in his own skills and abilities. From his past experiences visiting remote places in Scotland as part of his outward bound training, he knew what excitement was on offer in a remote and pristine offshore island. Oh yes, it would be a bit of a shock for folks coming from a big city, but he was sure that with a little help, he could get people motivated to enjoy the rough terrain and primitive camping conditions they would endure for the week. He also knew that his first aid training would be a plus. It was too damned easy for inexperienced climbers to get into trouble on the rocks.

"No worries though, I can bandage bleeding knees and elbows and deal out aspirins with the best of them." he told himself.

Justin decided that he would not have too high expectations for "the guests" as Stewart called them.

"They'll be a bunch of hick tourists." he said to himself. "No sweat for me to look after them."

On the plus side though, what if there was an attractive young woman amongst his group? Justin had a romantic heart, but also enjoyed his sexual encounters. Perhaps a cockney blond from London? Maybe a red head from Glasgow? The possibilities were endless. Per Stuart's instructions, he would have to keep his romance out of the sight of the rest of the campers. Quite honestly, that wouldn't be a problem. After all, once the rest of the camp had retired for the night, he could sneak round to his love interest's tent and offer her his services. Or perhaps there would be a more mature woman, hoping that the romantic Scottish Islands would be the place where she would meet the love of her life. She would be hunting for an Adonis figure, and Justin would fit the bill. She might even be prepared to pay handsomely for his services.

"Pull yourself together, Justin!" he told himself sternly. "Don't get carried away now."

Most likely, he thought, he would have to look after run-of-the-mill tourist couples of varying degrees of fitness and sanity. They would simply be along for the adventure and to escape the harrowing day-to-day tedium of the mainland. Well in that case, Justin would apply his shepherding skills to keep them from falling off cliffs, or tumbling down the steep peak of the Scottish Island.

"I'm pretty sure I can keep them all alive and well for a week." he reassured himself. "How tough can it be?"

But it would be more difficult to stem the disappointment that some of them would feel when Sandeagh Mhor turned out to be so far from the tropical island getaway that they mistakenly imagined it to be.

Justin had no major ambitions in his life, and was content to do what he did best. His only purpose in taking on this guiding thing would be to get free food and lodging for the week, and to make some money. Stewart would pay him well, and there might be some tips from the grateful guests. Perhaps he might even get a compliment or two, but he wasn't holding his breath. The money from the club gave him just enough to pay the rent on the bedroom he rented from a local farmer, and to pay for a beer or two at the weekend. He had a taste for the simple things in life, and as long as he could pay for his beer, he would be fine.

On the Friday before the trip began he gave Stewart a call.

"Hey, Stewart, tell me. What sort of a crowd will I have to deal with tomorrow?"

Justin wanted to have a quiet week, and the makeup of group he would lead could make or break that. Stewart obliged him by reading out the profiles of his charges over the phone.

"You have an unmarried young couple from Edinburgh, a married couple from Yorkshire, a single woman from London and four Boy Scouts on an outward bound course. That's a good handful. I bet they'll keep you busy."

Stewart chuckled down the phone line.

"No naughty business with the guest from London, Justin. I don't want any complaints now. And make sure you look after them all. I want them all home safely at the end of the trip."

Justin digested the information carefully. A single lady from London, eh? His blond perhaps? Four young lads doing an outward bound course. That sounded like trouble. The rest seemed pretty innocuous.

"Thanks Stew, I can manage. I'll keep them safe for you. I want them all to have a good time."

"You know I don't like being called Stew, Justin. Keep it to Stewart, OK?"

Justin thought of a few more things he could call Stewart, but the man was paying him. He bit his tongue.

"I'll call you Stewart to your face," he muttered under his breath, "but I'll be thinking stewed wart or stewpot."

He snickered at his own cleverness.

Stewart had informed him that the biggest risk to Island Adventures as a company was the injury of one of his guests. He might be sued, and there would certainly be a hike in his corporate insurance premiums. He was not sure if the company could survive with a tarnished safety image, and grossly inflated insurance payments.

Justin didn't care a hoot about the company, but he worried a little about what might happen to him if one of the guests was injured.

"I'll keep them safe." he said again to himself, with a little more confidence than he felt.

All that remained for him to do now was turn up the next afternoon at the Island Adventures corporate office. The office was housed in a disused seaside croft, where the business had its home. He turned in early that evening, as he knew just how strenuous the first days of any trip could be. The physical strain of setting up camp and his keeping a perpetual smile of encouragement would be physically draining for him. He fortified himself for the experience with a couple of beers that evening at his local pub. The potent locally brewed Scottish Ale had settled his mind and he drifted off to sleep. For some reason that night, he tossed and turned as he slept. Unbidden, strange thoughts streamed through his head. He was on a roller-coaster ride on Sandeagh Mhor. The roller-coaster had only one car, with ten seats, and all the seats were filled with smiling young people, strapped in to prevent any injuries. He and his companions for the ride, defied gravity as the car climbed to the peak of the island, and hovered there for a second. Without warning, the car then shot down a vertical precipice heading straight towards the ocean. Just as he thought they were all heading for a watery grave, with a mind-popping change in direction, the car skimmed the sea with a soaking splash, and resumed its skyward journey. Before long, the car and its riders were once more poised at the summit of the mountain.

"This is fun!" said Justin to himself in the dream as he reached the peak once more, and waited for the plunge seaward. Only this time, instead of taking a path to the precipitous drop to the ocean, the car moved inland on its unseen rails, heading towards what appeared to be a flat and boring plain.

"Well, the first part was exciting, but now it's a pretty tame ride." Justin thought to himself.

Without any warning, a hole in the plateau opened up directly in front of the car and its occupants.

"This is more like it!" thought Justin. The car accelerated and plunged deep into the cavern that had opened so suddenly in front of them. The car and its occupants fell into what appeared to be a bottomless mineshaft. There were three women in the car, and they all screamed as they descended at high velocity towards an unseen floor.

The temperature of the air surrounding the car became unbearably hot. Unexpectedly, they made an impossibly tight turn to the right through a hole in the mineshaft wall. The car slowed somewhat, but once again accelerated. In front of them, they could see a massive cave, lined with what appeared to be stalactites and stalagmites. Then two massive black eyes opened above an opening directly in front of the coaster. The hole morphed into the gaping jaws of what appeared to be a giant gorilla, his head crowned with horns, now approaching rapidly directly in front of them. They were about to be swallowed by the giant beast! Even worse, as they rapidly approached his mouth, the gorilla spat droplets of saliva at them. The drops landed on the roller coaster car, but where they landed, they sizzled, and scarred the paintwork. The gorilla itself seemed to be covered with a coating of fire, and it smiled maliciously at them as it closed the massive teeth in its jaws on the car. Justin woke up, terrified, and bathed in sweat. He looked around his room, and pulled himself together.

"It was just a nightmare, thank God!" he said. "Too much beer before bedtime doesn't work for me." Promising himself he wouldn't do it again, he drifted off once again to an uneasy sleep.

Jim Reilly, Colin Gardner, Peter Wu and Bruce Devlin

ROUNDING OUT THE GROUP DESTINED FOR the journey to the remote isle was a team of four senior scouts from Harrow in northwest London. They had all gone to the same school, and joined the scout troop on the same day. The young men were participating in the Duke of Edinburgh award scheme. They had already undertaken some community services activities and now they were participating in the expedition phase, planning, training for and completing an adventurous journey in the UK. They were going for Gold, a week away living in the rough and walking at least 10 miles daily based on a route that they had pre-planned. The scheme rewarded initiative and bravery in young people. There was a fine line between bravery and stupidity, but the scheme participants generally undertook the exercises without harm.

Jim Reilly, Colin Gardner, Peter Wu and Bruce Devlin had chosen the Island of Sandeagh Mhor to undertake their outdoor adventure experience. They were physically fit, and had worked hard at their chosen sports. Jim and Peter excelled at tennis, and Colin and Bruce were both avid cricketers. They all came from comfortable upper middle class families and lived in homes in the up market leafy Harrow on the Hill village, close to the green common land of Harrow Park. Peter and Bruce had recently celebrated their seventeenth birthdays, and Jim and Colin were both approaching eighteen. They were all close friends, but Peter and Bruce had always seemed to Colin and Jim to be especially close, and had been so since they first met over four years ago. They all had the enthusiasm and optimism of youth, and now they were raring to go to the island to gain the experience they required for the award. Bruce and Peter were both gay, although neither had as yet come out to their friends or families. It would be their first trip together away from their homes and more importantly their parental supervision. The two had early on signaled their interest in sharing a tent together to their troop mates, and as their homosexuality had not been revealed to the rest of the scouts, no eyebrows were raised, or questions asked. Bruce and Peter were looking forward to some intimate time together in the quiet of the Sandeagh Mhor night. They too had translated the name. Big Sandy had a special meaning for them, and they had great fun talking about being with him in Scotland!

Jim and Colin had no particular expectations for Sandeagh Mhor. It was a great opportunity to get out of their parents hair, and to enjoy some freedom. The boys both loved camping. Jim secretly hoped that by completing the course he might get to meet the Duke of Edinburgh in person. Colin on the other hand was more interested in earning more badges. He was particularly proud of the rows of merit award badges he had personally sewn on each sleeve of his scout shirt.

"I'm looking forward to doing some cooking on the campfire." he declared.

"Just don't burn yourself like you did last time!" said Jim. As he spoke the words, he felt an odd sensation in the pit of his stomach. His bowels were gripped by an icy spasm, and he thought he was about to mess himself. Just as quickly as the weird sensation appeared, it vanished. He shook his head, and dismissed the feeling as indigestion.

The four had signed up for the trip to the relief of their parents. Summer with teenagers could be tough, and the boys were at an age where experimenting with life could lead to trouble. What harm could come their way camping on a remote island in Scotland? What harm indeed!

2 Assembly.

June 16th, 2012

ROBERT SCURRIED AROUND HIS SMALL APARTMENT putting together the basics for the trip to Scotland. He was savvy about living in a remote location. He packed waterproof outer garments into a rucksack, and many changes of clothing. He was well aware of the harsh reality about the weather on Sandeagh Mhor. One could not predict from day to day if the sun would shine or if it would rain, and the temperature could fluctuate considerably within a single afternoon. Still, for Robert that made the whole experience more interesting. Sandeagh Mhor sat in the Irish Sea on the fringes of the Atlantic Ocean, close to the northern Gulf Stream. Prevailing winds scoured the island from the west to east, and there was a considerable amount of moisture and moist air bathing the island daily. The Atlantic brewed up storms on a regular basis, and they were ferocious, often with gusts of wind topping fifty miles per hour. Of all those who would be venturing forth to the island, Robert and Justin were the only two who really understood just how tough conditions might get. Even in summer they might have to survive heavy rain, freezing winds, and eke out an existence for days on the rough terrain, if a return trip by boat was hampered by weather and heavy seas. Robert had earlier called Julia on her iPhone to let her know what might be in store for them, and what he viewed as suitable clothing for the journey. He strongly encouraged her to pack similar resilient outdoor garb. Since he already owned a dual skinned tent with a top notch waterproof and insulating canvas and nylon floor, he had opted not to use tents supplied by the Adventure Island Company. Despite his warnings, Julia had remained extremely enthusiastic about the trip when he had discussed it once again with her on the phone. Robert grinned quietly to himself as he anticipated removing Julia's outdoor gear in the warmth of the tent. A sleeping bag for two was part of the deal they had agreed. Holy Cow, that was going to be fun! He would most certainly keep her warm, in more ways than one. For light reading, he packed two recently acquired adventure novels, and a survival guide that he would give to Julia as a token of his affection. If things panned out the way he wanted, he did not believe he would have much time to read the books. He had read the survival guide from cover to cover, and he had noted with relief that it contained no instructions regarding methodology to prevent his lusty sexual advances. Truth be told, Robert really believed that Julia was chasing him, rather than the other way round. That was just fine with him, and he would almost certainly let her have her wicked way with him as often as she wanted.

Julia also recalled their earlier phone conversation. According to Peter, this would definitely not be the trip for her to show off her Prada shoes, and parade around with a Coach purse. Even her beloved iPhone would be of little use to her for keeping in touch with her friends. She'd be better off waving semaphore flags from the summit of the extinct volcano. So she reluctantly placed it in its charge cradle to await her return. Mostly she packed shorts and figure hugging slinky tops, but forewarned as she was about the fluctuations in temperature on the island, she also made sure she had some cashmere sweaters and a waterproof jacket.

Once her packing was complete, and her backpack had been filled with essentials for the trip, she slipped out of her apartment door, and made sure it was securely locked. It paid to be careful in an Edinburgh tenement apartment as crime was rife in the area, and the entrance stairway was enclosed and too easily accessible to strangers. She then descended the dark and worn sandstone tenement stairs with their faint but recognizable odor of urine, with her backpack slung over one shoulder. She exited the common stairwell, and made her way the short walk to Robert's block. When she arrived, she whistled piercingly up at his window on the second floor. After a minute, he raised the sash and looked out at her, grinning broadly.

"Are you coming?" she yelled up at him.

"Try to stop me, Jules. I'll be down in a minute." he shouted back to her, and closed the sash. He grabbed his bag, and opened the apartment door. He wrinkled his nose at the tang of stale urine permeating the stairwell. He double locked the door behind him and ran down the single flight of stairs.

Julia was waiting for him in the warm June sunshine, and as he exited through the peeling painted door of the tenement, she rushed up to him and gave him a firm hug and planted a passionate kiss on his lips.

"Mmmm, it's so good to see you again!" she breathed in his ear as he held her close.

"You only left my bed this morning, you harlot." he replied, and gave her buttocks a squeeze.

Julia stuck out her tongue and made a face. Robert broke loose from her embrace. Hand in hand, they walked the short distance to where he had parked his car. Julia was not sure if she liked the rather battered green Ford Escort he had owned since University days. She had doubts as to its roadworthiness, but Robert clearly loved the tattered vehicle. The couple unlinked hands and split up to enter the vehicle. Julia squeezed into the passenger seat, and Robert took the driver's side. Robert was always happy to drive. It was one of the few times in life that he actually felt in control of his life. The couple set off in the glorious June weather into the side streets that led towards the M8 motorway, the main route out of Edinburgh heading over to Glasgow and the west. The traffic was light, and it only took a brief time for the Escort to reach the motorway. Several hours later, with two short stops for fish and chips, and a bathroom break, they turned off the motorway and hit the A82, a small two lane highway that took a very scenic route up Loch Lomond. From there they headed south on the A83 along the coast. Through the sea mists Robert could make out the faint outline of the Island of Gigha out in the Irish Sea on their right hand side. He shivered with anticipation. Soon they too would be on their island. The road meandered over the hills towards Campbeltown. Their only companions on the road were errant sheep, and the occasional car travelling in the opposite direction. In places the road narrowed to a single lane, and in order to allow cars to move in both directions, there were occasional broadenings of the road, labeled as passing places on small triangular signs. As they came to the brow of a hill, they could see the grey blue waters of Campbeltown Loch, and the string of houses along its edge that made up the town itself.

After descending quite a steep hill, they reached the coast road. Quaint stone cottages lined the sides of the road, and eventually morphed into larger houses and hotels forming the center of the town. After a short cruise down the High Street, they arrived shortly at the Campbeltown pier. Robert had done his research online. Campbeltown was a very quaint old Scottish royal burgh town and fishing port. It consisted primarily of small stone cottages set irregularly in a half moon shape around the sea loch harbor. Built of local stone blocks, the houses were designed to survive the harshest Scottish winter weather. Every year the houses experienced the ravages of gale force wind driven corrosive salt spray generated by the crashing waves pounding against the pier and the concrete harbor walls keeping the ocean at bay. Robert and Julia looked around. A row of drab brown buildings interspersed with more brightly painted houses lined the Campbeltown sea loch front. There were still the key Inns on the main road that had catered to the thirsts of the Whisky distillers in their heyday. The White Hart, The Commercial and the Argyll were now somewhat faded from their formed glory, but on a Saturday evening they still attracted crowds to listen to local Scottish ballads and accordion music. The loch of course he knew to be directly connected with the Atlantic Ocean. Guarding the natural harbor was the small Island of Deval. The seafront was solid stone, with a concrete post and thick metal link chain fence to prevent the frequent drunkards stumbling from the local pubs from falling into the loch. Robert thought the town was very picturesque. He doubted though that he could live in Campbeltown as he was sure it would be quite monotonous after a while.

Leaving the faithful Escort in a small parking lot, they headed over to the rendezvous point indicated in the materials they had received from their online booking. As they approached the small stone building indicated on the map, a young good-looking muscular man was standing at its door carrying a small wooden placard on a stick. He gave them a friendly wave, and a broad and infectious grin.

"I'm Justin with the Adventure Island travel company." he said.

"Let me guess, you are Julia and Robert?"

"Right first time, Justin." grinned Robert in return. "We're pleased to meet you."

Justin thrust out his hand. As they all shook hands, Julia examined Justin. He was a solid looking sandy haired youth, with a toothy and shiny white smile. Robert noted that Justin had a very firm grip, and he appeared physically to be in great shape.

The logo on the Adventure Island placard depicted a tropical volcanic island with stereotypical palm trees, and a red cap of lava dripping from the pointed tip of the volcano. Under the picture, in bright red lettering, the words "Island Adventures" contrasted the greenery of the palms. Peter laughed at the image. Sandeagh Mhor would not miraculously resuscitate itself from its current state of volcanic extinction. In fact, it hadn't erupted for several million years. He knew that from the perspective of any volcanic eruption, Sandeagh Mhor was as dead as a volcanic dodo. Justin motioned for the couple to enter the small sparsely furnished office. Around the unfinished stone walls there were wooden chairs placed to accommodate around a dozen people. Robert glanced at his watch. It was just after three o'clock. Robert and Julia could see that they were the first to arrive. The trip to the island was scheduled for a four o'clock departure. Having nothing better to do they settled down to wait for the arrival of the other members of the group. While they waited, they chatted amiably with Justin.

"You folks entertain yourselves for a minute. I'd better get back outside and see if anyone else is here yet." said Justin, and left the couple sitting together.

Marcia Greenwood had travelled up that morning from London by British Airways commuter jet from Heathrow to Glasgow, where she had rented a car. Fortunately, although it had a nagging female voice, the global positioning unit in the car had given her perfect directions to get to the office by the pier on Campbeltown's main thoroughfare. She also was greeted by the same friendly wave and smile from Justin when she approached him.

"You must be Marcia. I'm Justin. I'll be your guide for the week."

She thought she could detect a certain twinkle in Justin's eye, and when he shook her hand, his grip was soft and almost caressing. His hand lingered in hers a touch longer than she had expected. "Very interesting." she thought to herself and flashed a very warm smile in his direction. A little harmless flirting might spice up her adventure a little.

"He is a damned handsome lad." she said to herself. "This could be an interesting week!"

Justin's eyes traced the curves of Marcia's body.

"Things are definitely looking up." he thought. "This lady from London has turned out to be a real treasure. Better than that, she looks like she wants a little fun. If I treat her right, I might just have a chance to get laid this week."

"I am going to give her the best time of her life." he decided. Not that he wouldn't look out for the others too, but she deserved something really special. Fighting the urge to take her by the hand, he ushered her into the small rough stone building, and pulled out a chair for her.

"Marcia, meet Robert and Julia. They are from Edinburgh. They are going to be your camp mates for the next week. I want us all to be best friends by the week's end." As he made the comment, Marcia's eyes locked with his.

"I'll let you all get acquainted." said Justin. "The others will be along soon."

He broke away, and returned to his point of vigil outside the office.

The three made polite conversation as they waited for the rest of the party to arrive.

The four scouts had travelled to Scotland using the troop's minivan, driven by their scoutmaster, George Givens. Smelly Givens they called him behind his back, indicating the odiferous result of his infrequent encounters with soap and water. He was a grey haired, slightly paunchy man who dressed in worn khaki pants and an ill-fitting large shiny checkered jacket with worn elbows. The scouts at one time or another had suspected that he might have pedophilic tendencies, what with his desire to be with young boys all the time.

However, if he was cut from that particular cloth, he had not to their knowledge made any advances to members of the troop, and so the boys kept their suspicions to themselves.

It had been a long and tiring trip, with infrequent breaks for food, and to service other bodily necessities at the motorway service stations that dotted the roadside at regular intervals. Traffic on the M6 motorway had been particularly bad, with stop and roll conditions outside Manchester. However, they cruised into Campbeltown on time. Despite the breezy June weather, the lads were heartened to see that the sea loch looked relatively calm. Peter had been known to get seasick practicing kayaking in the local swimming pool. Justin greeted them with a perfunctory "Hi guys, how's it going?"

The scout group smiled at him in unison.

"Who's who?" Justin asked.

The scouts in turn shook hands with Justin and introduced themselves. Justin turned to the scoutmaster, who was hovering in the background, obviously eager to be somewhere else. The scoutmaster responded immediately to the attention.

"I'm George Givens." he said.

"Pleased to meet you, George." replied Justin. "I was told you'd be coming." Justin noticed a not so subtle odor emanating from the scout master.

"I'm in charge of these young ruffians." said George.

"You have all the paperwork?" asked Justin. Justin kept upwind of George, who smelt like overripe cheese and old socks.

"Right here." he replied, and handed over some large envelopes stuffed with paper.

"I'm sure we'll not allow these lads to get into any trouble this week, but just in case." said Justin, and took the envelopes with him into the office.

As they were all under the official age of consent, the scouts had been instructed to bring forms signed by their parents consenting to Justin acting on the boys' behalf in their absence. Justin in turn had signed a consent form the parents had provided him stating that he was qualified to supervise the lads on the trip. He hoped he would live up to their expectations.

The boys followed Justin into the office. In the waiting area, the four scouts joined the young married couple and an extremely attractive woman who appeared to be in her late twenties or early thirties. The three of them looked up as the scouts entered.

"I'll let you folks introduce yourselves to each other." said Justin, and trotted outside to wait for the final couple to show up.

"Can I go now, Justin? I have a long drive back down south." said George. "You've got everything you need, and you can get hold of me or any of the boy's parents, if there are any problems. The contact details are all in the paperwork."

Steering clear of the miasmatic cloud surrounding the scout leader, and glad to hasten his departure, Justin replied.

"Yes. Thanks George. We've got all we need. Have a safe trip back."

"You too!" replied George.

Having fully discharged his duties, he clambered into the scout van and started the engine. A cloud of diesel fumes poured forth from the van's exhaust as George and the van rumbled along the car park, and out into the main street of Campbeltown. Justin waved a grateful farewell to him, and scanned the quiet coast road for any other vehicles.

Inside the building, Robert looked up at the new arrivals. They were identically dressed in drab olive scout uniforms, with shiny buckled belts, and each had a row of cloth badges decking their arms. Robert was pleased to note that most of the boys had merit badges confirming that they had passed courses that were well suited for survival in a tough environment. One of the scouts had a row of badges down each arm of his shirt. From top to bottom, Robert's eyes travelled down the merit badges awarded for camping, climbing, first aid and nature, with the cleanest and latest badge at the bottom being wilderness survival. That was good. These boys could look after themselves.

Robert walked over to the boys.

"You lads look pretty fit to me." said Robert. "Any chance of you coming jogging with me while we're on Sandeagh Mhor? I could do with the company, and a bit of competition."

"Well I'd really like that." said Jim. "What about you, guys? Oh, and by the way, I'm Jim."

"Wouldn't miss it. I'm Colin." said Colin, and the other two nodded in agreement.

"Peter Wu's the name." said Peter, and shook Robert and Julia's hands.

"And I'm Bruce." said Bruce. He gave the couple a rather limp handshake.

"What brings you lads here?" asked Robert.

"We are all badgeaholics. As you can see." replied Peter thrusting out an arm. "We like to collect as many as we can. We're on the Duke of Edinburgh award scheme." he continued.

"We like doing new stuff." said Jim, rather redundantly.

After brief introductions, they all sat back to wait for the final members of the expedition to arrive.

Martin and Sadie Hoff had taken advice from their friends. Having never been far afield from home, they had been unsure as to how to equip themselves for the trip. James and Elize Thackery had been on a honeymoon trip to the Isle of Skye in the spring and had been a great help. The two newlyweds had undoubtedly had a wonderful time on the romantic Scottish isle. Their only gripe had been that the weather was a little unpredictable. In fact it had been downright chilly. And it had rained almost every day, although the rain came mostly as short, sharp showers. When the clouds did clear though, the scenery had been magnificent, and they couldn't wait to return. Martin and Sadie had turned to each other after Jim and Elize had left.

"I bet their love kept them warm." said Sadie.

"That and the fact they probably didn't set foot outside their hotel much!" Martin stated, and they both laughed.

Martin and Sadie heeded their friend's advice. They took the time to pack some comfortable waterproof garments in addition to more traditional summer clothing. Both hoped though that the rainy scenario painted by their friends would not materialize for them. They used matching fluorescent orange backpacks to pack up their stuff, and strapped climbing boots to the lower bar of the frame of the backpack.

"Come on, Sade. It's time to go. Let's get out of here."

They bundled themselves and their luggage into their car, a blue hybrid Toyota Camry Martin had purchased when fuel prices had topped five pounds per gallon.

The trip by road from Huddersfield had been uneventful. Their only delay was from a minor traffic accident involving two small cars that had collided at a road junction. From the look of the cars, no serious damage had been done, but the owners were arguing fiercely as to who was at fault.

"I was reading about automobile insurance scams." said Martin. "You know, Sadie, the one where the car in front backs into the one behind, and the driver in front claims whiplash injury and stuff from the victim's insurance company?"

"You have a very vivid imagination Martin. From what I can see, the old man with a flat cap in the Saab was probably not paying attention. Look at his glasses. They're broken, and taped together with a band aid. The old guy is probably not fit to drive."

"You're probably right, Sadie. Come on up there. Get the road clear. We'll miss our boat!"

The inevitable tailback of vehicles had occurred as onlookers gawked at the spectacle. Fortunately, neither of the drivers appeared to have suffered any major injury. The police had arrived shortly afterwards, and had helped transfer the damaged vehicles to the side of the road. One of the officers directed the traffic to keep it moving, and a few minutes later, the congestion had cleared. The couple set off again, keeping slightly above the speed limit to make up the lost time. The remainder of the trip passed quickly and without incident, and Martin and Sadie rolled into Campbeltown around three thirty, pleased that they had not been late. They parked next to a battered green Ford Escort in the local public parking area. Martin opened the trunk of the Camry and they both shouldered their colorfully loud backpacks. They marched in unison, hand in hand, towards the Island Adventures office. Justin gave a sigh of relief as he saw them approach.

"I'm Justin. I work for Adventure Islands. " he said, for the fourth time that day.

His infectious grin was undiminished. It didn't bother him much that he had to repeat himself. In fact, he found it very difficult to keep a straight face. He had seen the two matching fluorescent backpacks that Martin and Sadie were carrying. In fact it was impossible to miss them. Both of the packs glowed brightly in the afternoon sunshine.

"Daft buggers." he muttered under his breath. "They'll frighten the sheep."

They all shook hands cordially.

"Martin and Sadie, I am so glad you made it on time. I'd hate to leave anyone behind."

He released his grip on Martin's hand, conscious that Martin could have crushed his own rather powerful grip like an eggshell. The man was clearly an athlete, and very powerfully built.

"Let me be the first to offer you both a very warm welcome to Campbeltown. We'll be setting off shortly on the boat trip to Sandeagh Mhor. By the way, you two couldn't have picked a better day for a sea trip. The ocean out there is as flat as a pancake, and we're having a relative heat wave for this part of the world. Come this way and meet the rest of the group."

Justin led the way into the office. Martin noticed that the thick oak door could do with a lick of paint.

"It had endured too many stormy winters days." he thought, "but that didn't mean it couldn't be kept a little better."

Another concern entered his mind.

"I hope they didn't skimp on the supplies for the trip." he thought. "We are in the hands of this outfit, good or bad."

When they were inside Justin closed the door behind them. He stood in front of the desk.

"All right gang, we're all here. Welcome to Island Adventures humble office! Now I've got you all together, there are a few formalities to complete."

Justin rummaged through the single drawer on the desk. He pulled out some papers.

"Please can you each take a disclaimer form, and sign and date it. We are going to a remote island. I'll do my utmost to make sure we all have a great time, but this is just a reminder to you to be careful. If you are injured while exploring on your own, and not with me, you must agree that you will not be entitled to any compensation. I'm sorry I have to bring this up, and I do want to assure you that I don't intend to lose anybody on this trip."

There were a few nervous laughs. For some reason, Justin's comment had caused a wave of unreasonable fear to flow through the assembled party. As one, they shrugged it off.

Justin gave them all a few minutes to read the disclaimer.

"Any questions?" he asked.

"Looks pretty straight forward to me." said Martin. "Here you go."

Justin tapped a small spoon against a glass coffee mug to attract their attention.

"Before we get going, here are some basic rules for the week. Firstly, the boat trip. No horsing around please. I don't want to fish anyone out of the ocean today. The weather is calm, so it should be an easy trip. We have life jackets and all the safety gear we'll need on the boat."

Justin noted Peter visibly relax, and wondered if he had a phobia about the boat trip.

"Secondly, the island itself. We are going on a camping holiday, but it is absolutely not a holiday camp. Just treat the island with respect and you'll all do just fine. There are some precautions you'll need to take when you are out hiking. Robert, you told me you like to jog. There are plenty places where you can do that, but some of the cliff paths have crumbling edges. I would strongly recommend you keep back from the edge. When it rains, the jogging paths can get very slippery. It's not fun to have to wait for a rescue from the mainland when you have a broken ankle. And I know you all read the brochure. There's a very good example in the sorry tale of the drunken sheep farmer. He probably had a bit too much to drink and took a wrong turn in the dark. I don't want any of you to copy his swift plunge to his death off one of the sea cliffs."

His advice brought mixed reactions from the group.

"I have a terrible fear of heights, don't I Martin?" stated Sadie. "You won't catch me anywhere near the cliffs."

"Don't you worry my love, I won't be jumping off any cliffs with you." said Martin, laughing at her.

"Don't make fun of me Martin. The thought of that brings me out in a sweat."

Indeed Sadie had just felt a ghastly premonition. Martin's words had generated a fearful picture in her mind of them both leaping off a cliff, hand in hand. The picture slowly faded and she relaxed. Sadie gave Martin an aggravated look. It warned him that any more mucking around and he'd be denied his conjugal rights that night.

Justin looked at Sadie, and noticed the brief spasm of fear crossing her face.

"We're on a pretty flat part of the island, and you don't need to go near the cliffs." he said reassuringly.

"Oh, and by the way, there is no booze allowed on the island. There is none there, and we're not bringing any with us." added Justin. "We want you all back in one piece, and fit as fiddles. You can sneak some alcohol over there if you want, but just don't let me see it. Are you all fine with the rules? "

"Aye, aye Cap'n." said Robert, a touch mockingly.

"All right. Just remember, it's my job to make sure you're all here to have fun!" concluded Justin.

He was interrupted by the chiming of the bell in the church steeple in the small town.

"It's four o'clock folks, time to be on our way. If you are all ready, then follow me."

He stood up, and moved to the door, pulling it open. The bright afternoon sunlight made them all squint after the gloom inside the office. In single file, they followed Justin through the door.

He led the way across the parking lot to the harbor. Robert inspected the harbor wall with interest. He peered over the edge. The surface below was oily calm, and littered with the occasional empty beer can. The iron guard railing had rusted a deep red color from being frequently covered in salt spray. It could certainly do with a coat of paint, he thought. The cement joining the large square stone blocks of the wall had also been eroded in places. The top of the wall had several rough edged craters a few inches deep and filled with rainwater. An old man was leaning against the guard railing staring out to sea. He was dressed in a shabby dark suit, with a grubby woolen neck scarf, and he had an unlit pipe clamped in his mouth. As he saw the boat party approach, he pulled the pipe from his mouth and frowned at them.

"I wouldn't be going to that island out there if I were you."

He spoke in a distinctly unpleasant and disapproving voice, heavy with a Scottish burr.

"That's the home of Fionn mac Cumhaill, and hisself hates to be disturbed."

"Finn McWhat?" asked Marcia.

"Take heed, young lady. That's a disrespectful tone. Dinna mock the ancients!" the old man growled.

He hawked a gob of phlegm and spat it on the ground.

The old man rubbed his stubbled chin thoughtfully and continued.

"Fionn mac Cumhaill is part of our Scottish heritage. He should be revered as a god. It was hisself, that scooped out Loch Neagh with his bare hands. He threw the gigantic boulders he pulled out of the earth into the sea. Tis well known that those rocks became the Isle of Man and the island of Rockall. And now he and his kin are sleeping on that island. Ye tread carefully now, and ye be sure not to disturb his rest!"

"Finn McCool?" said Justin, using the anglicized form of the name.

"Damn local idiot." he thought. "He's getting a kick out of trying to frighten my clients!"

He turned to the old man and took a belligerent pose.

"You stupid old man. That giant is nothing but an old wives tail. He supposedly built the Giant's Causeway so he wouldn't get his feet wet crossing from Ireland to Scotland. And you believe any of that? He supposedly had all the knowledge in the world in his head just because he sucked his thumb one time! What's so credible about that?"

"I've heard a bit about him too." said Robert. "According to the legend, Finn met up with a leprechaun named Finnegas and helped him fish in an Irish lough. Finnegas was hunting a very special fish. You might ask why was this fish so important to him? Well, it seems that the beast was an enchanted salmon. It was said to have all the knowledge of mankind stored in its body. Whoever ate the flesh of the fish would gain all that knowledge and enormous power. So Finn helped Finnegas catch his fish. Then he helped him to cook the unfortunate salmon in a frying pan. While the fish was grilling over the fire, Finn carelessly touched the sizzling salmon's skin, and burnt his thumb. He strikes me as a bit on an idiot, but that was before he ate the salmon. Anyhow, what would you and I do? We'd stick the thumb in our mouths to take away the pain. That's exactly what he did. He stuck his singed digit in his mouth to take away the pain, and purely by chance he swallowed a piece of the salmon's skin that was sticking to his fingertip. Finnegas got his fish, and all the knowledge of the world, and so did Finn. I'm not so sure how he became a giant, but Finn supposedly ended up immensely powerful and omniscient."

Justin felt that the whole episode was going too far. He'd have some frightened clients to deal with soon.

"Don't encourage the old sod. He's just the village drunk." said Justin to Robert, and glared at the old tramp. If looks could kill, the man would be lifeless on the ground.

Justin turned to Robert.

"You did a nice job of telling that old wives tale, Robert. But we don't want our lasses to be frightened by a drunken old man, do we?"

"I'm sure Marcia, Julia and Sadie are too smart to be taken in by such a story." said Martin. "Am I right ladies?"

"Well I don't believe in Santa Claus, and I sure as hell don't believe in giant Irishmen throwing boulders about. I am partial to a bit of salmon though." Marcia smiled at Justin and Robert. "Don't worry about us ladies. We can take good care of ourselves."

"Don't you be getting yourselves upset now." said Justin, trying to lighten the moment with a pitiful attempt at an Irish brogue.

"C'mon, we have a boat ride and some hard work to do to get our camp set up on the island this afternoon."

"Hang on a minute, Justin." said Julia, her curiosity piqued by the tale.

"I'm always intrigued by a good story, Robert. I love hearing about anything to do with mythology and ancient legends. Is there anything more you know about this giant? Did he really live on our island? I mean, why would he choose such a barren place to live? If it were me, I'd have picked Dublin or Cork or some other more pleasant place to live. That would make much more sense."

Robert nodded at her amiably.

"The only other part of the story I remember is that Finn choose a deep cavern somewhere under Dublin city for his home. He hasn't been seen in a long time, if at all. As Justin says, it's an old wives tale. Nothing to worry yourself about."

"Hey Justin, let's get going. I'm dying to meet Big Sandy!" said Robert.

"Come along folks." said Justin. "You can tell stories around the campfire all night long once we get ourselves sorted out. We've got to go now."

Turning on his heel, Justin headed along the harbor wall, towards a set of steps inset into the stone block wall. The stone steps were uneven, and pitted with holes. They led steeply down to the waterline.

As Justin and the others turned away from him, the old man muttered "Stupid youngsters. Think you know it all, you do. You mind my words. Just you mind my words!"

Justin walked down the steps with great care. He had seen at least one unfortunate person slip and stumble, falling swiftly into the deep and very chilly salty water below. Although no harm had been done, and the lady in question had easily been fished out of the water, her soaking wet clothing had a put a real dampener on her day and the start of her vacation. The lower steps were extremely slippery with slimy green seaweed and had a crusting of barnacles. Justin had also seen people slip on seaweed covered rocks, only to have the skin of their hands ripped open by the sharp shells of the barnacles.

"Please take care going down these steps." he said as a result. "It's pretty slippery, and the barnacles show no mercy."

A small boat was moored at the foot of the steps. It was gently bobbing up and down on the wavelets of the sea loch. The powerful Atlantic waves they would encounter when they travelled westward beyond the Mull were considerably attenuated by the positioning of the harbor. Campbeltown harbor faced eastwards. On the west side of the Mull, breakers pounded the rocky shore relentlessly, but here their ferocity was tamed. The Majority of the party had little sailing experience. Julia had been sailing on the Firth of Forth with Robert, but the scouts being based in Harrow had had little opportunity to sail. Marcia was also a landlubber. Martin and Sadie had accompanied some friends to a fabulous holiday on a three masted schooner sailing around the Greek islands, but that hardly counted.

"It looks pretty peaceful, doesn't it?" said Marcia to Justin, seeking reassurance. "The sea I mean."

"Doesn't get much better than today, Marcia. It's almost dead calm out there."

Justin and Robert were both excellent sailors and had been through many episodes of bad weather at sea. Both were well aware of what the Atlantic Ocean might do to them on a rough day. Of the two, Justin was the expert, having crewed and Captained racing vessels as the fought the fury of westerly winds, and enormous waves. He knew without doubt that once they had passed beyond the confines of the sea loch, they would be exposed to a little more swell. But today it was really quiet, in some ways too quiet. Normally he would have to face a variety of wave heights produced out in the open sea, and pushed eastwards and magnified by the prevailing westerly wind. Today at least though, the forecast was for mild swells only. That was a real blessing, because there were many such trips where he ended up swilling out the boat to remove vomit.

Peter eyed up the thirty four foot wooden boat with a little trepidation. She looked solid enough. She had a twin screw inboard diesel engine, and a covered area to prevent the worst of the sea spray and the elements from assaulting them. However, she really was not what he had been expecting to see. The boat looked somewhat ancient and frail to battle against the ravages of the Irish Sea.

"Are you really sure this boat will be able to stand up to the worst this ocean can throw at us, Justin? I mean, she's pretty small, and well, she looks a little frail?" he asked.

"This boat'll be around long after you and I have left this planet." Justin replied, mindful that swearing at his guest would not earn him any Brownie points. Stewart had instructed him well. "You may feel like saying it, but "bugger off you stupid dork" doesn't cut it when you have paying clients."

In order to put their minds at rest, Justin thought it would be helpful to share a bit more information with them about the boat. It would probably help them understand just how sturdy his boat was. He turned to Peter, and rattled out a few facts about the boat.

"She was built in the forties in one of the best shipyards in Scotland. Her heart is solid oak and she has a most beautiful frame. Don't let her fool you, she's a tough old cow. She has survived some unbelievably bad weather in her time, and always she and her crew came home in one piece. Caught her share of herring in her day too, but now she's retired from fishing and we use her as the local ferry out to the island."

Peter still looked doubtful.

"Come on Justin." he said. "Just what makes you so sure we are going to make it there and back in that tub?"

Peter was willing to assume that Justin knew what he was doing, although he seemed not much older than Peter. He still didn't trust the seaworthiness of the boat.

"She is definitely not a tub, Peter. Please don't insult the old lady." Justin answered firmly. "I have trusted my life to her on several occasions. But I understand that you might be nervous. Before I tell you more about her, take a close look at the boat."

Peter examined the ship more closely. She was painted a cheerful fire engine red, with a black stripe running along the waterline, and she was named the "Aquaholic".

"Damned tourists." Justin thought to himself. He was after all the expert sailor. "Why not leave the worrying to the folks who know what they are doing."

Still, in order to make his life easier, he could tease his cargo a little, then give them all a bit more of a background on the boat. After all, he had spent many, many hours with her, and knew all her intimate secrets.

"Peter has raised some concerns about this lovely lady in front of you. He is worried that she can't get us out to our island and back. I have no such concerns. Let me explain."

He caressed the hull of the boat with his hand.

"She is my one true love in life. I have known her for many years, and we have a special bond. Let me tell you a little bit more about her."

As he spoke he looked at each of the group in turn to ensure he had their full attention. They were all paying very close attention to his words.

"It is advisable to be honest, Justin." echoed in his head. These had been Stewart's parting words to him.

Justin assured them all again that they had nothing to worry about.

"This beautiful boat was born in the shipyards on the Clyde River over fifty years ago. In her early days," he said, with admiration in his voice, "she was a regular fishing boat. Quite frankly, she was the star of the local fleet. There were many days she would bring back several hundred pounds of herring to the harbor."

While he was talking, Justin noted out of the corner of his eye that Marcia was staring at him. He turned and smiled a deep and warm smile at her and she blushed.

Marcia had decided she was in love with Justin. He had a very melodious voice, and it tugged at her heart strings. She had seen small fishing boats many times on vacation trips with her parents to the tiny coastal towns in Cornwall. This craft was very similar to the small brightly colored fishing boats she knew from her childhood. She visualized a large net full of flapping silvery fish emerging from the water behind the boat, gulls circling overhead in search of a cheap meal if one of the fish escaped the net. Then she sniffed deeply, and her nostrils searched, in vain, for any tang of old fish coming from the boat. No matter, she still had the boat trip to the island, and a whole week with Justin.

Justin cleared his throat, snapping Marcia out of her reverie.

"Her original name was the "Second Bounty" in honor of her ability to take the local fishermen here in Campbeltown to the best mackerel and herring grounds in the area. They were, quite rightly, proud of her. Of course, she was retired a few years back, when her planking started to warp, and she had sprung a few leaks."

"That'll get their attention." Justin thought to himself, trying to mask a laugh.

Peter looked aghast at Justin.

"We're setting out to sea on a leaky retired tub? You've got to be kidding!"

Justin just smiled at him and shook his head. Maybe the joke had gone too far. It was time to put them out of their misery.

"Honestly Peter, you've got nothing to worry about." he suggested.

"Two years ago I was part of a youth project to restore the old tub. We rebuilt her from the keel up, and made sure she was totally seaworthy again. We all think we did a first rate job. As a result, I'd trust her with my life. Look, I don't think we'll have anything to worry about. Do you think I'd be sailing her if I didn't believe she can be everything we need?"

"I suppose not." said Peter, and backed off.

"That's enough of a history lesson. You'll all enjoy yourselves on Sandeagh Mhor, and this veteran will get us there and back. All right, it's time for us to get going."

Justin leapt aboard the boat, and took a broad, rough plank of wood from the stern of the boat and bridged the small gap between the stone steps and the boat with it.

"One at a time, please," he asked, "and if you need to, take my hand as you come aboard."

It was a pleasant summer afternoon and the seven young men and three attractive women embarked enthusiastically for the short boat trip to Sandeagh Mhor to commence their adventure.

The boat floated quite steadily in the calm waters of the harbor. Justin gently aided each member of the party with a guiding hand as they walked slowly and carefully along the short distance separating the boat and the harbor wall. One-by-one, they jumped off the plank and onto the raised locker along the edges of rear of the boat.

"This is the first time I've walked the plank." joked Martin. "I hope it won't be the last."

The others laughed, unaware of the predictive significance of his words.

Once onboard, they found that the fixed teak wooden bench seating provided for them was surprisingly comfortable. There was a large brass ship's wheel up front, and some modern navigation equipment stacked in a rack. The satellite navigation system seemed somewhat incongruous to Martin as he examined the wooden planking and brass fittings, relics of an older age of seamanship. Once they all were comfortably seated, Justin pulled the plank onboard and stowed it aft. He then released the mooring rope, and started the engine. The diesel engine sputtered noisily to life, and belched a huge cloud of black soot into the clean sea air. After a few moments of stuttering, the engine rhythm became a regular deep pulsation. Once the engine was running smoothly, Justin turned the wheel and pointed the boat toward the center of the sea loch. The Aquaholic gently cruised out of the harbor, and immediately started to rise and fall with the gentle swell. The sea was a greenish blue color, and a little murky, so nothing much below the surface could be seen.

"It'll take us just over an hour to get to the island." Justin told them. "We're all pretty lucky today. The sea is really calm."

"Make yourselves comfortable. Anyone for some bottled water or a can of soda?"

He opened the cooler built into the shelving at the front of the boat. Marcia grabbed a diet soda from the ice chest, and the others followed suit.

"Island Adventures is based on customer service. We know how to look after our clients. We want you all to enjoy yourselves." said Justin. "It probably comes as no surprise to you. We've done this trip once or twice before."

What Justin did not share with the others was that this was indeed the first trip with clients to Sandeagh Mhor that he had supervised. He didn't think it mattered. He had visited the island earlier in the year with Stuart to familiarize himself with the topography and the campsite, but never as team leader.

"If you are anything like the rest of the folks I've had with me on these trips, I know some of you might feel a little seasick on the boat today. Don't worry though, I have the best meds. These little green tablets should do the trick for you."

He pulled out a small clear glass bottle of antihistamine tablets.

"These beauties are the minty fresh melt-in-the-mouth variety. They should take care of any seasickness before it starts. They might make you a bit sleepy though, but I reckon that's better than barfing."

Justin passed around the bottle.

"OK guys." said Jim, who had taken on the role as unofficial leader of the group of scouts.

"We agreed we'd all do this together, and that means the motion sickness stuff too."

The scouts popped the antiemetic tablets into their mouths. It would be better to put up with a little drowsiness than to have to stand the smell of puke. They were all well aware of Peter's ability to throw up in a swimming pool if it got too rough.

"I'll get by. No need to worry about me." he had assured them, as they travelled northward in the van.

Jim and the others didn't buy any of it.

"That's enough of your crap, Pete." he said. "You could vomit just looking at a boat. Remember, this is going to be a shared experience for us. What one does, we all do. Unless of course it's something really stupid. So let's start this trip off right. What do you say?"

"Didn't the musketeers have a saying for that?" asked Bruce. "All for one and one for all!"

"You want us to be musketeers? We don't have muskets. We don't serve a king. " said Jim.

"But we want to impress a Duke, and we do have knives." countered Bruce.

"All right, we'll be the knivesketeers." said Jim. "I know it's a bit uncool, but let's do it! We can still do the all for one thing. All together now."

Feeling a bit daft, but happy to work as a team, in unison, the four lads shouted: "All for one, and one for all!"

"Now that is cool." thought Peter. "A bit more of this team building and the four of us can rule the world. Well maybe England. Just like the musketeers, we'll live, die and win together too." The dying bit didn't really appeal to him, but just like the Dumas denizens it would be part of the knivesketeers credo too.

After a few minutes, Jim opened his mouth in a huge theatrical yawn.

"I could do with a nap." he said. "It's those damned tablets!" He placed his head in his arms, and shortly thereafter commenced snoring softly.

As she ploughed quickly through the foam, the boat rocked gently, lulling her occupants to doze or daydream. The waves were gentle, and that afternoon, the sea was at its most benign. A few lazy looking black headed gulls drifted expectantly near the boat. They soon discovered that although the boat had a long fish producing history, fishing was not on the agenda today for this crew, and they wheeled away, crying out to each other, as they moved off to better hunting grounds. The coastline receded rapidly behind the wake from the boat, and soon all that could be seen of the mainland were the tips of the hills of surrounding the town of Campbeltown on the horizon. The sun hung softly in the air, its heat muted by the breeze generated by the boat's forward motion, and the constant currents of air cooled by surface contact with the chilly waters of the Atlantic.

As their journey progressed, Justin relayed the boat's position to the coastguard at fifteen minute intervals. He also took the time, as he had been instructed, to call his boss. The conversation was brief, and provided Stewart with an update on the progress of the journey, and the state of their clients. When they had arrived at the island, Justin would send a final notification to the coastguard and Stewart that they were all safely ashore and were in great shape.

During the last thirty minutes of the journey, the dome of Sandeagh Mhor Island could be seen rising from the waves. In the distance, it seemed somehow soft and mellow, the slight sea mist obscuring its harsher features. However, as the boat neared the island's tip, the tall columnar lava columns of the cliff face stood out like teeth in a skull, giving them the impression of an inverted jawbone of some gigantic mammal. The peak itself was majestic and despite the softness imparted by sea mist, had a definite intimidating appearance. Its resemblance to a hunched gorilla was startling. The angle of the afternoon sun created two shadowy areas on the rocks that could be easily mistaken for eye sockets. Sparse grasses and bent and twisted bushes were scattered across the rocky slopes of the peak where windblown sand had combined with sea bird guano to form pockets of fertile soil. The plateau above the cliffs could not be seen from their low lying vantage point, but from a distance it appeared to have a benign, almost flat surface, gently sloping from one end of the island at sea level to the shoulders of the volcanic plug. The sky remained impressively blue as a backdrop to the picture, and Justin could sense a rising tide of excitement in his team. Martin and Robert let out whoops of joy as the boat eventually bumped into the crude stone jetty reaching out like a parched tongue from the rocky foreshore. A rusted heavy metal ring was cemented into the surface of a particularly large rock near the seaward tip of the pier. Justin dexterously leaped the narrow gap between boat and shore to land on its surface, clutching a tether in his hands. He picked up the ochre colored ring and tied the anchor rope to it with nimble fingers. His long hours of practice had not only perfected his knot tying skills, but had also made him extremely fast at the task. Once the boat was securely tied to the anchor point, Justin prepared to disembark his passengers. Once again, Justin bridged the distance from the boat to the pier with the plank. It perched somewhat precariously across the gap. In contrast to the mirror calm in Campbeltown harbor, this time the waves moved the plank with a slight rocking motion. Despite the ocean swells pounding into the westward side of the jetty, and losing most of their energy, they still had enough power as they washed around the large boulders at the tip to create an unstable undulation on the boat deck.

"Come on!" Justin yelled. "We haven't got all day!"

He busied himself steadying the plank as much as he could. There was some stirring in the boat, but the boy scouts were the last to stand up. Peter had nodded off as the boat had approached land.

"At least we didn't have to deal with him throwing up." said Bruce, as he made his way unsteadily towards the plank.

"Come on you adventurous bunch, we have a lot to do before it gets dark." said Justin. "Get your butts over here."

"He's a goddam cheerleader." said Martin to Sadie. "All he needs are pom poms and a skirt."

"Shut up Martin! He's got more oomph than you do."

"Fancy him, do you?" he teased her.

"Shut up Martin."

As before, Justin helped each of them clamber across the plank onto the jetty and they clustered together on the uneven rocky surface without mishap. His next task was to bring the boxes and sacks of provisions and supplies from off the boat. There were several large boxes of tinned food, and two sacks of potatoes. He laid their week's worth of food in a large pile on the jetty, and grinned mischievously as he handed out orders to the scouts to shoulder a burden each. They looked pretty fit, and he was sure they would take orders.

"You lads are young and fit. I don't think you'll mind doing the lion's share of shifting this stuff up to the camp. Any problems with that?"

"Na, we can do that, it's a piece of cake." said Jim, and shouldered a sack of potatoes. The other scouts followed his lead, carting assorted boxes of tinned food and fresh vegetables up the mountain.

Once he had loaded up the scouts with various boxes and sacks, Justin divided the remaining packages equally amongst the couples. Despite having the feeling that they were being used as human pack-horses, there were no protests from anyone.

"Why don't we have any water in our supplies, Justin?" asked Marcia. She had taken note of their fodder for the week, and hoped that Justin could cook.

"The island is blessed with a plentiful water supply." Justin explained. "There is a stream on the island that is topped up with snowmelt in the spring and by rain storms all year round. There are many areas of the island which are basically bog land. You'll be able to bathe in one of the small ponds scattered over the island's plateau, and most are interconnected by fresh water rivulets. A few years back, Island Adventures had the streams and ponds tested for bacterial contamination. Luckily for us, there were no pathogens detected, and we confirmed that the local water is totally safe to drink. Any other questions?"

There were none. Justin nodded with satisfaction.

"It makes our life much easier really. All we have to do is bring canned and dried rations, and a cooking stove. We will be totally self sufficient for the whole week. And by the way, I love campfire cooking. You'll all eat well, believe me!"

A path of sorts ran gently upwards along the beginnings of the plateau, and the party snaked up the gentle slope towards the camp site.

Island Adventures had a limited budget for the basic consumable supplies, but one area where Stewart and his team had excelled was in the provision of the best in outdoor camping gear. Justin had brought along a tent for each camper, with the larger ones reserved for the couples and the scouts.

While not up to Seyntex military standards, the tents were of the highest quality fabric, and of extremely high durability. There was no need in Stewart's mind for his tents to be capable of withstanding bullets. However, they had been constructed using TurtleSkin puncture-proof technology, and were designed to thwart the worst weather that Scotland could offer. Robert and Julia declined the offer of a tent having brought their own. The one remaining nylon bag containing the redundant tent was stowed by Justin back on the boat. After a hike of a few hundred yards uphill, the campers-to-be reached a clearing in the middle of the plateau, with a circle of stones at its center blackened by previous campfires.

"This must be the campsite." said Julia.

"Right first time, Julia." said Justin, and he supervised the unloading of the supplies from the weary shoulders of the scouts and the couples. It took two trips up the path from the jetty to bring all the supplies and the camping gear to the camping ground. Justin rubbed his hands together, satisfied with their progress.

Somehow Marcia had escaped from having a major burden to bring up the path.

"That's favoritism! I'll bet these two have something going by the end of this trip." muttered Julia. Martin looked at Marcia's beckoning curves amusedly, and then nodded in agreement.

By the time the sun was settling along the western seascape, the tents had been erected to Justin's rigorous standards, and brushwood had been collected by the scouts to make a fire. Marcia wished she had had the forethought to bring marshmallows for toasting over the blazing logs.

"Got any marshmallows?" she asked Justin hopefully.

"As a matter of fact I do." he replied, and pulled out a bagful of the pink and white confectionary cubes. He handed Marcia the bag, and smiled at her.

"Sweet things for a sweet lady." he said. "Leave me a few will you?"

Martin rolled his eyes skyward.

"He could be a bit more subtle about it." he whispered to Julia.

The excitement of reaching their home for a week was beginning to settle a little. Now was the opportunity to plan out their evening. Robert and Martin joked about taking the boat back to the mainland to search for the nearest pub. The scouting group set off to explore the plateau. As they went about their ways, Justin regarded each of the party thoughtfully, attempting to size up where trouble might emerge, and who would be the first one to cause him some grief. He couldn't put his finger on why he thought it, but he believed it quite likely that the scouts would somehow get into trouble. They had way too much confidence, and lacked the maturity and common sense of the others. However, the tranquil scene surrounding him did appear idyllic, and neither he, nor any of the adventurers had any immediate sense that there might be trouble brewing. Justin cautioned the scouts to be back in the camp before full darkness fell. There were flashlights available, but the chances of stumbling off a path and into ankle wrenching rocks were really high after twilight faded, and besides, he had no desire to waste the flashlight batteries without due cause.

The four boys set off up the rocky pathway at a good pace. They were determined to climb the peak before nightfall. As they climbed, they egged each other on to go faster, to push each other to their limits.

"Slow down." said Jim after a while. While all the scouts were fit, he was now out of breath.

"Wimp." said Colin amusedly. "You're holding us up."

"Colin, mind your tongue. A chain is only as strong as its weakest link. And right now, you might be that link. We support each other, dummy."

As unelected leader, Jim delighted in attempting to assert his authority.

To be fair to the supposed weakest member of their group, they all slowed to a fast walking pace. As they neared the rocky cliff path leading to the summit, Jim called out.

"See that hole in the rocks over there? It looks like a mineshaft. I didn't know there was any mining on this island."

The four crowded round the rough circular opening. It was deep, about eight feet wide, and they could not see the bottom of the pit. From the rough edges of the shaft, it was apparent that the opening was natural, most likely the result of erosion from below. Faintly, they could hear the sounds of waves percolating up from below.

"It must've been caused by a rock fall. The sea probably eroded a cave right under us." said Bruce. He gathered up a small rock and flung it into the opening. They heard it clatter noisily down the rocky walls of the pit, ending with a slight splash as it hit the bottom.

"You hit the nail on the head." said Peter, and he too threw a rock down the shaft.

They all took turns throwing rocks of various sizes into the pit.

"Let's push a real boulder down there." said Jim, and they all looked around for a suitable sized rock. Over towards the rocky cliff of the summit peak, a promising candidate sat about twelve feet away from the pit. It was almost four feet wide, smoothed by the elements and dappled with moss and lichen. It appeared to have rolled down from the cliff after winter ice had shattered its tenuous hold on the rock face. Using all their strength, the four young men leaned shoulder to shoulder in an effort to push the large rock into the pit.

"We need some leverage to get this monster rolling towards the hole." said Jim. He looked around for a tree branch or some other pole like object to act as a lever. Peter placed a flat rock next to the boulder. By pure chance, Jim found a piece of old two by four planking in a gulley close by.

"This will do the trick." he said. "It must've been left behind by that crazy sheep farmer."

He placed the tip of the plank under the rock and slid it on top of the flat stone. The four leaned on the plank, the flat rock acting as a fulcrum. Their combined weight shifted the stone. It moved hesitantly towards the pit. Slowly they inched the rock closer to the gaping hole. They had to replace the flat fulcrum rock twice as the boulder inched nearer to the hole. With a final heave the rock reached the edge of the pit. They all dug their heels into the turf, and placing their shoulders against the boulder, they gave a final heave. Success! The boys had the satisfaction of watching their missile entering the dark opening. It crashed and smashed its way down the tunnel, and bounced at an odd angle off a spur of rock, entering what looked like the entrance to a side tunnel in the rock wall. Peter thought he heard a distant grunt as the boulder disappeared into the earth.

"Did you hear anything?" Peter asked the others. "I thought I heard something."

"You heard something?" said Jim. "Like what?"

"I don't know what I thought I heard."

"It was just the sound of the rock bouncing off the walls of the pit?" suggested Colin.

"I guess so." said Peter. He was sure he had heard the noise of an animal deep below, but there wouldn't be any animals in this cave on the island, would there? He shrugged it off.

"That was teamwork, guys! High five!" he yelled.

The four scouts raised their hands, and slapped them together.

"Yes! We are a team!" said Bruce, elated by their success.

"Come on guys. Let's get back to the camp. It's getting dark. We've had enough fun for the evening." said Jim.

"Perhaps." said Colin under his breath.

The boys turned around and moved away from the pit, down the path towards the encampment. If they had taken the time to look back, and look downwards into the darkening stone orifice, they would have been surprised to see a faint ghostly orange glow deep in the dark depths of the cavern.

Back at the encampment, Robert and Julia sat on a blanket. They had found the perfect spot, supported by the wiry tufts of a clump of heather beneath them. They had also positioned themselves close to the fire for warmth, and now they sat together, arms around each other's shoulders. Both stared dreamily at the sparks drifting skyward on the thin smoke issuing from the blazing logs. Martin and Sadie had also positioned their blanket on the ubiquitous heather. Now they held hands and whispered to each other. Marcia, feeling left out, kept making sidelong glances at Justin, all the while pushing her blond hair back behind her ears. Such subtlety did not escape Justin's keen eyes, and when he glanced in her direction, this time she was the one who rewarded him with a broad smile.

"I can play this game too." he thought to himself and he returned the smile, turning up the heat a notch with a not so subtle wink. There was a powerful sexual tension developing between the two single campers.

The evening slowly and peacefully drifted onwards, and the sun finally set behind a distant bank of clouds. The golden fringe of the clouds faded to pink then to grey as the sun sank below the horizon.

"I think I'm going to call it a day." said Justin, and picked himself up from the boulder where he had been sitting. He yawned.

"We can have a lie in tomorrow. At least until six. The seagulls start shrieking around then."

Julia and Robert walked arm-in-arm towards their tent. Marcia sidled over to Justin, and whispered something in his ear. Justin snickered, and slapped her rump provocatively.

Suddenly, a loud female scream dissolved the peace of the night. Startled, Justin, Marcia, Julia and Robert all paused in their tracks.

"What the hell was that?" asked Julia.

They all looked at Justin, as if he might have the answer, which he clearly did not. Justin turned and ran with powerful strides towards the source of the sound.

"I'll bet some damned Boy Scout adventurer has fallen into a gorse bush." he muttered to himself.

"You folks stay here. If I need any help, I'll yell."

The origin of the scream was from within the camp. It had come from a tent Justin had helped erect earlier in the day. He remembered which couple had chosen that tent. It belonged to the Hoff's.

Reaching the tent, Justin thrust aside the tent flap. He thought he would see some bug attacking Sadie. After all, the island's fauna was limited to sheep, seagulls, and occasional spiders. But something had caused the commotion in the tent. As his eyes adjusted to the dim light in the tent, he was intrigued to see that Martin and Sadie were locked together in a very compromising position. Unnoticed by the others, the couple had crept giggling into their tent to satisfy their lust. Sadie lay on her back, her legs splayed open. Martin was servicing his wife's needs. Sadie's head was thrown back, revealing her soft white throat, and she was panting noisily. The shriek that the whole camp had heard was indeed from Sadie. But it was obviously not a scream of pain. Martin had worked his male magic, and Sadie had achieved an explosive orgasm. Panting, the couple, in some embarrassment, separated and looked up startled at Justin. They scrambled to cover themselves up with the sleeping bags.

Justin blushed.

"Sorry guys. We heard a scream and thought maybe one of you was in trouble. I didn't mean to disturb your, ah, rest." he said, his face scarlet.

He quickly turned to leave. Pulling aside the tent flap once more, he stepped outside and then closed it behind him. Moving at a more leisurely pace, he returned to the fireside and the questioning looks on the anxious faces that were flickering orange and red in the glow of the fire.

"It's a false alarm." he said, with a mischievous grin on his face. "Mrs. Hoff had an encounter with a, er, snake in the tent".

Marcia and Julia turned pale.

"Snakes?" they asked. Both had a morbid fear of reptiles.

"Just kidding guys." Justin replied. "There are no snakes on this island, least not the kind you were thinking of."

He picked up the first aid pack and returned it to its customary home in his tent. Whistling a Scottish ditty, Justin made his way back to the fire and warmed his hands over the blaze.

As he did so, the four boy scouts materialized out of the gloom, walking closely together in single file down the path. As they entered the camp, they crowded round the fire to warm themselves. They were all grinning broadly.

"That was fun." said Peter, holding his hands over the flames.

"Woo-hoo, we are the greatest, you guys!" said Peter.

"Perhaps we can explore the cave tomorrow?" said Colin, his eyes wide with excitement. "There's probably an entrance down near the cliff base."

"Better make sure there are no stupid scouts up top though. I wouldn't like to get hit by a boulder down there!" said Peter.

"I'm ready to call it a day." said Bruce with a yawn. "We all put in a lot of energy today."

"Me too." answered Peter.

The four scouts split off in two pairs and walked quietly to their respective tents.

An hour later, as the fire died and the full moon lit the landscape with a ghostly glow, all that could be heard in the darkness was snoring from the tents, and a whistling tone as a growing wind from the west caused the guy ropes of the tents to vibrate. The cool breeze ruffled the nylon seams along the ridges of the tents, and added a fluttering vibration to it.

The weather forecast for that night had been for calm weather, and cool but pleasant temperatures. But the weather off the west coast of Scotland can be extremely unpredictable. Slowly but surely, the wind gained in speed and intensity, with scudding clouds now racing over the island, from time to time obscuring the moon. Unknown to the campers below, the clouds were the silent harbingers of some severe weather that would shortly be moving into the area.

3. The First Disappearance

June 17th, 2:03 am

ROUND TWO O'CLOCK IN THE MORNING, the moon was totally obscured behind thick clouds, creating pitch black conditions in the camp. The fire had died, leaving only a few gleaming embers, and casting almost no light on the tents or the campsite.

Out of the blackness, a second scream pierced the air. Unlike Sadie Hoff's climactic outburst earlier in the evening, this was clearly not a scream of passion. It was unholy, a horrible shrieking and wailing of pain and fear that rose and fell before rising to a crescendo, then abruptly ending in silence. The intensity of the sound, and its soul destroying hopelessness, split the night apart. The screaming had terminated swiftly, but not before it had penetrated deep into the brain of every person in the camp. Almost as one, the frightened faces of the campers peered out of their tents.

Justin disentangled himself from Marcia. She had quietly joined him, giggling softly, after all others had turned in for the night. She had wanted to get to know him better, and she had not been disappointed. He could do particularly delightful things with his tongue, and as a result she had been totally sated.

Justin pulled on a pair of jeans in the dark, then rummaging through his rucksack, he found a flashlight. He scouted round quickly once outside, flashlight in hand, to seek out the source of the scream. He checked first on the post coital Hoff's. They were bleary eyed through lack of sleep, but unharmed. Next he checked on the scouts in their tents. He noted with passing interest that Peter and Bruce were both naked and had been sharing one sleeping bag. There would be time to explore that conundrum later. Then checking inside Robert and Julia's tent, he found it completely empty. There was evidence that they had been sleeping there, but they weren't there now. The sleeping bags were rumpled and disheveled, but of the couple there was no sign.

Feeling that there was not much he could do in the darkness, but determined to try, Justin made an exploratory search around the campsite. He yelled out Robert and Julia's names repeatedly as he searched. There was no response. At length, when he had determined that they were not in the camping area, he moved up the path on the slope towards the peak. There was no sign of Robert or Julia there either. As he moved upward, glancing around, and finding it difficult to concentrate on the path in front of him, he tripped over a rocky outcrop. He stumbled, and just caught himself before he fell. It was too dangerous in these conditions to do a broader search, he decided. Still, Justin thought he'd take a look around the path leading towards the pier. Passing back through the camp, he hit the stony trail towards the landing area. He trod carefully now, the beam of the flashlight cutting through the raindrops now descending from the leaden sky, and illuminating his path. He yelled loudly.

"Julia!"

"Robert!"

Once again there were no replies. At least, Justin thought, there had been no more screams. That could be good, or bad. On reaching the stony jetty, he turned around. Of Julia and Robert, there was no sign.

Once again, he made his way carefully back to the camp.

On his arrival there, he encountered the sleep-befuddled campers, huddling together in a group. They all looked at him questioningly.

"We've lost Julia and Robert." Justin said. "They are not in their tent, and I couldn't find any trace of them on the path up the plateau or down by the jetty." he explained. "I looked around as much as I could, given that it is pitch black out there, and I almost broke a leg navigating the rocks on the path, but I couldn't see them anywhere. Look. I'm sure nothing serious has happened to them. We know they're out there somewhere and we'll need to find them soon. The weather this time of year is relatively mild, but there's always a danger of exposure, especially if somebody is injured. It's too dangerous for us to go exploring now."

He stopped, and ran his fingers through his wet hair. Then he continued.

"It'll be light soon. Dawn breaks around five am this time of year. I think we should wait until dawn, and then we can find them more easily."

Bruce looked at Justin questioningly.

"What could happen to anyone on this island, Justin? That scream was real, and I don't know about you, but it chilled me to the bone."

"I don't know Bruce. Maybe Julia or Robert tripped over a rock on the path. I almost broke a leg doing that just now. Jim and Peter, you can climb the peak when it gets light. I'm sure we'll find them then. You know, they probably went off to have some quiet time alone. The tent walls are too thin to stop much noise! And they, ah, were in the mood to make some noise. If they are in any trouble, if I were in their shoes, I would likely lay low until dawn. If we all head out now as a search party, we might have additional people getting lost. That path is extremely slippery and it would be really easy for one of us to sprain an ankle. Look, I'm sure they are fine. It's just that they can't hear me calling with this weather."

As if to answer him, a howling gust of wind blew through the members of the party, ruffling hair and clothing. A spattering of rain accompanied the icy blast causing them all to shiver. Justin had an alarm watch strapped to his wrist, and he set the alarm for two hours later.

"Look we're all tired, and we'll search for Julia and Robert at first light. I've set my alarm and I'll rouse you all when I need you. Get some sleep." he ordered.

"But that scream sounded close and so full of pain." Marcia said, almost hysterical. "It sounded like it came from the mountain."

"Don't worry, we'll find Julia and Robert at first light." repeated Justin. "That's only two hours from now. Now please can you all try to get some sleep? I'm sure we'll find them in the daylight, and we can laugh about it all tomorrow night."

Reluctantly, they all returned to their tents. With the exception of the whistling of the rising wind, an uneasy peace returned to the campsite and its occupants.

4. Robert and Julia:

June 16th, 2012 11:55 Pm

OBERT AND JULIA HAD RETIRED TO their tent shortly after the Hoff's. They had quietly disrobed and clambered into a single sleeping bag. Together they had enjoyed passionate and fulfilling sex, but to avoid another embarrassing encounter with Justin, they had managed with difficulty to keep their lovemaking silent. Wrapped in each other's arms, and bathed with sweat, they had both drifted into a deep sleep. All was quiet. Towards midnight, they both awoke suddenly in the pitch darkness. Julia sat up, and gathered the sleeping bag around her naked body. She was trembling. Robert also sat up, and put his arm protectively around her shoulders.

"Jules, what's wrong?"

"It was awful! I had a terrible nightmare, Rob. It was really, really bad."

"What happened?" Robert was on edge. "Tell me all about it."

"Well, I...I don't want to talk about it."

"Oh, go on Julia, you can talk to me."

"Oh, well, all right then. But it was so vivid! I was on the path leading up to the plateau with you. I was feeling really hot and as we climbed over a ridge, there was a sinister orange glow ahead of us. As we walked upwards towards the glow, I felt like my skin was on fire. I looked down at my arms. The hairs on my arms were starting to shrivel up with the heat. Worse than that, I felt an intense pain in my legs. When I looked down at them I could see them turning black and starting to smolder! The pain intensified with each step I took, and it became unbearable. Oh God, it was unbelievably bad. I turned to you for help. You were sweating profusely, and I could see a deep fear in your eyes. I put my hand on your cheek. You felt like you were burning up. When I looked more closely at you, I saw the skin on your arms blistering and then the burnt skin started to peel off your arms. You started to scream. Ahead of us, the orange glow increased in intensity until it became unbearably bright. There was a flaming figure in the center of the glow, and it strode towards us. I tried to look away but I couldn't! I couldn't move. As the figure in the fireball came closer, it took the form of a giant ape, at least thirty feet tall. But it looked unlike any ape I had previously seen. It had flickering flames all over its body instead of a hairy pelt. And it had horns! It came closer and closer. The thing was radiating so much heat that I couldn't stand it. And then it reached out and touched me. The pain was excruciating! I screamed, and then I woke up. Oh Robert, it was so real, and...and please, I don't want to talk about it anymore."

Robert just looked at Julia, beads of sweat covering his face. He too was shaking.

"Jules, this is uncanny. You won't believe me, but I was with you up there on the path tonight. No, it can't be. It was a dream. But I was there. You were there with me. " he said.

"It was just as you described. I was on the path leading up to the peak. You were there and we were holding hands. I saw the orange fireball, and when it came closer, it looked like a giant fiery ape, but it had horns, and eyes that pierced my skull. I felt like I was on fire. I suffered the same burning sensation. When the beast came close, I couldn't move. I wanted to protect you, but something it did to me kept me from moving. The beast reached out to us. I felt its paws touching me on the arm, its fiery skin scalded me, and I was in agony. I turned to look at you. Your face was contorted with the pain. Julia, I watched your skin peeling off you in folds as the creature scorched you with its flaming breath. You screamed, and then I woke up. Oh my God, what a horrible coincidence!"

Julia was dumbstruck. "You saw it too? How can that be? You're making it up!"

Robert shook his head slowly. "No Jules. I saw that beast and I felt the heat pouring off its skin. I felt my body burning. And that monster. I couldn't look away from it. It had coal black eyes that stared right into my soul. I couldn't make that up now, could I? Now do you believe me? "

"Yes", whispered Julia, "His eyes. His eyes captivated me. I couldn't move! "

"Jules, I don't feel so good right now." Robert said. His face had turned beetroot red, and he was dripping salty drops of sweat onto the sleeping bag on the floor of the tent. "Let's go outside for a moment to cool off?"

"All right. I don't feel great either, Rob. Maybe some fresh air will clear my head."

Robert undid the zip on the tent flap. A cool breeze fanned them as they stood, naked and sweaty together.

"Ahhh." The cooling breeze on her face made Julia felt so much better.

"That feels so good. I was suffocating in that tent. The night air will help both of us dry off this sweat. Come on, let's go up the mountain. There'll be nobody around to see us. Besides, I don't want to try to sleep right now. I'm not sure I can face another nightmare like that again tonight!"

"You're crazy Jules, but I love you. You're the boss. Let's go."

They set off into the dark up the mountain path, hand in hand. Despite the horrors of the fiery vision they had both experienced, both Robert and Julia found that they had become sexually aroused. Robert stared at Julia's bare breasts, barely visible in the gloom, and the soft dark mound of her pubic hair. Unbidden, visions of Julia's state of ecstatic bliss earlier in the evening flashed through Robert's head. He swiftly became erect. Julia too had a flashback to their early evening encounter. She remembered clawing Robert's arched back as he had climaxed inside her, collapsing onto her heaving breasts, breathing heavily. As she replayed their passionate encounter, unbidden another vision entered her mind. She could see them both making love in the open air on the mountainside. Yes, the ideal place would be up in the wooded copse perched above the camp. Robert looked at Julia. She seemed much more relaxed now and although she appeared flushed, now it was the flush of sexual excitement. He smelled her musky scent as they stood together on the rocky path.

She looked up at his face and smiled. She twined her arms around his neck and placed her lips against his. Their mouths opened and their tongues entwined. Separating, they walked further up the path. The weather was cool and damp, but they both felt calm and refreshed.

"Let's go up to the foot of the peak." said Robert. "We'll have a bit of privacy up there, and no-one will see us."

"Yes, Rob, there's a small wooded area up there. But it's strange, I haven't been up there yet I know what it looks like. Oh, Rob, I feel so horny. I want you to make love to me again!"

Together, they walked closer to the peak.

There was no moon, and the night was dark. The sound of the ocean crashing against the rocky circumference of the island was a soft and whispering backdrop to the silence of the night.

As they strolled upwards along the rudimentary path, Robert moved his had to Julia's buttocks, and gave a quick squeeze. Although they were both nude, neither felt any embarrassment. Strangely despite their exposed location and the late hour neither felt the chill in the air. The rough pebbles, ground by many icy winters, and polished by feet over the years, felt like a carpet under their feet. Robert and Julia felt totally at ease. The sheen of sweat both had exuded after their lovemaking had disappeared and now was present only as salt speckles on their skin.

"Rob, I want you." said Julia, a deep burning feeling developing in her groin.

"I need you Julia. I want to make love to you." panted Robert, partly from the exertion of walking up the path, and partly from his mounting desire. "Quickly, we're almost there."

"Oh God, yes!" said Julia.

Neither paused to think how strange it was that they should know the topography of a deserted island they had never visited before. Julia felt unbelievably good. And yet, she was experiencing a strange numb feeling in her extremities. They were warm and tingling. As she walked up the path, her limbs seemed to float along the pathway.

"This is all so weird." she thought. "Why am I not worried about what are we doing up here? And the visions I keep seeing." It was as if she had been given some powerful narcotic mixed with an aphrodisiac.

"This feeling I have isn't natural." she decided. "Rob must've slipped something into my drink."

She felt euphoric, but without any rational reason. As a student she had tried marijuana under peer pressure from her girlfriends in her University dorm. She had not particularly enjoyed the experience. But this time, whatever she had been given, she felt a buzzing high, and along with the buzz, her sexual desire kept mounting. Both the feeling of being high and her desire to make love to Robert grew as the couple ascended the plain. Although it was extremely dark, they both sensed when they were approaching the wooded area. Perhaps it was the wind whistling through the leaves, or the creaking of the boughs. Robert pushed his way through the undergrowth, and pulled Julia in behind him. Gingerly, they made their way into the middle of the small copse.

Julia gently placed her hands behind Robert's head and drew him close to her. She kissed him lightly, and then she whispered in his ear.

"You didn't put any sort of aphrodisiac in my food this evening did you, you naughty man?" she asked in a low growling voice, lust making her eyes shine.

"I was about to ask you the same thing." he replied, nuzzling her soft neck. "But why would you think I would do that?" he asked her.

"I feel strange." she said. "Good strange though, like I am walking on air. I feel revved up and very horny, but otherwise very much relaxed."

"Me too, Jules. Oh God, I want you so much!" said Robert, and moved his tongue over her naked body.

"Make love to me, Robert!" she gasped, and pulled his head into her bosom.

They lay down together on the carpeting of soft moss on the floor of the small grove of trees. They made love with an urgency both felt, but neither could fully understand.

As they lay together on the mossy carpet, with the trees a canopy above them, Julia's euphoria slowly evaporated. It was so dark, and the wind had picked up, shaking the trees above them. Suddenly, none of this felt right to Julia. She shuddered with fear, and a blossoming chill. Robert was dozing gently by her side.

"Robert, wake up!"

Robert opened his eyes. "What's up Jules?" he said groggily.

"Rob, I have an awful buzzing in my head, and something is up with my eyes. It's just like someone gave me fogged glasses to look through." Julia said. "I feel really weird."

Robert rubbed his eyes. Something was clouding his vision too.

"What happened?" he said, rubbing his eyes in an attempt to clear his vision. "I feel like somebody threw a handful of grit in my eyes. Oh Lord, what are we doing up here at this time of night? We have to get back to the camp. We'll have to be really careful Jules when we go back down that path. If we miss our way, we'll be over the cliff edge like that drunken farmer."

Robert remembered their contract. The Adventure Island policy had been very strongly communicated to them in what they had signed. Strictly no alcohol or illicit drugs. Stewart had been firm with his instructions to the lawyer who drew up the contract.

"I'm not losing anyone through drunkenness. It would be very easy for someone under the influence to get carried away, and fall off a cliff."

Julia and Robert dissected their evening. They thought back to their last meal. They had cooked it together. Nobody else had been involved in making their meal.

"I didn't put anything in the food." said Julia, "And you said you didn't."

"No, I most certainly did not. It must be something else."

"But what?"

Julia looked down at her arms. She was surprised to see that she had developed extensive goose bumps there. In fact her whole body was covered with them. She shivered again, and then shook more violently, as she realized that she was not only cold, but getting damp from a light rain that had started to fall.

"Robert. I'm getting really cold." Julia's teeth were chattering.

"We have to get back to the tent... " she added, "...and soon. I really need to get warm. I'm freezing!"

Robert remained somewhat dazed by whatever force was affecting them. His mind was so confused that he did not notice that he was naked, and in no way appropriately dressed for a mountain climb in the dark in forty degree temperatures.

Then slowly his head cleared a little. Julia was moaning close by him. Julia was obviously in some distress, and her soft moaning penetrated the fog clouding his eyes. He jumped to his feet and shook his head to try to clear out the fog in his brain. His ploy worked to some extent. His mind felt a little clearer. But not completely clear. Reaching out with his hand, he pulled Julia up to her feet. Her skin felt cold to his touch, and she had a bluish tinge on her lips and fingernails. She was shaking uncontrollably and he wrapped her in his arms to try to warm her up.

"You're heading for hypothermia, Jules. Let's go back then. Quickly. The exercise might warm us up a bit." suggested Robert. He was still trying to digest why they had both acted so peculiarly. Nothing came to mind.

Now he too began to shake uncontrollably with the cold.

They turned around to head back to the camp. In the dim light, Robert wondered how they had managed to make such a tricky climb in the dark. And how could they have been so stupid as to go rambling in cold and damp weather without clothes. The rainfall had not disturbed them much, but now the rain started to fall much harder, fat and heavy drops, and they were both very quickly soaked. It all still seemed very strange. The path was slick with rainwater, but thankfully their bare feet seemed to offer some grip on the stones. They had reached a cluster of boulders the size of small cars that bordered the path on their right hand side. The feeling of muzziness in their heads reappeared alarmingly as they approached the boulders. One particularly large and rough stone covered with lichen looked different from the others. It was streaming with rainwater, but steam seemed to be coming in clouds from somewhere behind the stone. The steam appeared ghostly white at first, whispering around the rough surface of the rock, and dissipating as it moved skyward.

They both eyed the plume of steam warily. This was not right.

As they watched, the steam plume changed color slowly from dull white to a glowing orange. The steam metamorphosed into what appeared to be a thick sulfurous yellow cloud. Spatters of liquid headed upward from the cloud like tracer bullets. They could both smell the fumarole stink of sulfur blowing from the cloud on the wind.

"I don't like this." said Robert nervously. "I saw this sort of thing once before on a National Geographic television program. It was a documentary about a volcano in Iceland. They were talking about a volcanic eruption.

That yellow cloud and that glow could be the beginnings of an eruption. But it can't be, this island is just rock. There's no volcano here!"

At least they both felt much warmer now. In fact, Julia felt herself start to sweat with the heat.

"Julia, I think it would be a good idea to get out of here, right now!" Robert stated, as the glowing yellow cloud billowed out towards them.

But Julia seemed mesmerized by the cloud, and stared at it with glassy eyes.

"We need to stay here. The cloud is telling us to stay here." she whispered in a dull monotone, hypnotized by the apparition, and what lay behind it.

Robert too felt the strange attraction of the cloud. There was now a curious fluorescence coming from behind the rock. As they watched, the glow intensified. Robert tried to hold on to his senses. What on earth could cause this glow? Perhaps one of the miscreant scouts had set off some kind of a firework behind the rock to frighten them, but he knew all the scouts were back in the camp. The magnetic pull of the cloud became intense, and they both moved towards it, their discomfort completely forgotten.

The glow brightened insidiously as they walked slowly towards the rock. Both Julia and Robert had an uncanny sense of déjà vu that was decidedly unsettling.

A halo of flame emerged from behind the boulder. Two coal black pits of eyes stared at them. The eyes seemed like bottomless pits in the orange face, and they had a hypnotic effect that was unshakeable. Julia screamed again and again as the enormous creature vaulted over the rock to confront them on the path.

Too late, they realized that they were trapped. The creature opened its mouth and roared. Even from a distance, they could feel the creature's hot breath burning on their faces. Slowly, with dreadful purpose, it closed in on the paralyzed couple. Their last recollection was of a pair of enormous flame covered arms embracing them in a furnace blast hug of death.

5. The Storm

June 17th, 2012 5:00 am

USTIN AND THE SEARCH PARTY SET out at first light. Half the party headed down to the jetty, and the others went up the path to the plateau. Two thirds of the way up the mountain, Justin, in the lead, noticed some smoke coming from a blackened pile of sticks on the path. His curiosity piqued, he made his way cautiously toward the smoldering ashes. As he approached the edge of the blackened area, he could see that the sticks were piled up in an unusual formation, with two of the piles being capped with structures having a globular appearance. As he came closer, with a sickening feeling in his stomach, he recognized eye sockets and teeth in what looked like bone. There was no doubt. These were without doubt human skulls. There was no-one else camping on the island. These burnt remains had to be all that was left of Julia and Robert. Justin bent over and threw up. After a few deep breaths, his composure returned. He straightened up, and once again was faced with the accusing grins of the skeletal remnants of his clients.

"What the hell happened here?" Justin was shivering with shock.

He stirred the ashes with a stick, an attempt to work out how long they had been there. Given the rainfall that night that would have contributed to the cooling of the ashes, Justin estimated that their deaths had probably occurred around or shortly after the time they had heard the scream early that morning. There was nothing to indicate what had caused the conflagration, but there some curious burn marks on the path, and on a boulder close by. Justin shivered. He called out to Martin Hoff, who had just caught up with him on the trail.

"Martin, stay back!"

"What's up, Justin?"

Then Martin saw the skulls.

"Oh no, oh God, what happened?"

"Poor bastards." said Martin, after he had got over the shock of seeing the human remains.

"Do you have any idea what might have happened, Justin? These bones do belong to Julia and Robert don't they?"

"It could have been lightning. I mean, it must have been. What else would cause them to be so horribly burned?" Justin offered.

Something about the story didn't ring true for Martin. If it had been lightning, they would inevitably have seen the flash, and there would have been an almighty clap of thunder that they could not have missed.

Martin just shrugged his shoulders, and refused to speculate.

He had heard of the concept of spontaneous combustion, where people apparently burst into flame without any identifiable cause, but to happen to two people at once, and here on this island? That was very unlikely.

"I think we'll have to leave the scene for a forensic specialist. We should call the mainland." he said. "Someone smarter than us can work this out."

"Perhaps we should cover up the bones in case animals carry them away. You stirring up those ashes with a stick won't have helped a forensics expert much, Justin." he added.

"Look, none of us had anything to do with this." said Justin angrily.

"We were all accounted for in the camp when we heard the scream."

With a common understanding that there was nothing else they could do immediately for the deceased couple, Justin and Martin rounded up the remainder of the plateau search party and broke the news to them. Totally dejected, the search party returned to the camp. Marcia and Sadie sat huddled together weeping. There were no words of comfort to help them.

With all that had happened, they had been ignoring the weather.

The sunny start to the morning was being rapidly eroded by a huge bank of black clouds scurrying in from the west.

A sudden flash of lightning and a deep rumble of thunder in close proximity, warned them of the rapid approach of the storm.

The recent mild temperatures on the Scottish west coast were about to end, and in a most violent way. Hot and moist Mediterranean air had been streaming northwards over the British Isles leading to a heat wave in the south of England and balmy days and nights in the usually chilly Scottish summer. But now, a much colder air mass was approaching from the Arctic. The moist southerly winds clashed with the approaching cold front bringing a rapid uprising of warm air, driven by a wedge of cooler surface air into towering thunderheads. The winds on the island escalated from a mild summer breeze to churning, ferocious gusts, bordering on hurricane force. The tent city was not likely to be in danger thought Justin, given the strength of the material and the extensive anchoring provided by stout guy ropes, but he had some concerns about the boat. The stone jetty might hold off the worst of the waves being generated by the storm force winds, but it really didn't provide Justin with the comforting strength and stability of the harbor on the mainland.

"I'm going to go make sure the boat is anchored, and I'll radio for some help at the same time." Justin shouted to Martin above the howl of the wind.

"I'll organize the coast guard to take us all back to the mainland, and I'll let the police know about the deaths. You stay here and look after the group."

Worse than having to let the police know what had happened, Justin was dreading telling his boss. With his jacket over his head to protect him from the worst of the water streaming from the sky, he made his way slowly along the path on the lower plateau, dodging the deeper puddles and thick mud churned up by the rain. As he arrived at the shoreline, he was astonished to see waves smashing over the jetty, pounding the boat where it was tethered to the rocks. His heart in his mouth, Justin realized that their ability to get off this barren rock was in deep jeopardy. Running rivers of seawater flooded the decks of the sturdy craft.

"If I cut her loose," Justin thought, "but tether her to these stones, she stands a better chance of survival than being pounded against the rocks where she is."

Soaked with salty sea spray from the crashing and rolling surf, and the teeming raindrops flooding from the heavens, he finally reached the stone with the ring where the boat's mooring rope was attached. The waves flooding over the jetty threatened to spill him into the sea, and he clung, cat-like, to the seaweed strewn rocks while the thrashing ocean vigorously attempted to dislodge him. At last he reached the mooring rope, and loosened the reef knot he had established to keep it in place. Suddenly a massive breaker rushed over the rocks, pushing him relentlessly into the churning waters, and freeing the boat and mooring rope in an instant. A second equally impressive breaker pushed the boat two hundred feet off the coast of the island in seconds. A third foaming wall of water crushed the boat like an eggshell. Justin floundered in the churning foam. With skills borne of many years of white water rafting, he started to work with the current and the waves to bring himself towards dry land. It was a momentous struggle, and at times, Justin feared he had breathed his last. After a supreme effort, he grasped hold of a rock above the waterline and hauled himself onto the rocky shore. He had suffered little more than bruising from being slammed into the rocks. Exhausted, he lay on a small shingle beach. After a few minutes rest, he had enough strength to get up. He looked towards the mooring, then further out to sea. With utter dismay, he could see the boat's rudder and propellers as they slowly sank into the maelstrom. Now they had no communication system, or way to get help from the mainland. There was no way he could recover the radio, even if it had survived the sinking of the boat. The sea depth increased rapidly off the shore and it was likely that their craft rested in over one hundred feet of water. It was all they could do to survive until the coastguard realized they had not returned on schedule, and sent out a search party. And he had lost two of the team. He felt drained, and deflated. He desperately hoped that nothing worse could happen to them, but his gut told him otherwise. There was something suspicious about this island. Despondently, he battled the fierce wind and waded through the rivulets of water on the path back to the camp.

Eventually, the lightning receded, and the grumbling thunder faded into the distance. The rain slowed to a steady downpour, and as the evening approached softened to a light drizzle. It had become noticeably cooler.

6. One by one

June 18th, 2012 5:05 am

AWN BROKE ON THE THIRD DAY. The previous day's storm was a distant memory, and once again the sun cast a baleful glare on the stones and glistening trees of the water slick plateau. The survivors huddled together in a damp mass as they collectively pondered their situation.

"Where do we go from here?" asked Marcia, her eyes still bloodshot from crying. Too late she had realized that their link to the mainland had been cut.

"Look, it's not as if nobody knows we're here. A boat will be along soon." said Justin. "I radioed our position to the coastguard and to my boss Stewart at Island Adventures before we landed, and they'll be suspicious if I don't call again soon."

"Just how soon?" asked Sadie, who was also clearly still shaken by her experiences of the previous day.

"Depends on the coastguard and Stewart." offered Justin, unsure if they would be worried before the entire week was up.

"But look, we had that storm last night. That might be the trigger for them to try to contact us, and when they can't?"

Justin tried in vain to settle them all, without letting them know he hadn't a clue what to do. It didn't work.

"You think we're all stupid." said Sadie, and turned away. "We're not. You have no more of an idea than we do when help will turn up. Look, Justin, we've got to be honest with each other. We are in deep trouble, and we have currently no way out of here. Why don't you just admit it to yourself and to us and we can try to work something out."

Marcia just put her head in her hands.

"We are all stuck here until help arrives, unless you want to swim eleven miles across a freezing ocean." Justin told them all a little coldly. He was upset by their lack of trust in him, but in truth it was totally justified, and he was feeling very guilty.

Justin's words did nothing but reinforce Marcia's fears. A tear trickled out of the corner of her eye.

"I'm so frightened." she said, her face crumbling.

Justin wrapped a consoling arm around her shoulder.

"So am I." he admitted to himself. "So am I."

The third evening was a somber affair. The scouts hunted around for wood for the fire. They had made an attempt to climb the peak to determine if they could establish a fire on the mountain top. Their attempt to light a signal beacon was a dismal failure. The intermittent showers of rain, and strong gusting breeze, prevented them from establishing a blaze. Disgruntled, they traipsed back down the steep trail to the camp as the light began to fail.

Martin observed the general disquiet of the group with growing concern.

"No-one will come looking for us until we are late getting back to the mainland." he said. He sounded very subdued.

"Maybe Justin is right. They'll check on us because of the storm?" Marcia offered.

"We can only hope so, but I wouldn't count on it." said Martin. He felt a real heel for being the pessimist in the group, but they had to try to sort things out for themselves, or they would all succumb.

The fear was contagious. One by one they had all attempted to use their cell phones to reach out for help, hoping for a miracle, hoping that a distress message would get through. Despite the fact that there were no indicator signal bars displayed on the screens of the phones, each of them prayed that an SOS message would reach listening ears somewhere. Their hopes were dashed. There were no responses to any of the distress calls. The batteries on their cell phones had finally given up, and so did they.

With nothing else to do but wait and make the most of their

predicament, the weary group of campers retired to their tents to seek some relative comfort, out of sight of each other, and away from the thin damp mist of the evening. Marcia was feeling particularly drained. She decided not to seek the solace of an evening with Justin. Instead she crept to her own tent. Her only desire was to try to cope with her misery by getting some sleep. Surely things would feel better in the morning. As she expected, it took a long time for her to finally drift off into a troubled slumber. When she did eventually nod off, she found herself having a very strange dream. Not so much a dream, more of a nightmare. In her dream state, she left the safety of the tent and headed out of the camp. What had started out as a pleasant ramble on the island had morphed into something much less comfortable. It was dark, but the weather was kind that evening. She found herself walking up the plateau path on her own. That in itself was unusual. She had always been a gregarious individual, and hated solitude. So being alone in the dark on a path to nowhere really unsettled her. But she was drawn upwards by some unseen force. She had been feeling anxious from the start, but as she moved steadily up the path, she became more and more disturbed. As she came close to the final assault on the peak, she started seeing strange jets of mist or steam pulsing from tiny fissures in the rocks. The whole experience was surreal. Beneath the steam, ghostly orange lights flickered in the cracks in the rocks. In her dream, she could feel herself sweating, and she looked down on her limbs and noticed the sheen of sweat on her arms. It was curiously warm on the mountain, given the cold temperatures they all had experienced that had pervaded the island that day, after the arctic front had moved through. It felt almost like the temperature on the island had reverted to the previous day's balmy highs. Despite her anxieties, and knowing that this had to be a dream, she felt compelled to keep climbing. Somehow she felt certain, without knowing why, that the answer to all her problems and questions resided at the peak of the mountain. It was a totally irrational feeling. She questioned herself why she felt that way, but it was a distinct and compelling obsession for her to have to climb the mountain peak. Strange voices echoed in her head as she walked. Mostly they were so quiet as to be almost inaudible, and she could not understand what they said. The quiet voices were interspersed with louder ones, apparently to her ears speaking gibberish. As she focused her on the voices, on occasions she thought she could made out the words "curse you, you devils" and "you are all evil" and "you'll all die for this" and "hateful vermin" repeated endlessly. But why would anyone be whispering these words in her head? The words were filled with so much hate. She would never do anything to provoke such hatred. She could think of nothing better than to get off the island and to go home right now. She knew that subconsciously, her rational mind was trying to get her to think of a way to get off the island. Marcia tried to ignore the voices in her head, and concentrated instead on the climb she felt she was being forced to make. After several hundred yards of walking up the steep gradient, and sweating profusely from the exertions of her ascent and the odd heat that surrounded her, she reached the base of the cliffs forming the volcanic plug. Ahead of her she saw more steam rising from cracks in the ground. At least she thought it was steam. When she really looked closely at the vapors, she could well believe it might be smoke, but she could see nothing burning. The smoke or vapor had a sulfurous tang. She reached out and touched the rock face in front of her. It was hot to the touch, and rapidly drying despite moisture applied to the rock from the thin rain that was still falling. Why on earth was the rock warm? She tried to put all the pieces together, but other thoughts intruded on her concentration. She felt an even stronger compulsion to keep climbing the peak. Bravely in her fugue state, she stepped onwards up onto the steep summit path.

"If I pinch myself, I'll wake up." she thought to herself.

She hummed a tuneless song to bolster her flagging spirits, but it did little to help her feel better about what she was doing. Step after step, she moved upwards, coming ever closer to the summit. Occasionally she tripped over a rocky ridge, or an uneven stone in the path. However, nothing stopped her inexorable march towards the summit. As she neared the top, a strange radiance illuminated the summit stones. The stones themselves had taken on an imbalanced hue, as if an impressionist painter had obscured their form. Marcia felt like she had taken one of her sleeping pills, and as a result she couldn't quite focus on the world. Looking around, and shaking her head to try to clear it, she noticed a previously unseen small cave in the rock face under the tip of the mountain. The cave glowed inside with a flickering orange phosphorescence. She shivered once, thinking back to a video game she had played with friends. The game was a virtual reality first person exploration of an alien world. It had been set underground, and in each cavern there were glowing mushrooms that had provided the light for people to follow subterranean paths into the labyrinth. Unable to resist and pulled as if by a magnet, she moved towards the cave. It was around four feet in diameter, and ducking her head to avoid injury, she made her way inside. Inside the cave, in sharp contrast to the dark night outside, the cavern was almost as bright as day. As a result, she had no difficulty moving deeper into the mountain. The cave twisted and turned, and then turned sharply downwards where the light seemed even brighter. To facilitate her passage, there was a set of roughly hewn steps carved into the floor, leading deep down into the mountain.

Still driven by the same unseen force, she descended carefully, frightened but curious to find out what lay below. Strange that Justin had not mentioned that this cave existed, she mused. Surely someone else has been down here exploring before her? She had descended around one hundred feet when, as she turned yet another corner, the narrow cave tunnel suddenly opened out into a larger chamber. The light that pulsed from the walls of the cavern grew stronger, and she shielded her eyes from the radiant cliff walls. She also felt the heat inside the cavern in the mountain increase, and her body poured with sweat.

Moving around a large rock wall in the center of the cave, the voices in her head became louder and more distinct. Again she heard comments that were spoken with a distinctly hostile intonation. This time there were more words that she could understand. Against the background cacophony, distinctly she could hear the voices shouting "Devils!" and "Puny apes!" and "Vermin!" Then there also were short sentences which produced goose flesh all over her body. The voices echoed through her head. Again and again, she heard the voices saying "How dare you disturb us!" and "How dare you wake us up!" Most chillingly, she heard "You will suffer for this!" from a deep and dark rumbling bass voice. As she moved forward, she could see what appeared to be a narrow entrance to yet another tunnel at the far end of the chamber. From this tunnel, a steaming cloud spilled out and curled along the floor towards her into the cavern. Distantly, she could now hear sounds of what she thought to be people talking in a strange language. A spasm of fear gripped her intestines. Despite her trepidation and a strong desire to turn and run, she made her way towards the smoking tunnel. Its walls were circular solid rock but strangely smooth, with a flat floor. Despite her vision being blurred by the vapors issuing from the tunnel, she could see that the floor of the tube sloped downwards. The tunnel reminded her of the phenomenon known as the Thurston lava tube. The lava tube had been formed when liquid lava had poured forth under the cooled and solidified surface lava flows, keeping its heat, and its ability to move at high speed in its insulated environment. She had strolled down the solidified lava tube on a visit to the Kilauea volcano in Hawaii big island, but this particular tube was much broader. The walls of the tube were very warm to her touch, and she could sense the heat of the floor being conducted through the soles of her shoes. She groped with trying to understand the significance of what was happening to her, but it all still failed to make sense. Annoyingly, she felt the strange illogical magnetism drawing her further downwards into the depths of the mountain. Again, as she progressed across the smooth cave floor, she continued to experience frissons of fear. Her nerves were distinctly on edge. Then, as she made her way towards the light, she was startled abruptly by a loud grinding noise, and a heavy liquid gurgling behind her, which made her turn round. With horror, she realized that the walls of the tunnel she had recently traversed had turned from steaming rock to molten lava. Now glowing rock walls flowed together like closing curtains. The heat was intense. She felt the bare skin on her arms begin to burn. She had no choice but to move forward to avoid being roasted alive. As she stepped rapidly forwards out of the tunnel to escape the heat, she could hear the deep rumbling bass voice, and the cacophony of counterpoint tenor accompaniments growing ever louder.

After running rapidly forwards for a few more yards, and narrowly escaping being trapped in the liquid rock, she reached a glaringly bright chamber, lit with a pulsing orange glow from an unseen source. As she eased herself into the immense cavern, at one end, over two hundred yards away, she could see a group of glowing and flickering figures. She was reminded vaguely of a nativity scene she had seen as a child, but the figures did not have that peaceful and friendly look about them. Given the intense heat, she certainly did not feel like she could in any way be part of that Christmas scene. As she moved warily towards the group, she could see just how enormous each figure was. The center figure resembled a large male gorilla with incongruous sharp pointed horns sprouting from above each ear. The creature was at least six times as tall as she was.

"He must be over thirty feet tall!" gasped Marcia.

But there was something totally wrong with his skin. In place of hair, flickering flames flowed over his body. He glowed a deep orange color, like an orangutan, with twisting yellow snakes of flame pouring from every inch of his skin. He exuded power, and she could not take her eyes off him. Gradually, she also took notice of his entourage. An equally large female gorilla hunched next to him, and stared at her with baleful coal dark eyes. Smaller creatures, clearly subordinate to the pair, stood a respectful distance behind the imposing couple. Marcia wanted to run, but she did not have that choice. She was drawn step by step towards the group, as if she was being reeled in, like a fish on line. As she approached the towering monsters, she felt them all train their eyes on her in unison. She was now frankly terrified, yet amazingly despite the adrenaline surge she experienced and the urge she had to get the hell out of there, she felt she had no ability to flee. One thing in particular disturbed her immensely. The monstrous gorilla's eyes were mesmerizing, shining black diamonds in their flickering orange faces. Her heart hammering in her chest, she urged her recalcitrant limbs to move, to run, but to no avail. Step by burning step, she was pulled closer towards the group. The heat in the cavern, and the stench of sulfur emanating from the figures was overpowering. A sensation of extreme pain pulled her gaze down to her arms. Looking downwards, she realized that the fine hairs on her skin were beginning to singe and crisp with the intense heat emanating from the cavern walls. Still, unable to resist, she found herself walking towards the glowing group. Her ability to turn around and run had vanished. She had been completely intoxicated by the hypnotic stares of the giant beasts. She could sense their intense fury. She wanted to run, needed to run, but she could not resist the magnetic pull of these staring beasts. At length she found herself within ten feet of the glowing apes. The leader bared his teeth at her. His teeth were brown and yellow fangs, each one as long as her index finger, and dripping with smoking saliva.

The great ape spoke in a deep rumbling voice, repeating the words she had heard in her head during her descent into the cavern.

"You are a puny and meddlesome insect. You have absolutely no idea what you have done, how much harm you have caused. How dare you disturb our peace!"

He paused, and spat a ball of flame at her feet. She realized with awe that it was corrosive acid that dripped from the corner of his mouth. Each drop created a small smoking crater on the cave floor where it landed.

He continued, his voice rising in concert with his fury.

"We needed our sanctuary here to recover from our past battle. We were disturbing no one here on this island, and now you come here and throw rocks at us to wake us up. Your actions are unfathomable. You and the other miserable insects in your tribe. How dare you disturb the rest of the gods! How dare you!"

He spat at her again, and now she felt intense pain in her right foot, as the flaming acid that was his saliva burned through her shoe. This could not be happening! How could she be feeling real pain in a dream!

The great flaming horned ape moved closer to her. She could now feel the intense heat radiating from his body. He stared deeply into her eyes.

"Your folly will not go unpunished. For your presence here, and your interference, now you must suffer. You all must suffer. All of you. Your entire feeble race."

He lifted his knuckles from the floor and stood upright, towering over Marcia. He opened his mouth and let loose a powerful roar, full of anger and hatred. Unbelievably quickly, he reached out a huge hand and grabbed her arm. Her skin instantly blistered and crackled and a stench of burning flesh assaulted her nostrils. In a flash she realized that the intense pain in her foot and now her arm were real, and she was most certainly not dreaming. She writhed with the excruciating agony she felt all over her body. Her vision started to flicker and she knew that she was on the verge of fainting. The fiery beast leaned in closer to her. She could feel the skin on her face catch fire. The pain was unbearable.

He whispered in a deep and menacing tone.

"I am Tibran. You are not worthy of my time. No creature on this planet disturbs my rest!"

His flaming breath seared her skin, and acid sprayed from his mouth over her ruined body. Baring his fowl brown teeth once more, he drew her, screaming, into a final fiery embrace.

7. Discovery.

June 18th, 2012 5:15 am

I N THE GREY LIGHT OF THE early dawn on the third day, Justin patrolled the tents to make sure that the remainder of the group had at least had some sleep that night, and was safe. The four scouts sat dejectedly in front of their tents as they spooned down mouthfuls of rehydrated porridge mix. Martin and Sadie Hoff held each other for comfort.

Marcia was not in her tent. She was not with the others having breakfast. Justin called out her name, but there was no response. A growing knot of anxiety twisted in his stomach.

"Have any of you guys seen Marcia?" he asked.

There were no replies.

"Anybody?" he asked again.

"Last time I saw her was yesterday evening." said Julia.

With a growing sense of panic, Justin decided to form a search party.

"Martin and Sadie, could you go down to the pier and see if she's there?"

"Bruce and Peter, head on over to the north cliff path. Jim and Colin, you take the south side. Sadie, you stay here in case Marcia comes back. I'll head up to the peak."

They split up and went off to search for Marcia.

Martin almost tripped over a tree root in his haste to travel down to the water's edge. He called Marcia's name frequently as he went. He listened intently for her voice. There was no response.

Justin raced up to the plateau. He decided to head for the peak, with the aim of getting to a vantage point where he could scan the whole island. There was still no sign of Marcia.

"Marcia!" he yelled out into the wind. "Marcia!"

Just as he approached the final approach to the cairn of stones perched on the summit ridge, he noticed a blackened area of vegetation at the foot of a steep cliff. In the center of the blackened area, he thought he could see the bones of a sheep. Once again, as he got closer, he could make out that the pile of blackened bones was too large for a sheep. Feeling a renewed deep sense of horror and disbelief, he slowly approached the blackened and still smoldering pile. Within the ruined remains of a skull, melted fillings confirmed that the remains were human. The only person unaccounted for on the island was Marcia. Justin wept openly. His world was coming apart. He mourned the loss of his lover, and also, yet another of the persons who had depended on his leadership. Wearily, and feeling sick, he walked back down the path to convey the news to the rest of the group. Of the happy group of ten who had set out for adventure on that sunny June day, a mere three days later only seven remained. Worse, he had no clues as to what was happening or why.

From a distance, Sadie could see Justin's dejected posture as he approached the camp. Almost intuitively, she knew something bad had happened.

"Justin." she called, "Did you find Marcia?"

Justin said nothing. He nodded slowly.

"She's dead." he said morosely, "Burned beyond recognition, up near the summit. I don't know what happened. I don't know what's going on. This has never happened to me before."

Martin noted the rapid decline in Justin's mood with concern. He knew that someone needed to keep them all together through this or they would all die.

"Get a grip, Justin!" he said, "Pull your damn self together. You're the one with the local knowledge to get us all through this crisis. We need you to lead, not to act like a cry-baby and run off to your tent. We need you as our leader. Do you understand?"

Justin looked up at Martin, and shook his head.

"I'm no leader. I don't know what we need to do to get out of this mess. I'm no better than any of you. Damn, why did I have to be part of this?"

Martin had taken a course in survival training. If a group didn't have a leader, it would fall apart. This party needed a leader and it needed one now! He decided to take over.

"All right Justin, keep your head screwed on. I did some survival training a while back. I can at least keep us going until help arrives, but I'll need your help. Are you up to it?"

Justin nodded.

"First thing we should do is we should bury Marcia's remains. I don't know what killed her, but if the wildlife here gets to her, it'll make it a darn site tougher for the forensic detectives to work out what happened."

Justin looked up at Martin.

"You're the real leader here, Martin. This whole episode has scrambled my brains. But I can help you. I have something we can use to dig a grave for Marcia. Then we can pile rocks on it to keep the scavengers away."

Now that they had a plan of action, Justin felt that he had a pan of action, and that he could do something positive. He and Martin returned to camp, and Justin retrieved a small field shovel from his tent. The two of them then climbed back up the hill to Marcia's remains. In a small clearing next to the rock face they took turns to dig a shallow grave for her. It was hard work given the unyielding nature of the stony ground, but eventually it was completed. Both men were silent. Marcia's charred remains were transferred to a tarpaulin they had brought for the purpose, and they carried her body over to the pit they had dug. After her charred bones had been interred and covered to prevent seabirds from scavenging them, Martin said a few words in her memory, and placed a pile of small rocks at the head of her temporary grave.

"Once we get home, the police and her next of kin can come here to collect her remains. Then they can arrange a proper burial service for her on the mainland." said Martin.

Justin stared morosely out to sea. He really wanted to be

somewhere else right now. No amount of training could help with the first time that anyone experienced this sort of disaster. Sensing his lack of experience and his discomfort, Martin just clapped him on the shoulder.

"Never give up, Justin. It's never over till it's over. Keep yourself focused on our survival. I know you have a trick or two up your sleeve."

"I'll be OK." said Justin.

"Damn right you will. We've got to keep our spirits up, and more importantly the spirits of the rest of the group. We can't lose hope. We must keep going. Are you with me?"

Justin nodded his agreement. Both men knew it was going to be a real struggle to keep them all sane and working together over the next few days.

Justin picked up the muddy shovel and they both descended once again to the camp. There, they joined the dejected group of campers, clustered around the remnants of the campfire. In an effort to raise spirits, Justin prepared the best lunch he could with their dried and canned supplies. Although they could hold out for many days on what they had brought to the island, none of them dared to mention that the supplies would go even further now with their reduced numbers.

Justin noticed that the supplies of combustible material for the fire were running low.

"Why don't you guys go off and see if you can find us some driftwood?" Martin suggested to the scout group, who were on their haunches next to the fire.

Knowing that any diversion might provide some relief from their collective feeling of gloom, the teenagers quickly agreed to search for some firewood. Besides, it would offer them a chance to get some exercise. The scouts split into two pairs.

"That way we'll have each other's company, and if anything strange happens, we can help each other out." said Colin.

"All right." said Bruce. "Let's go down to the shore. We should be able to find some driftwood if we look carefully. We can circle the island now because the tide is low. I know I saw a few broken crates when we arrived here. You know how messy sailors are. Any junk, they just throw it into the sea. There are so many ships passing these islands. It's so much easier to throw the junk into the sea than to have to cart it back to port and dispose of it."

The scouts tossed a coin to choose which pair would go in which direction. Peter and Bruce called heads and won, and chose the east side of the island. Jim and Colin would take the west coast.

They all followed the narrow path that ran to the pier. Once they arrived at the pier, they clambered down the rough grassy bank abutting the rocky shoreline. The sea looked benign, and waves lapped at smooth rocks ten feet below them. The rocks were covered with a white crusting of barnacles, and bladder wrack seaweed. Both pairs of scouts moved nimbly along the wet and slippery stones, now fully exposed with the retreat of the sea. The water sucked and slopped in between weed covered boulders, now partially exposed by the ebb of the tide. They moved purposefully in opposite directions around the island's rocky shore. The further they went from the jetty, the higher the cliffs and the basaltic ribs of the island extended skywards to dwarf them. Soon they could not see the tops of the columns at all.

A chorus of seabird cries descended from the nesting areas high above. When the two pairs of scouts were out of sight of each other, Peter and Bruce held hands. This maneuver served not only to help keep their balance, but also to cement their growing relationship. Perhaps the trip would not be a total disaster after all. As they approached the steepest cliff face near the towering flanks of Sandeagh Mhor's peak, they noticed a fissure in the cliff. It looked like one of the columns had broken off at the base, revealing a deep cave, which the sea had exploited over the years, pummeling and pounding until the softer interior rock had been eroded.

"I'll bet it connects with that pit we saw up above on the peak." said Peter.

"Let's explore a bit." Bruce added, and despite the horrors they had experienced that week, he had a hint of excitement in his voice.

"After all, we are on an outward bound course."

Peter agreed.

"Let's go then."

They walked over the rock to the smooth sandy base of the cave and waited until their eyes had become accustomed to the gloom. They peered into its depths. The cave seemed to stretch deep into the mountainside, and as their eyes became better accustomed to the gloom, they could make out the walls of rock, arching ribs of rock like giant teeth. As they walked deeper inside, the sandy floor transitioned to a jumble of small boulders, overlying hexagonal blocks of stone.

"There's not much in here, so far." said Peter, and they moved further into the cave.

As the light from outside faded, they reached a curve in the cave. The bend in the tunnel obscured their view of its end. They decided to keep going further into the cave.

Suddenly a deep rumbling could be felt under their feet. It reverberated in the enclosed space of the rock walls. A dull booming echoed sonorously as the harsh vibrations elicited a deep, bone shaking harmony in the rock ribs surrounding them.

Peter and Bruce stared at each other, unsure of what they should do. The rumbling deepened and the floor of the cave began to undulate alarmingly under their feet.

"Let's get out of here!" shouted Bruce.

"Oh shit!" said Peter.

Cautiously, given the difficulty in moving forwards on the shuddering stones, they started to make their way towards the mouth of the cave. Their feet were shaken loose by the tremors in the rock around them. Pieces of rock began to rain down in front of them from the ceiling of the cave.

"It's too dangerous, Bruce. We can't go back, we need to go deeper into the cave." said Peter.

More uncertain now, they turned back into the cave depths to try to find some shelter from the falling rock. The pattering of splintered stone became a steady roar. The light from the mouth of the cave was extinguished as a curtain of rock closed off their way out to the beach. Seeing that their exit was blocked, they pushed on deeper into the cave. In the depths of the cavern ahead they could see a glimmer of light, and they rushed towards it hoping for the opening that might lead them to the surface. The deeper they penetrated into the bowels of the mountain, the brighter the light became.

In due course the rumbling dwindled and eventually ceased. A strange silence, interrupted by occasional falling rocks smashing against the cave floor, settled in the cave.

"I guess it was an earthquake?" said Bruce. Peter looked perplexed, as he had been sure that his geography lessons at school had mentioned nothing about geological instability in the region.

"Maybe, or maybe it was something else." Bruce did not elaborate on what he thought something else might be.

They decided to press on. Rounding the final corner in the cave, and facing a solid stone wall, the boys looked around for the source of the light. Looking upwards, they could see that the fracturing rock wall had created a new opening about ten feet above the floor of the cave. It looked large enough for them to enter, and the bright orange glow pulsing from the opening gave them hope that there might be an exit. Peter gave Bruce a lift up with clasped hands, and he managed to grab a rocky knob protruding from the edge of the cave wall. His gymnastic training helped him pull himself upwards, and he eventually found himself, panting, in a sitting position on the ledge. Once Bruce had regained his breath, and had settled himself into a safe position, he removed his shirt, and used it as a rope to help pull Peter upwards. Soon both were safely lodged on the ledge of the opening. They had both suffered minor scrapes and bruises from pebbles descending on them from the rock fall, but were otherwise unharmed.

The glow was much brighter in the opening, and they could see that it came from the opening in the far end of a short passage. They crawled forward until they were positioned at the far entrance of the opening. To their surprise, a large cavern extended in front of them as far as they could see. At last the source of the illumination that had pulled them into this cave became apparent. A bright golden light was visible at the far end of the cavern, behind a rock formation. Looking upwards they could see reflections of the light on the rocky cave roof, amplified by the sheen of moisture on the rock. Out of the silence, strange noises echoed through the cavern. The sounds reminded the scouts of Native American Indian chanting. But the language was not one either of the boys had heard before. They clambered down the short drop from the connecting passage onto a smooth stone floor. The chamber was oppressively hot, and they could detect a sharp sulfurous tang that irritated their nostrils. The two boys looked at each other questioningly. Where were they, and why was the cavern so hot?

"Pete, let's get the hell out of here." said Bruce, a sheen of sweat on his forehead.

"I'm with you." answered Peter, nervously. "Which way should we go?"

Looking around, they were encouraged to see another opening in the rock about two hundred feet to their left, well away from the flickering orange glow. A paved path seemed to lead up from the opening, and cool air wafted in their direction from the new tunnel. Gingerly, they made their way gingerly towards the new opening, not sure why caution was the best approach. Both felt intimidated by the nature of the deep chanting they could hear ahead of them. As they neared the entrance of the opening, the cadence of the background noise changed. The speech became louder, developing into a sonorous rumbling, and had taken on a sense of urgency. Separate from the chants, a new and overwhelming sound blasted outwards towards them. It was a separate deep and growling voice, and its owner was clearly displeased. And now they could hear voices in their heads, repeating the words, "you are evil intruders" and "you have disturbed our rest" and "now we will kill you all". The last phrase struck terror into the hearts of the boys. As with most young adults, they believed themselves to be invincible, but now they were not so sure.

"Make a run for it." whispered Peter. "I have a really bad feeling about this".

"Go!" yelled Bruce. "Into that tunnel!"

They both wasted no time in charging towards the ascending pathway.

Reaching the first few steps to freedom, they made the mistake of turning round to look at the source of the sound. As with Marcia the night before, what they saw stopped them in their tracks. To their right, a group of giant gorilla like creatures with curling spiked horns, and snaking flames in place of hair, were hunched over. Most noticeable about the beasts were their deep set coal-black marbles of eyes. Their collective gaze penetrated deep into the two boy's souls. The largest of the flaming beasts stared intensely first at Peter, and then did the same with Bruce. Both boys were rooted to the spot, and could not move. The ape slowly stood up to his full twenty foot height, and lumbered slowly towards the scouts. He was in no hurry to do what he was going to do. The terrified teenagers noticed that wherever the ape had placed one of his gargantuan feet, a pool of molten rock bubbled and hissed.

The cavern had gone totally silent.

"Know me as Tibran!" rumbled the ape, flames issuing from his mouth and nose as he spoke. Drops of superheated acid sprayed from his mouth as his words resonated around the cave.

"Your kind has called me the devil, a leviathan, a monster, but I am far worse than that. I am your worst nightmare. I come from a place so alien to you that you would not survive there. My race has fought many battles over time, and we are weary. I even fought with my own son for the right for our race to have peace. And now, after we have been hiding away, sleeping in the safety of this deep place, you have chosen to wake us. You are like mice in our food closet. You are moths in our clothing. You are gnats on our flesh. Yours was not a wise decision to come here. Your kind is weak and feeble, and we are infinitely strong. We were birthed in the molten core of this planet. We are immortal. And we will crush those who would disturb our rest.

But one of you will survive to take a message to your pitiful tribe. One of the ten humans who desecrated our sanctuary. I have not yet chosen the survivor. Is it one of you two? Tell me what you believe might be your redeeming qualities. Tell me why I should spare one of your miserable lives so that you can be an emissary for us? Tell me!"

As he spoke, Tibran extended his arms forwards, and then beat his fists upon his chest. As he did so, ferocious flames flowed around his body like a mantle, before slowly dying as they hit the rock walls of the cavern. He roared his disapproval at the boys, and bared his glowing brown fangs.

"So, you will not even speak when I command you to do so."

He stared threateningly at the cowering duo.

Still neither boy could reply. Both were terrified out of their wits.

In absence of an answer, and indeed expecting none, the giant flaming horned ape strolled in a leisurely fashion towards the helpless boys.

"Then that is my answer." he concluded, and reached out to the boys with both of his huge hands. He pulled them into his arms as if they were toy dogs. Peter and Bruce felt a searing heat penetrate their bodies where Tibran touched them. His skin was hotter than a flaming coal. Both screamed as they were slowly cooked alive.

The screams rapidly ceased. Both boys had been fused into a congruous pool of boiling gore, crisped flesh, and charred bone. In death they became joined together, forever. It was ironically what they had been seeking for each other in life.

Tibran disposed of the smoking carcasses by throwing them forcefully up the stone staircase. Such was the power of his muscular arms, the smoking remnants of the two former boy scouts flew up the passageway, bouncing off the walls as they went. Their corpses flew out of the cave on the peak before rolling in a blackened pile to come to rest at the foot of the cliff. Tibran brushed the sooty remnants from his hands and returned to his family. His wrath was growing, and he smashed his fists into the rocky walls of the cave, splintering off shards of rock, and leaving glowing fist marks on the stone.

Back on the plateau, Justin and the Hoff's had heard and felt the rumbling of the earthquake. In fear, Justin had rushed to the cliff edge to see if he could see the scouts. Eventually, he made out two lone figures returning to the jetty. He ran down the slope, unmindful of the treacherous boulders and roots that were omnipresent, and always attempting to trip him. In a few seconds he reached the jetty. Jim and Colin were marching purposefully toward him.

"Did you meet up with Peter and Bruce?" Justin asked, mindful that the group had been supposed to have a rendezvous at the far end of the island.

"No." said Colin, "We didn't see them. We thought they had turned back."

Jim looked perplexed.

"We walked right around the island and we didn't' see them." he added. "Did they come back by a different route? We felt the tremors of the earthquake, but the ground only shook briefly, and it didn't really bother us much. "He looked quizzically at Justin. "Do you think something happened to them? They are tough lads, and they'd stick together if they were in any trouble. And they are trained in survival tactics."

"You know, we did see a fresh rock fall on the far side of the island, near the bird colonies." said Colin. "You don't think...."

Justin could only stare at the two boys. With a feeling of dread, he took off for the peak in a rush. Once again as he came close, there was a smoking pile of bones to be seen. This pile also had two skulls in its midst, and he turned and vomited as he realized their source. His vomiting became unproductive, and turned to dry retching. His mind overloaded, he fell to the ground in a dead faint. After a short time, he began to regain his senses. His hands and knees were in contact with the rocky path. He noticed that the ground had become unbearably warm. Looking around he saw plumes of steam issuing from gaps between the rocks. Worse than that the rocks seemed to be dissolving. As he watched, a tongue of smooth pahoehoe lava emerged from between two boulders. The flow started as a trickle, then welled up and travelled towards him. He could feel its intense heat as it consumed the surrounding vegetation with fiery flashes and flame. In no time the flow had covered the remains of the two boys with a silvery flaming layer of molten stone.

Understanding immediately the danger he was in, Justin stood up and raced down the mountainside. This could not be happening, he said to himself. This mountain, this island could not be an active volcano. This whole area may have been volcanic once, but now? Lava in Scotland? The whole area was supposed to be geologically ancient and dead.

He ran down the treacherous path as fast as he could without falling. Occasionally, with great trepidation, he glanced behind him. He did not like what he saw.

From several points on the hillside, lava gushed forth. Tongues of red hot and indomitable molten rock poured out of the ground. Where the glowing streams coalesced, the resultant shimmering rivers gained momentum and flowed rapidly towards the campsite, and towards his precarious position. As the flaming lava touched them, the bushes in the path of the fiery rock burst into flame. With no exception, the lava consumed everything in its path.

Justin raced down the treacherous path to the camp, nearly killing himself in the process. At last Justin could see the camp ahead. As he neared the camp, Justin yelled out a warning to the others.

"All of you. Get the hell out of here! Make for the jetty!"

Glancing up the mountain, Sadie and Martin could see a roiling wave of molten rock powering its way towards the camp, flash frying everything in its path.

Sadie turned to Martin.

"Martin, what do we do?" she asked, her voice trembling with terror.

"We have to try to get out of the way of the lava flow." Martin said, with more confidence than he felt. "Come on Sadie, this way."

He pointed to the path heading towards the cliff on the eastern side of the island. Both took to their heels, and ran along the grass bordered path to the eastern cliffs. It had been a tough choice. Martin was convinced that the slight upward slope of the hill he had seen as it rose towards the east would divert the lava past them, and down to the jetty and the western shore. He hoped he was right.

The two remaining scouts took Justin's advice and ran downhill towards the jetty. Both reckoned that they could swim into the ocean next to the pier if necessary, and watch the lava being quenched by the cold ocean waters from the safety of the ocean.

Justin himself was paralyzed by fear. Winded by his headlong flight down the mountain, he could not make up his mind what to do. He stared up the plateau at the rapidly approaching fire front of the silvery lava flow. A bubbling and gurgling below the camp drew his attention. Too late he realized that a further upwelling of molten rock had commenced from a fissure that had opened immediately below the camp. He was trapped. There was no escape. Believing he was doomed, he sank to his knees, and prayed for deliverance.

The silvery pa'hoe 'hoe flows moved swiftly down the mountain, and traversed the plain with ease. In defiance of gravity, the flow split into two tongues, completely bypassing the camp, but pursuing the Hoff's to the east, and reuniting beyond the camp with the lower flow to chase the scouts who had now reached the pier.

Justin remained isolated by the lava in the camp, surrounded by the two divergent flows, but seemingly in no immediate danger. He cowered next to the tents.

"This can't be real!" he said to himself. "There is no way that the lava would flow uphill. And why would this island have turned into a volcano?" It made no sense to him. Feeling defeated, he sank down to the ground to await his fate.

Martin and Sadie Hoff found themselves cut off from safety as the flows approached. They had moved close to the cliff top as the twisting ropes and pools of lava approached them. Hand in hand they watched as their destiny approached them. There was no escape. Relentlessly, the lava coiled and twisted, pouring off the cliff below and above where they stood in silvery ropes, generating explosive clouds of steam where the molten rock met with the frigid waters below. Martin and Sadie clung to each other as they perched on a rough pile of ancient volcanic rock on the edge of the cliff. As a refuge, it offered brief respite from the inevitable march of the lava. Martin and Julie could both feel the incredible heat radiating from the incandescent surface of the lava. Inexorably, the rivers of molten rock flowed towards each other in a pincer movement. Feeling their skin singe, Martin and Sadie looked at each other in desperation.

"This is it, Martin? We don't have any way out, do we?" Sadie sobbed. Plucking what remained of her courage together, she stood up straight.

"I love you, Martin." Sadie said to Martin and reached out her hand to him.

"I love you too, Sadie." Martin replied, fear draining the energy from him. He linked hands with his wife.

Holding hands in the age-old ritual of love, the couple jumped together off the cliff edge, just before the flood of rock assailed their cliff top bastion. They fell, screaming, and smashed into a bloody pulp on the jumble of sharp rocks far below. Lava continued to pour over the cliff face in glowing gobbets. The lava created Martin and Sadie's tomb as it covered their twisted and shattered bodies on the exposed boulders below.

The two remaining scouts were having the first and last real adventure of their lives. They retreated along the pier. Both could see the advancing wall of flaming rock as it demolished all in its path and headed towards them. Surely the ocean would extinguish the flames? They watched helplessly as the fiery fluid stream advanced on several fronts over the seashore and into the ocean. Huge clouds of steam exploded skywards as the lava advanced into the water. Then thin slivers of golden liquid glass fired outwards as the rock boiled the sea water. The strands of molten glass arced towards the boys. As the glass cooled in the air, it showered the boys with coils of shimmering strands.

Jim and Peter had reached the edge of the ocean at the pier.

"I'll be damned, it's Pele's hair." said Jim. "I read about that when my dad and I went to Hawaii last year. I never thought I'd see it in person, and now I wish I hadn't." Jim was referring to the Hawaiian islander's belief that the volcanic glass strings produced when lava hits water were the hair of Pele, the goddess of the volcano. But now it was too late for the boys. Glowing puddles of rock expanded towards them, and surged forwards over the stones of the pier. The landward side of the pier soon became covered with flowing toes of pa'hoe 'hoe lava. The lava inexorably approached the two scouts standing on its tip.

"What do we do now?" asked Jim, desperation clear in his voice. "Do we try to swim for it?"

The sea surface around them was steaming ominously. The lava was also emerging from under the sea surface, heating up the water to boiling point. The sea was indeed cooling the lava rock forming pillow like shapes under the waves, but the heat from the liquid rock before it solidified was transferred to the sea water. The lava continued to pour forth from under the ocean and now piles of molten rock spurted forth from the surface of the ocean. It was much too late for them to move anywhere. The choice they had was to wait for the fiery lava to consume them, or to boil alive in the sea. The situation was hopeless for the boys, and they both knew it.

"Pete, we are going to die! There's no way out! Oh God, I don't want to die like this! Will you do something for me? Please? I saw a movie about Joan of Arc when I was very young. She was burned to death at the stake. I was badly burned when I was young. It was my own damned fault; I held a firework in my hand. But it was so painful. Pete, I am terrified of fire now. Please, don't let me be burned alive! Please!"

Tears ran down Peter's cheeks, but he understood what they both had to do.

"Only if you do the same for me." he sobbed. "All for one and one for all?"

Knowing they had only seconds left to live, the two friends looked at each other. Jim pulled out his scout knife. It was long, and he had honed it to perfect sharpness. Peter did the same. His blade was equally sharp. They stared hopelessly at each other.

"We could have had so much in life. It shouldn't have to end like this. Jim, I am so sorry. I wish I could have done more for you. We have to do this. We'll save each other so much pain." said Jim. "Pete, please. Make it a quick death for me. I'll do it for you. We have to do this now!"

For a few more seconds, Peter wrestled with the concept of killing his best friend. Then he nodded.

"Oh Lord, Jim, why are we here. I don't want to die."

"Jim, I don't want to do this either but it's the best way for us. Let's do it. On the count of three." said Peter, trembling with fear. "Three, two, one, now!"

Facing each other, sweating in the intense heat, and separated by inches, the boys simultaneously plunged their finely honed knives into each other. Both boys fell immediately to the ground. Spurts of blood pulsing from their chests sprayed onto the hot lava as it closed in on them, turning the bloody streams into puffs of black vapor. Mercifully both boys had lapsed into unconsciousness. The lava poured over their bodies. Both dying boys were consumed in flame before being buried beneath the unforgiving flow.

8. A message for the world:

June 18th, 2012 4:00 Pm

USTIN GLANCED AROUND IN AWE AT the destruction caused by the lava flows. He seemed to be safe at least for the moment in the camp. However, without too much thought it was clear to him that he had no means of escape from his tenuous place of refuge. He still didn't understand how or why he had been spared. The lava flows had slowed somewhat, but still glowed brightly, radiating intense heat. Justin had dwindling supplies of food, no fresh water, and no means of communication with the outside world.

As he stared at the mountain above him, a terrible rage consumed him. This was all not supposed to happen. His life was supposed to be easy and care free. For God's sake, Justin was just a group leader for a travel company offering tame adventures for tourists, he was not James Bond. He cursed Stewart for leading him into this mess.

A sudden movement caught his eye. Something strange was happening on the peak above him. In the distance, he could make out a group of six figures emerging from a glowing cavern in the mountainside. Although they were still very distant, Justin could see that they were heading in his direction. With disbelief, he saw the figures splashing though the lava flow like it was a mountain stream. They came closer and closer. These were not people, they were giant beasts. The beasts were the stuff of nightmares, tall and broad, and resembling giant apes with horns. They wore no clothing, and their bare skins seemed to be covered with a living carpet of fire. They continued to move purposefully in his direction. The largest of the group led the way. It stared directly at him with deep jet black eyes, and Justin's skin began to crawl. Immediately, he sensed a voice in his head. The damn thing was talking to him! The beast's voice rumbled deeply as it spoke to him.

"You have been chosen."

"You are the one who will carry our message to your verminous tribe."

"You will be spared for now to do this."

The creature's voice resonated through Justin's skull like an immense foghorn. It was unbelievably powerful and blotted out all of his thoughts.

"I am Tibran, leader of the Fire Tribe. You have disturbed our rest. We sought peace and tranquility in the bowels of this mountain. You roused us with your stupid games, and now you and your race will suffer the consequences. We are all powerful, and your meddling will not go without punishment.

You will bring this message to your people. You disturbed us as we slept. Now we are all awake and we will bring your so called nations to their knees. You are vermin, and we will obliterate you from this planet, our home. We will crush you like the worms you are. You have only seen a tiny fraction of our power, and you were powerless to stop us. You are feeble and you will all die. Now you will go and tell the rest of your puny race that we are watching and will strike soon. You cannot resist us, and you will all die horrible deaths. This is the revenge of Tibran and the Fire Tribe!"

Justin fell to his knees, unable to stand as he was mentally cowed by the awesome power of the beast.

"Do you understand, pitiful human?"

"Yes." said Justin. "Yes, but why are you doing this? Why did you kill all my friends? Why?"

"Your so called friends were stupid. We were resting peacefully on this island. Your friends pushed a boulder down a shaft and into our home, awaking us from a vital sleep we needed to recover from our injuries. Damn you all to hell. You have no respect for the Gods. We will be done with you."

Tibran stood up, and slammed his fists into his chest.

"Now take our message to your feeble tribe. We are coming to get you. You will all die!"

With the message delivered, the glowing primates turned their backs on Justin and the camp, and loped away up the whorls and rivulets of the lava field. Tibran turned and stared back at Justin, boring into him with his impossibly dark eyes. Tibran sent Justin one final crushing thought.

"Have no illusions, you will all die!"

Quickly ascending the newly minted lava landscape, they disappeared into one of the lava vents. Immediately, the flow of lava from all the vents ceased, as if someone or something had turned off the supply. Slowly the silvery mountainside lava streams began to crust over, and to cool. Justin shivered despite the ferocious heat generated by the cooling rocks. He had been given a message to give to the world, and he did not relish the thought of passing it on.

9. Containment

June 18th, 2012 8:42 Pm

A FEW HOURS LATER, AS JUSTIN SLUMPED in a fetal ball next to the remnant of the tents, he heard a distant thrumming of blades cleaving the cooling late evening air. Faint glowing dots in the sky to the east resolved into the powerful beams of search lights as two large twin rotored Chinook helicopters approached the island. They slowed, and hovered warily as they surveyed the scene below. The searching beams illuminated the devastated landscape, creating a silvery glow where they touched the lava surface. As the aircraft approached, Justin could see men in uniform sporting video cameras. They were quietly recording the island's new topography. After a few minutes, one of the huge Chinook choppers drifted over to close to Justin's position. The pilot could see the island of vegetation and the tents. This would be one of the few areas of the island considered as a safe drop point for the soldiers on board the craft. Above Justin's head, climbing ropes snaked out of the rear of the chopper, and hit the ground close to his feet. After a few moments, six well armed marines rappelled down the ropes, landing dexterously on their feet in the jumble of small stones near the camp. The tents near Justin rustled and flapped in the downdraft of the massive helicopter blades. Justin peered upwards at the craft, happy to see his rescuers. A nagging doubt crossed his mind though that they might have another agenda. While in his heart he believed that the appearance of the helicopters and troops signaled they were on a rescue mission, somehow the fact that the troops were heavily armed set his teeth on edge. The six soldiers deployed rapidly around the edges of the camp site. They scouted around the edges of the lava flow, prodding the rock with temperature probes.

"It's cool on the surface." said one of the soldiers into his headset.

He had positioned himself close to Justin. "There are a few thermal hot spots on infrared, but the vast bulk of this lava is cool enough to touch."

Seeing that everything was at least for the present secure, the tall and burly soldier, obviously by his bearing and uniform markings the group's leader, approached Justin cautiously.

"I'm Flight Lieutenant James Farquhar of Her Majesty's armed forces." he started. "You are?"

"I'm Justin Hardwick, with Adventure Island Holidays." said Justin, although he had a curious feeling that the Major already knew who he was.

"What the hell happened here, son?" asked the Flight Lieutenant quietly.

"Sir, I have absolutely no idea." Justin started, then added "But I do have a lot to tell you."

"Justin, my job is just to get you the hell off this island, and back to some people who can make sense of this all. I don't need to hear your explanations right now. Come with me."

He took Justin gently by the arm and led him over to the rope still dangling from the helicopter.

"Grab hold!" instructed the Flight Lieutenant, and he helped Justin attach himself to the lead rope from the craft. Together they were hoisted back into the belly of the helicopter.

The remaining troops were left to explore the island, with strict instructions to report back if they found anything of concern. The lava had cooled sufficiently to be traversable on foot. The soldiers proceeded warily, and walked cautiously across the smooth lava surface. They had been told that the rock crust might be thin in some places and that pockets of liquid rock might still linger below, ready to crisp any unfortunate person who fell through.

The lead Chinook banked away from the island and headed straight to the military base in Lanark. In the cabin, Flight Lieutenant Farquhar remained silent for the twenty minute journey. Justin listened to the roar of the engines and the beating of the rotors, and thanked an unseen God. Justin was grateful for the lack of chatter, as he was not sure he could steel himself for what he had to say.

The Chinook touched down on a landing pad at the Royal Air Force's Prestwick base in Lanarkshire. Justin was immediately escorted by two burly Corporals to a featureless office building sitting next to the large cross marking the landing area. He was then ushered into a sparse office. He looked around to get his bearings. It was a small room, lit by a single light fitting in a mesh grill on the ceiling. There was a desk, and two chairs, and a medical gurney in one corner.

"Why am I here?" he asked one of the Corporals, who stood to attention next to the door.

"Sir, you'll be meeting Group Captain Sikorsky. He is the head of the military intelligence unit here."

"Military intelligence? Why?"

"Sir, I can't answer that. Please wait for the Group Captain."

Unbeknownst to Justin, the highly unusual volcanic activity on Sandeagh Mhor had been relayed by a military satellite to the British defense headquarters in Cornwall. A team of military and civilian investigators had been dispatched by the UK government to determine its source. There was a furious buzz of activity to learn more about the remote island. Further investigation by the military intelligence unit had uncovered that the island was uninhabited, and typically deserted. This week however, a small travel company called Island Adventures had ferried a group of tourists to the island for a camping adventure. The tourists and their guide from Island Adventures were supposed to stay on the island for a week. Although there seemed to be pure coincidence between the occurrence of the geothermal activity and the tourists being on the island, Group Captain Sikorsky decided that they would need to debrief any survivors to make sure. At this point, it appeared Justin was the only one who had survived.

The Group Captain had taken it upon himself to undertake the interrogation. He burst into the office and threw his enormous bulk into the chair behind the desk.

"Sit down, Justin." he ordered.

Justin complied. He had a pretty good feeling that what this man wanted, he got.

The Group Captain was a giant of a man, towering six inches over Justin's not inconsiderable height. He had a deep scar on his left cheek as a result of a climbing accident. He was not one to concern himself about his appearance, and he forgone reconstructive surgery. The scar now pulled his mouth into a permanent sneer. His presence alone would have been intimidating to Justin, if Justin had not recently been exposed to a huge fiery horned beast that dwarfed this man. He thought back again to the instructions he had been given. No one would believe him, but he had to try to get the message through to the authorities.

Justin was extremely concerned that for some unknown reason he was being held accountable for the events that had unfolded. He also felt intense resentment about the way he was being treated. He had come close to death, and no-one seemed to respect that. All he wanted now was a luxuriously hot shower, and to drown several beers and crash into bed. Somehow, though, Justin was pretty sure that his agenda and the Group Captain's were not the same.

The officer lit up a cigarette, and stared at Justin.

"Mind if I smoke?" asked the Group Captain.

Justin said nothing. He had a feeling his answer would be ignored anyway.

"You know why you're here?" he asked Justin. "Speak up lad, we haven't got all day."

"Well, I guess it has to be something to do with what happened on the island?" said Justin.

"Funny man, eh? Of course it has to do with what happened on the island. Tell me exactly what went down over there. Don't miss anything out. The report said you had nine companions. What happened to them? You were supposedly in charge."

Group Captain Sikorsky stood up, and walked round the desk until he was directly in front of Justin's chair. He leant forward and whispered in Justin's ear.

"You will tell me everything, and it will be the truth. Now!"

"I don't know what happened to all of them, but I did see some human remains." said Justin. He felt his bowels loosening with fear, and hoped he wouldn't disgrace himself.

"From the beginning, Justin. Exactly what happened?"

Justin proceeded to give an in-depth review of the events that he had witnessed as best he could remember them. He took the colonel through the meeting in Campbeltown and ended with the appearance of Flight Lieutenant Farquhar. The colonel listened thoughtfully, with a stony face. When he got to the part about his encounter with Tibran and his family, the Group Captain raised a hand and motioned him to stop.

"A giant flaming gorilla with horns?" he said mockingly. "And this gorilla gave you an ultimatum for humanity. You expect me to believe that crap?"

He shook his head, and turned around to speak with the marine who was smirking quietly next to him.

"Sir, it's all true!" said Justin aggressively. "Why would I make it up?"

"Why indeed?" countered the Group Captain.

"Your story was fine until you started finding charred bodies. Did you murder them, then create a cover story to try to cover your tracks? Its immaterial anyway, I don't think we'll find any bodies on the island. The lava flows took care of that. I think we'll have to find out the real truth another way."

He motioned to the second Corporal, who had a medical insignia on the sleeve of his jacket. The Corporal advanced purposefully towards Justin, carrying two hypodermic syringes. One was empty, and the other contained a clear amber fluid.

"We can make this just as simple or as complicated as you want, Mr. Hardwick. The orderly here will take a sample of your blood for analysis. I am particularly interested in finding out if you are taking drugs. Then we will give you a mild sedative. If you resist, I'll have you strapped to that gurney over there and we'll do it the hard way."

"The only way he could have made that all up is if he had been taking some hallucinogen." thought the Group Captain. Will Sikorsky believed that all of Justin's generation was dope fiends and drunkards. He believed that Justin's story was a classic example of a drug induced fantasy. No way was he going to let Justin off the hook lightly. "But we have ways of making him sing like a canary." he mused, a wicked gleam in his eye.

Justin felt that he had no choice but to cooperate. He was friendless in this room, and he knew he would have no chance of getting a lawyer. He also had no desire to be hog-tied and forced to submit by this military muscle man.

"Do what you have to do." he said.

The Group Captain smiled a cold and amused smile and nodded to the Corporal.

"Roll up your sleeve, sir." the Corporal said, brandishing an evil looking cannula. "This won't hurt much if you keep still."

The medical orderly swabbed Justin's left elbow with an ethanol pad. A rubber tourniquet was applied above his elbow, making his antecubital vein stand out prominently. Swiftly, the orderly took the polyethylene cannula and stainless steel trocar, and with a quick stab, positioned the venous access port into the bulging vein. He then took a Vacutainer, an automated blood sampling vacuum filled vial, and connected it to the port in Justin's arm. Justin's bluish venous blood flowed vigorously into the tube, sucked in by the vaccum. When the tube was full, the orderly removed it from the port. He packaged the dark tube along with some supportive paperwork, and set it aside. Later it would be sent to the local hospital laboratory for analysis. The orderly now brought the second syringe and its contents and injected the amber liquid slowly the port in Justin's arm. Justin could feel his grip on consciousness slipping as the powerful sedative penetrated deep into his brain. In seconds, he had developed a complete inability to resist his captors, physically or mentally.

The Group Captain asked him the same questions again. Even if Justin could have lied, after the neuroleptic and anxiolytic cocktail he had received, he would have been totally unable to do so. He repeated the answers in a low monotone. When the Colonel asked about his drug use, he repeated again that he had never taken any psychedelic substances on the trip, or in his life.

Will Sikorsky was becoming increasingly frustrated. The cocktail always worked. He had to have a lunatic to interrogate today. They'd get nothing of much use out of Justin Hardwick. His brain was wired wrong. It had to be. This whole damn escapade was a waste of military time and resource. The events on the island had been a natural phenomenon, nothing more. And that story about a giant flaming ape? Pure fantasy. Well, he would document what had been recorded, and pass the information on to his superiors. He gave strict instructions to his subordinate to keep Justin under highest security lock and key for the present.

"Look after him, and lock him up. We don't want any fanciful rumors spreading about aliens invading the planet, do we?"

He left the room and slammed the door.

10. Briefing.

June 19th, 2012 8:30 am

ENERAL HAYDON PORTER HAD HASTILY ASSEMBLED a group of experts in Colchester Garrison to discuss the phenomenon. They met together in a large room, secured from the outside world. It was a gloomy room, with a large rectangular metal table in the center, painted a dull military green. Some of the visitors sat on the uncomfortable chairs surrounding the table. Others paced nervously round the room.

"Professor McLeod, give us your thoughts." said General Porter, bringing the meeting to order.

Professor Iain McLeod, the expert geologist co-opted on the military evaluation team, shook his head.

"There is no way on earth that this extrusion of lava on Sandeagh Mhor is a natural occurrence." he said.

"Firstly, there has been no seismic activity detected in the area, with the exception of one isolated small localized tremor in the immediate vicinity of the island. A single small tremor! This event is completely atypical of what we would expect leading up to a major eruption. Volcanic eruptions are always preceded by a crescendo of increasing seismic events. You can't have an eruption without magma welling up from a fault or hotspot in the earth's crust."

Professor McLeod looked intently at his colleagues. He continued, scratching his jaw thoughtfully.

"Secondly, the eruption appeared to have been of a very brief duration. It wasn't accompanied by the usual degassing of lava we see at Pu'u O'o or any of the other erupting volcanoes on the planet."

The Professor was referring to a volcanic vent on the flanks of

Kilauea on the Hawaiian Big Island that had been erupting now for almost twenty five years.

He frowned again as he continued. "There was no release of sulfur dioxide. In fact, apart from a tiny residual trace of sulfur in the lava we tested on the surface flows, there was almost no evidence that this was indeed terrestrial magma. Our sampling of the local air revealed almost no pollutants."

There was an outbreak of muttering and shaking of heads in the group of scientific experts.

"Thirdly, the eruptive flows were generated by several simultaneous outpourings of lava from localized fissures all over the surface of the island. That is again totally atypical of any eruptive pattern we have observed in the shield volcanoes of the Hawaii Island chain or the composite volcanoes in the Pacific rim of fire. Indeed, in any of the volcanoes that we have studied in the last hundred years."

Professor McLeod paced restlessly, his hands clasped behind his back.

"It is just impossible that this eruption was a natural event." he muttered.

"Well, if it wasn't natural, what was the cause?" asked General Porter. The General had been appointed as the military leader of the investigative team by the Prime Minister.

Group Captain Sikorsky and Major Archibald Brandon also listened attentively.

The Group Captain had spent an hour that morning debriefing the scientific team about his interrogation of Justin. Justin had spun a highly fictitious yarn about spontaneous combustion consuming the visitors to the island, or more likely bolts of lightning incinerating them. Then he had rambled on about a giant fiery talking horned gorilla horde. The chief gorilla had commanded him that to tell the world authorities about the imminent destruction of mankind. It all seemed extremely far-fetched.

"Group Captain Sikorsky, you questioned the witness. Do you believe what he told you?"

"We used standard interrogation techniques, and I'm certain he told us what he believes to be the truth. However, do I believe what he told us? No. I think the young man was under the influence of narcotics, and fantasized the whole thing."

"Thank you, Group Captain. I think we are all of the same opinion. Giant fire breathing gorillas with horns don't seem to be commonplace in the Scottish highlands."

There was muted laughter in the room.

"But that does leave us with an unexplained volcanic eruption off the coast."

The General looked directly at Professor McLeod.

"You have some more investigations to conduct I assume?"

The Professor nodded.

"My colleague Professor Kevin Mitchell is on the island right now with an investigative team."

"Then report back to the group once you have concluded your investigation. I need to brief the PM."

The General made his way out of the briefing room, and picked up a phone. He was connected immediately with the British Prime minister.

The Prime Minister of Great Britain, the Honorable John Marsden, had requested an update as soon as possible after the debriefing. The General spoke cautiously.

"Our conclusion is that we cannot form a conclusion at this point in time, Prime Minister. The volcanic eruption seems have been a singular and isolated, and as yet inexplicable recurrence of volcanism in an area where volcanic activity has been extinct for many millions of years. No evidence of military or other threat to the United Kingdom has surfaced. A crack team of geologists is examining the recent eruption site for any evidence of previously undetected geothermal activity, but as yet has not reported any rationale for the pyroclastic events. Professor McLeod and his team will report back to us once they have gathered additional information."

"Keep close to this, General; I have a bad feeling about what is going on here."

The Prime Minister put the phone down, and turned to watch the television coverage of the event.

11. Firestorm

June 19th, 2012 3:44 Pm

A T THE SAME MOMENT THE PRIME Minister had been talking with the General, a team of ten hand-picked of highly qualified scientists was combing the island of Sandeagh Mhor, complete with a military escort. Unusually, they could not find a single source for the lava flows. They had observed pillow lava formations under the ocean near the rocky beach, but these flows were limited to a thirty foot distance from the shore, and were capped by pa'hoe hoe low viscosity flows running over their surface. The whole geological event just did not make sense, and there were no clues as to why it might occur.

"I don't believe the data." said Professor Kevin Mitchell, the lead geologist, with a puzzled frown.

"It all makes absolutely no sense. And yet our instruments have all been recently calibrated, and they don't lie. All our sensing devices indicate that this lava flow was of an extremely low viscosity, the hallmark signature of an ultramafic eruptive event. The viscosity of the lava flows was approaching that of water. The residual heat beneath the surface of the lava flows indicates that the lava had a temperature of at least one thousand six hundred degrees Celsius. This is unbelievably hot for a modern lava flow. This type of eruption has not occurred since the Proterozoic era over five hundred million years ago. The earth's mantle is just too cool these days to allow this type of lava flow to occur. The flows we have seen in Hawaii and other shield volcanic regions are hot, measuring in at around twelve hundred degrees, and they flow smoothly in pahoehoe formations, but this stuff is unbelievably fluid. The spatter cones indicate that the height of the fountains of lava reached over three hundred feet high, and thousands of tons of molten rock erupted per minute. The whole eruptive event is unbelievable. Just unbelievable! There is no evidence of Felsic flow, no a'a a'a clinker, and the cooling rock mineral signature is high in iron and magnesium. This is just not possible!"

"What on earth is he talking about?" asked one of the soldiers who had assigned to protect the scientists.

Dr. Mervyn Wylie, an associate Professor, and the most senior of the assistants to Professor Mitchell took the time to explain the scenario to him. He peered through his thick spectacles at the soldier who had asked the question.

"The Professor is concerned that the molten rock in these lava flows is inconsistent with any lava flow we have experienced on earth in the last few hundred million years. Such flows existed in pre-history when the earth's core was much hotter, but there is no way they can exist today. Today's lava is cooler, and forms Felsic lava flows, thick and short lava flows consisting of rhyolite or dacite rock rich in silica, aluminum, potassium, sodium and calcium. The ultramafic flows of prehistoric times would flow like water, and were richer in magnesium and iron, hotter and much less viscous than standard lava flows."

"Professor, there has to be some reasonable explanation for this event, don't you think? There is incontrovertible evidence in front of us all that a major eruptive event occurred on this island. I am well aware that today we don't have an explanation. However, that is based on our current knowledge. We really haven't had time to digest the data we have gathered at this point. Yes, there's no doubt this eruption was real. The evidence is incontrovertible. Even stranger, the flows were limited in extent and involved a type of lava not seen since the dawn of time. We have to believe our analyses. There has to be a rational explanation. As surreal as a super-fluid lava eruption seems, without the hallmarks of typical lava flows we all have observed worldwide in recent times, as we all can see, it destroyed all life on this hell forsaken island."

"With the exception of one fortunate young man."

Junior geologist Dr. George Garcia took no offense. His experience had been limited to date to the typical pa'hoe hoe flows on Hawaii. They were so predictable. The lava was hot and fluid and tended to pour across the older flows. When the surface flow cooled, the flowing rock formed lava tube expressways where the molten rock, insulated from cooling air, poured in golden incandescent rivers following the force of gravity. The tunnels of lava remained molten, pouring seawards at a high flow rate, eventually emerging either as fresh surface flows, or causing eruptive mounding and cracking of the cooled and solid surface lava. Recently, he had stood, sampling ladle in hand, before jagged a'a a'a flows. These were less impressive manifestations of an eruptive episode, but they had an inexorable ability to push everything ahead of the aside, and bury and burn whole towns. The a'a a'a flows were slow moving crumbling walls of semi solidified rock that eventually cooled into a glassy, crusted, razor sharp field of broken rock that would slice the flesh of the unwary soul who dared to cross them.

But there was absolutely no evidence of such flows here on the island. The impossible had happened, and it was up to the scientists to explain it. As yet they though, they had no clue to the origins of the phenomenon they had witnessed.

The Professor and his team had continued to sample the rock flows leading from the summit, and also the newly cooled lava beneath the sea's surface. Mostly they searched for signature elements to help them attempt to reveal the origins of the rock. Having done all they could, the team commenced packing up their instruments and samples to board the transport helicopter loaned by the military for the occasion. Suddenly, one of the geologists, Alistair McEnroe, a red headed burly bearded Scot from Aberdeen, noticed a curious red glow under the restless waters near the curved remains of the jetty.

"What do ye reckon that is?" he enquired of his colleague, Dr. Bill Garland, a sassenach ex-Cambridge whiz kid known to his friends as Bill, who had undertaken his Ph.D. in Hawaii.

In addition to enjoying the pleasures of the tropical paradise, Bill had spent most of his time deep diving and studying Lo'ihi, the underwater volcano building a submarine summit close to the shores of the Big Island. Lo'ihi had many thousand feet still to climb in the next fifty millennia before it was likely to become the newest Hawaiian real estate.

Bill looked intently towards where his colleague was pointing. He noticed with horror the golden glow beneath the waves.

While he watched, the ocean surface began to spin off swirling clouds of steam, and an ominous bubbling of boiling sea water accompanied the brightening glow penetrating the surface.

Bill guessed in an instant the likely cause of the disturbance. He had seen similar eruptive events in his Scuba gear while circling above Loi'hi's submarine summit. But this underwater upheaval was of a much greater magnitude. There was an enormous submarine eruption beginning, very close to the island.

"Oh, God, we have to get out of here!" he yelled.

He attempted to keep his voice calm, to avoid any panic with his colleagues, but his fear rapidly overcame reason and he blurted out:

"It looks we are about to experience an underwater eruption of some sort. A really big one. I really think we need to get out of here. Right now!"

He turned, yelling to his colleagues to follow him, and ran towards the helicopter. Without any hesitation, the others scientists and their military escort took his lead and rushed towards their only means of escape. Ten scientists and four marines clambered rapidly into the twin rotor USM C CH-46 Sea Knight helicopter, and Bill closed the door.

"Get us airborne, Captain. For God's sake get us out of here!" shouted the Professor to the pilot. Once the door was closed, the huge rotors of the helicopter began to spin lazily, and then with increasing speed.

While the pilot did all he could to get the helicopter airborne, Bill picked up the transmitting video camera, and began streaming a continuous live picture and the sounds of the emerging undersea volcano to the command center near the coast of Scotland. In the military base, remote and secure from the emerging action, the assembled team looked on with wonder and then with growing horror as they saw the glowing orange incandescence expanding then exploding from beneath the waves. Within seconds, sputtering steam roiling in furious clouds off the surface of the sea, and gave way to shrieking fountains of fiery lava, reaching many hundreds of feet into the air. A thunderous roar and high pitched hissing of steam drowned out all other extraneous noises. As the glowing lava globules reached their fiery peak, and started to descend through the air they were caught by a strengthening wind. The breeze pushed them in the direction of the island, causing them to land in great smoking piles of red hot rock. Like hailstones in a storm, the spherules of molten rock piled up on the ground, creating spatter cones and ridges.

"That lava is heading right for us!" yelled Bill. "Get us out of here. Now!"

The lava fountains did appear unnervingly to be under some sort of malevolent control. The direction the spattering molten rock was taking became alarmingly apparent. Like jets of water out of a hose, it appeared that fiery fountains were all being aimed towards the helicopter. In the helicopter, there was a growing sense of panic. The pilot, who could see that his craft was in dire peril, applied full power to the engine. The blades were turning, but still alarmingly slowly, as the huge jets of fire increased in diameter and effortlessly doubled in height. Deadly tear drops of magma rained closer and closer to the spinning rotor blades. As the pilot pulled the vehicle into the air, the myriad of red hot droplets descended on the rotors, and began to stick to them like cement. As more lava adhered to the blades, they began to spin erratically. Then, the blades began to melt, completely destroying their ability to lift the massive machine. The troop carrier abruptly fell to the surface of the island. The collision damaged the landing gear and shook the occupants. They were stunned. It was now obvious to everyone in the helicopter that the machine would not be able to get them out of here. For those watching in the command center, the video stream flickered and weaved and bobbed around the inside of the machine. Worse still, screams were heard inside the craft as gobbets of molten rock peppered the hull, hissing though the metal and landing directly on the bodies of the science team and the pilot. Fabric charred and caught alight as the hellish volcanic rain became more intense. One by one, the scientists succumbed to the intense heat, and molten firebombs, with the video camera faithfully recorded their death throes. It was only when a massive explosion occurred, caused by the demise of the helicopters fuel tanks, that mercifully the video feed to the command center ceased. Fragmented, and with no remaining living occupants, the rapidly melting remnants of the helicopter were buried under an accumulating pile of ash and slag.

12 Attack!

June 19th, 2012 4:15 Pm

AN AWED SILENCE CLOAKED THOSE IN attendance in the Colchester Garrison command center. The whole destructive episode had lasted just seven minutes. The events that all present had just witnessed seemed truly beyond belief.

General Porter broke the silence.

"Oh my Lord!" gasped the General. "What on earth just happened?"

"It appears our men were killed by lava from a volcanic eruption." stated the Major bluntly.

"There isn't any reason for any type of volcanic activity to occur off the coast of Scotland. And, I know it can't be true, but if I can believe my eyes, that eruption looked as if it was deliberately designed to take out our men."

The General had witnessed carnage before in battle, but on those occasions the enemy had always been a tangible force. This time he was totally blindsided by the events he had just witnessed. There was no logical reason for what had just transpired. He had faced many demons in battle, but on this occasion he had no idea of just who or what he and his troops might be facing.

He replayed the events in his mind over and over again. Something unusual flickered at the edge of his consciousness. He ordered the technician to replay the video, this time in slow motion. He was sure he had seen something stirring in the fire fountain just before it had doubled in size.

The technician reset the recording to when Bill Garland had first turned on the video camera. The glow was already present, and was beginning to rise to the surface. Slow motion helped them see what had happened prior to destruction of their colleagues. Just before the lava streams had erupted, they could see several discrete glowing shapes moving in the lava under the water surface. By their motion, and seeming purposeful activity, they were clearly independent of the melted rock. Then the boiling water and steam cloud had obscured the view. The mist cleared when the giant lava fountain had punched upwards. As the orange and red geyser had emerged from the glowing surface of the bay, a vague shape of what appeared to be a large beast was visible. The General ordered the technician to stop the playback and to enhance the image. Now, as the whole group looked on, the figure became clearer. They could see all see a huge horned gorilla-like being. The creature had black coals for eyes, and in place of a pelt, its skin surface shimmered with flickering flame that resembled burning fur.

It had turned in the direction of the helicopter, and stared malevolently directly into the lens of the camera. With an upward wave of the beast's arms, the lava spurting from the ocean doubled in volume, and reached high into the air. The creature was clearly directing the lava flow in the direction of the craft.

There was pandemonium in the room.

"Silence!" commanded the General. "There is something very evil on that island. You all saw what I saw. I know it's beyond belief, but we may indeed been invaded by aliens."

"We need to alert the War Office and the Prime Minister. Immediately. Those things must be stopped!"

13. Assault

June 20th, 2012 2:00 Pm

HE US ARMY AMPHIBIAN ASSAULT CRAFT approached the island of Sandeagh Mhor very cautiously. From its original dark appearance, with tufts of green vegetation, Sandeagh Mhor had metamorphosed into a silvery gray whale, with a distinct tail where a spatter cone had formed where the helicopter had been. Even the basaltic columns were streaked with rivulets of silver, where lava overflowing the cliff edge had attached itself to the broken ledges and dribbled over into the sea. The rocks beneath the cliffs had been covered with a combination of pouring lava from hidden fissures on the ocean bed, and then coated, like icing, with semi-fluid ribbons of rock splashing down from above. The place was eerily silent. No bird cries could be heard, as the local seagulls, terns and cormorants had fled the island for safer pastures. The lowly bleating of sheep was no longer a part of the background noise. All the local sheep had been driven either to jump off the cliffs to their doom, or had been cornered on the plateau, and had been roasted into oblivion.

Still, the island seemed preternaturally silent, as if someone or something was watching their arrival, and had a surprise waiting for them. The commander had ensured that his troops were equipped both with the latest assault rifles and grenades, and that back-up mortars were available. Unusually, they had also been equipped with a variety of fire extinguishers, and no explanation was forthcoming for the deployment of such tools. In the briefing the marines had received, they had been told only that there was some kind of animal activity on the island of Sandeagh Mhor, and they were to be alert for anything out of the ordinary. They had also been told of the recent volcanic activity, and what to do in the event of an eruption. The latest technology in particle filtering gas masks had also been issued as routine, in case of sudden venting of toxic volcanic gases.

The craft landed at the northern end of the island, close to the huge spatter cone that had now cooled sufficiently to be safe to touch. The cone reached over one hundred feet into the air in a rather discrete pile, with a ridge of solidified lava extending towards the beach.

Private Jenson Graham thought the hill resembled the sand castles he used to make on the beach on vacation in Italy, where he had scooped out a hole in the sand near the water's edge and waited for it to fill with filtered sea water. Then he and his brother would cup their hands and dip them into the water and sand mix. The hard pan surface of the beach was the perfect building base to create towers and castles of dribbled sand. Given that they were vacationing in Italy, the towers of rippled sand had been named the Dolomites, after the rugged mountain ranges in the north of the country. Jenson was a typical naval recruit, with close cropped hair, and rugged good looks. Like his comrades, he was dressed in camouflage gear, with heavy boots. Like half the men on his team, he wore a strange green device strapped to his back. The device resembled a large tank, and had a tube and nozzle hanging from it. It was extremely heavy, and he was glad that he did not have to carry a gun as well.

He and the rest of his platoon leapt out of the boat and onto the smooth and slightly rippled lava surface at the edge of the island. It was easy to traverse the lava, as it had covered all the pebbles and boulders with a smooth stream, and there were no bushes to impede their progress or line of sight. Here and there, there were miniature lava trees, where a particularly tough bush had resisted the lava long enough to create a carbonized column supporting a covering of rock. It was a barren and alien landscape, now quite out of keeping with the rest of the islands in the area.

As they slowly and warily advanced up the smooth plateau surface, all eyes in the platoon were open to trouble. But seemingly there was nothing to cause them concern. However, they all had an uncomfortable feeling of being watched. Worse than that, their nerves were set on edge by an unseen crackling energy in the air, akin to the feeling prior to lightning striking. Whispering voices suddenly flew unbidden into the heads of the marines. As they approached the base of the volcanic peak, the voices became increasing loud.

"Do you hear what I'm hearing, Captain?" asked Private Pietro Sgherza, as he tapped his earphone. "I feel like I'm picking up radio noise in my headset, but it doesn't go away when I pull out the earpiece."

"I'm getting that stuff too, Private, and the rest of the guys are reporting weird noises in their heads. It's very spooky. Keep your eyes peeled."

The noises became progressively louder as they climbed up to the base of the volcanic peak. Strange lights started playing along the surface of the newly deposited lava, golden, then red and white. In an instant, fierce beams of intense white light streaked out from minute cracks in the surface of the newly minted rock. With a growing concern, the Captain debated briefly what to do. It was time to regroup and consider their choices from the safety of the landing craft.

"Marines, move on out to the landing craft! Now!" ordered the Captain.

The platoon of marines started to retreat to the safety of the landing craft. The Captain continued to monitor his surroundings. He was deeply suspicious of this terrain, but as yet there was nothing to target, nothing to destroy. As the men approached mid plateau, near the abandoned encampment, the same flickering and glowing lights played over the rocks they were approaching. Beams of bright white light shot out from linear cracks now criss-crossing the congealed lava in front of them, blocking their view of the coast and the landing craft. The whole island lit up like a Christmas tree. The only area of the island that looked normal was the abandoned campsite. For no reason apparent to the Captain or his men, the area had been spared the complete domination of the landscape and destruction produced by the lava flow. They could even see a small copse of trees curiously undamaged by the heat from the surrounding flows. The tents clustered around an old campfire had also all survived intact. Trusting the normal looking campsite over the flickering and glowing lava fields, the Captain ordered his men to move on the double to the island of vegetation.

"Men. Get your asses over to that copse of trees! I don't trust this lava any further than I can throw it."

The platoon ran en masse to vicinity of the campsite. The lava field was unstable. Anything could happen. It was obvious to the Captain and his troops that they had a much better chance of dealing with an enemy in a territory they understood, rather than on the treacherous lava field.

As the beams of light flared ominously in the lava flows surrounding the campsite, bubbling pools of orange lava welled upwards out of cracks in the ground, signaling the commencement of a new and deadly eruption.

"Oh hell, we're in deep shit now!" the Captain said to no-one in particular.

He looked around at the bubbling lava. The size and shape of each of the lava pools was strangely symmetrical. The pools expanded outwards until they touched each other, then the molten rock streamed upwards and outwards towards the camp. In seconds, a circular band of molten stone, hissing and steaming ominously in the afternoon air, surrounded the soldiers in the campsite.

"Hold your ground!" ordered the Captain.

"Against what, Captain?" said Private Sgherza, totally fazed by the rising wall of hissing rock.

"I'm going to get us out of here boys. There's nothing to fight, and I think we're in bad trouble."

"No kidding, Captain. Let's get the hell out of here!"

The Captain required no further prompting. He radioed for help from the support helicopters circling the island. This was no random volcanic eruption, it was a coordinated attack.

"I'll be damned." he thought, going over in his head the briefing he had been given by his superiors. "Those idiots in central command know what they're talking about after all."

Two key points stood out in his head, and one order he had been given. As he had listened incredulously to the story, the Major had continued.

"There may be fiery creatures on the island. If there are, these beasts may be able to control the movement of molten volcanic rock. If you encounter any of the creatures, take them out!"

"Sir, I don't mean to question you, but do such things exist?" he had said, his astonishment clear in his expression.

"Soldier, I don't lie, and I don't fabricate monsters. If anything bad happens, kill as many of the creatures as you can, then get you and your platoon out of there. We'll be standing by to pick you up at the first sign you're in trouble."

Per his orders, the Captain ordered half of his troops to make ready the large green canisters that had been strapped to their backs. Circular valves on the sides of the canisters opened their contents to garden hose sized tubing, with a control trigger and handle at its tip. The platoon members carrying the containers turned on their valves and grasped the handle, fingers itching to pull the triggers to release the contents of the containers. They had rehearsed this procedure endlessly, but none of the men had ever thought they might have to use this novel weapon. For the remainder of the platoon, the Captain ordered them to lock and load their conventional AK 45's.

"This is it!" he thought to himself. "This is where we find out if we can beat these things."

He still couldn't bring himself to believe in fire monsters, but the heat singeing his eyebrows was pretty damn convincing. At least the command had attempted to provide them with some means of defense. The canisters were full of a new and powerful refrigerant which could be directed as a powerful stream against a close target. He trusted bullets over a souped-up fire extinguisher against any enemy any day, but the canisters and their contents was the best that they had right here and now. Something even stranger was happening to the lava surrounding them.

From various points around the camp, the marines could see glowing golden heads, complete with sharp spiral horns and intense coal black eyes slowly rising above the hissing molten lava in each of the ponds. Then they were horrified to see huge muscular arms and torso's, covered with flame, emerging from the puddles of molten rock. There were twelve monsters in total, horrible beasts towering above them. But now they had targets!

"Open fire!" yelled the Captain.

The troops swiftly complied with his order. Immediately they were all deafened by the rattling of automatic fire emerging from multiple machine gun barrels. The high velocity rounds whined through the air as they headed towards the beasts surrounding the camp. Two of the marines placed mortar tubes in position, and they poured a stream of shells into the air towards the monsters.

In the distance the troops could hear the sound of the support helicopters battling through turbulence caused by heat rising from the rippling lava pools across the island, and they redoubled their efforts to defeat the menace in front of them.

"Come on guys, get your asses in here." yelled the Captain over the radio. "I don't think we'll win this one, and we need to get out of here! For Chrissakes get the hell out of this unholy battlefield!"

The barrels of twenty sub-machine guns poured forth concentrated streams of high velocity rounds, concentrating on the ungodly monsters in front of them. The troop's training kicked in, and with tight precision they channeled grenades in the direction of the flaming apes. Mortar rounds pounded out of their launchers and zeroed in on the gargantuan beasts.

"Come on men, let's crush these apes. Shoot their damn butts off!"

The encircled soldiers in the camp fought with fury and determination to attempt to eradicate the enormous fiery predators.

"Surely it can't get worse." groaned the Captain.

It was clear they were losing the battle. The thousands of bullets pouring forth from the automatic weaponry melted as soon as they came close to the evil beings, leaving transient silver and copper puddles on the flickering skins of the creatures. The molten bullet drops occasionally coalesced and then slid down the monsters bodies to the lava surface like raindrops on a window pane. There, they were rapidly subsumed and disappeared into the molten rock below. The mortar rounds that were to have rained death from the sky on the beasts suffered the same fate, and exploded prematurely in mid air as their casings melted, and their high explosive contents ignited.

The grenades they had thrown too suffered a similar fate, and proved useless against the beasts.

After what seemed like eternity to the troops below, the choppers finally hovered overhead, getting ready to touch down to evacuate the troops.

The Captain issued one last command:

"Use the extinguishers!"

The ten marines carrying the large canisters pulled their triggers in unison, concentrating on the tallest beast, most likely the leader. If they could just knock out one of the beasts, then they knew they could eventually win this battle. Thick streams of frothy white coolant foam gushed forth from the souped-up fire extinguishers, coating the largest beast as he towered above the troops.

"Is it working, Captain?"

The tinny request for information buzzed in the Captain's earpiece. It had come from the Major who was hovering safely in one of the helicopters several hundred feet above the island, and well away from the lava flows.

"I don't know yet, sir. I'll let you know once the foam clears."

The hissing streams of foam frothed forth from the nozzles of the ten fire retardant cylinders that were aimed at the giant creature standing unmoving on the silvery rock surface.

The Captain looked on intently, hoping for a miracle. But what he saw confirmed his fears. The foam evaporated as it touched the burning skin of the beast. The Captain observed the roaring horned attacker for any sign of it slowing down, or any sign of it developing any weakness. None was visible. "Our damned counterattack was as effective as us pissing against the wind." The Captain realized that his troops were in deep trouble. For a third time, a human expedition to the island of Sandeagh Mhor was in full retreat. Again, as had happened previously with the team of scientists, the attempt to retreat turned out to be futile. The helicopters descended towards the troops, blowing hot gusts of air against the tents, and rustling the leaves and branches of the few trees remaining on the island. Such a tactic had been anticipated by the apes, and they scooped up huge globes of steaming hot lava. As the helicopters came close to landing in an

175

attempt to load the marines for evacuation, the giant apes hurled their flaming fireballs at the rescue craft. The balls of molten rock splashed against the metal and glass walls of the craft, and quickly coated the whirling blades of the choppers. Wherever they landed, the material dissolved into red hot puddles. Huge gaping holes appeared all over the craft, making them lose the ability to remain airborne. Their twirling blades picked up the majority of the molten rock, and quickly eroded into useless nubs of metal. After a few seconds of this tumultuous assault, each of the choppers in turn burst into flame and crashed into the lava surrounding the camp. They exploded on contact with the superheated rock, the fragments dissolving immediately in the newly emergent liquid lava pools. One by one, the fragments of the rescue helicopters disappeared as they were consumed by the fiery hell surrounding the stricken marines.

With the escape attempt by the helicopters thwarted, the attention of the beasts was turned on the remaining troops. Long streams of flame shot out from the fingers of the demons, pouring liquid hell into the beleaguered encampment and turning the soldiers, one by one, into crisped cinders. In a few heartbeats it was over. The former campsite, like a green blot on the landscape, had been converted to a silvery tomb for the troops, now covered by a fused dome of magma.

The military commanders, who had observed the debacle from an observation helicopter close to the center of the island, were totally stunned. The best of the best of the most prestigious and feared fighting corps in the world had been wiped out like insects.

14. A Plan of Action

June 21st, 2012 10:00 am

ENERAL PORTER PUT HIS HEAD IN his hands, and then rubbed his temples. His craggy face looked very grim.

"These things are deadly, and I have no doubt they will attempt to carry out their threat." he said angrily.

"All right men, what the hell are we going to do about these killers?" he asked, looking in turn at each of his subordinates in the room.

"Nuke the bastards!" said Major Hinkson. "We just saw how much our conventional weaponry did to these bastards. Absolutely nothing!"

"How the hell do you nuke an island off the coast of a populated country, Major? We'd have to evacuate half of Scotland. And how do you know it would work? These things look pretty indestructible to me."

"Look, you saw how much damage we did in Hiroshima and Nagasaki, and we've got weapons way more powerful than that now."

The conversations in the room became passionate. After a few interchanges regarding possible options, General Porter called a halt to the discussions.

"Look." said the General. "This is getting us nowhere. I'll call the PM's office and we'll put together a task force to work out the plan. We must wipe out this incredibly serious threat to mankind, and soon."

The General made his way from the briefing room to his private office and picked up the phone.

"Get me a secure line to Number One." he ordered. A few minutes passed and then the General heard the voice of John Marsdon on the phone.

"What's the latest, Haydon?"

"You know what's happened, sir?" asked the General.

"Yes, I do, General. I had a feed of the entire catastrophe from the observation helicopter beamed to my office. I am so sorry for the loss of your men."

"This is without doubt the most serious threat our nation has faced, sir." said General Porter.

"In my humble opinion, and in the expert opinion of most of my top advisors, something radical must be done to fix this problem, before it gets out of hand."

The Prime Minister agreed.

"Jesus, General, these things are playing in our back yard, and we've already lost way too many people. We don't even know what they are and how to stop them."

"What can we do to contain these abominable creatures?" asked the Prime Minister, his hands gripping the edge of his chair tightly.

The General did not mince words.

"Sir, these abominations have not been damaged or reduced in their ability to fight in the slightest by our conventional weapons. A short sharp surgical strike might do the trick. But we're going to have to pull out our biggest guns. I am urging you to support us in annihilating this menace using extreme force."

"You mean nuclear weapons, Haydon? That's radical all right. But we have several million people in Scotland who would be affected. We haven't the ability to make a limited nuclear strike that would blow apart that island, and believe me, I think they are holed up deep in that damned rock."

"If we obliterate the island and these creatures," said the General, "we will probably purge the earth of this fiery menace before we are all destroyed."

"Oh Lord, what a mess. You are right. We can blow apart the

island, but what about the local population, the wildlife, the long lasting effects of a nuclear strike. Radiation exposure. Fallout. The economy. Talk reason, damn it? What about the longer term consequences for the world. This is not just a tactical technical exercise! Taking the nuclear approach will wipe out more than just these sodding beasts!"

"Sir, if we don't do something, I firmly believe we will not have anyone left on the planet to worry about the economy, or the environment."

The Prime Minister was a man who had shown himself to be extremely capable of making difficult decisions under pressure in the past. But first and foremost he was at heart a politician. While the security of the people of the United Kingdom ranked top of his priorities after his self interest, he also remained cautious about doing anything that would decrease his or his party's popularity and chances of reelection. Old habits die hard.

The General was not stupid, and had been through his own share of political turmoil in his time. He took no offense to the verbal riposte he had just encountered. He had fought enough battles with politicos and had won on many occasions.

"Sir, with all due respect, we have no time to be thinking right now about how your electoral voters will react. We need decisive and active leadership. This event is without precedent in history. If we are still around to be judged, how do you want your name to go down in history? We cannot be weak in our response to this major threat to humanity. No doubt there will be an element of collateral damage. This is war." retorted the General. "We can't afford to wait, sir."

"Collateral damage, General? You mean citizens? We'll just go in and blow up a Scottish island without worrying about the Scots? I can see that being written about in history books, and I don't think you and I will look too good."

The General was persistent.

"Sir, this situation is extreme. We need to do something right now to limit the risk to not only the people of the United Kingdom, but also the world. These creatures want to eliminate the human race from this planet. You heard about their threats. Do you think they can't do what they said they would do?"

"No General, I believe after what I saw today that these creatures over enough time would be able to carry out a systematic eradication of the people of the world. But we must have some less radical options for starters?"

"Sir, once again, it is our belief that these beasts will stop at nothing. You just told me you believe they can wipe us all out. I know you are not suggesting we shouldn't try to prevent that!"

The Prime Minister was silent for a moment.

"Haydon. I need some time to think. Let's get a few more minds behind this. It's a hell of call to make, and I want to be absolutely sure we have no more options. I trust your judgment, but if we screw this up, we are both history, or toast."

In his heart, the Prime Minister was torn between agreeing with the General that something urgently needed to be done, and fear of alienation as a result of his making the wrong decision. He felt to an extent that the General had been acting in an insubordinate manner, pushing him towards a radical decision that he was not sure he had the strength to make. But he also knew deep inside him that the General was right.

"All right, Haydon. Let's move on getting a plan in place. Get yourself to Aldershott and get our military advisory group assembled immediately. General, that's an order. I'll join you all after conferring with the cabinet. But understand this. I'll be with you every step here. I believe just as you do that we do indeed have no time to lose!"

"Yes, sir." acknowledged the General, and put down the phone. He made another quick call and arranged for a military jet transfer to the Aldershott military base.

Back in number ten Downing Street, the Prime Minister ran his fingers through his thinning grey hair. He had the reputation amongst his cabinet and staff of remaining calm during challenging times, and this grooming gesture was his only sign of stress. He was well aware that he was facing the most difficult situation of his three years of leadership. He thought back to what his predecessors had faced. War had been tough for Churchill, and Atlee and several earlier prime ministers, but at least the conflict situations at that time had been somewhat predictable for them and their troops. Men fighting against men he understood, but they were facing a totally new and unpredictable threat now. Worse still, they had a total absence of concrete information about the nature of the beasts. He sighed. His cabinet and the United Kingdom military forces were looking for his decisive leadership. Doing nothing, in his mind, was not at present an option, and he would not let them or his fellow countrymen down.

Carefully, he ran through again in his mind everything he knew about the current threat to the country. Once again, he realized he had very little information to process, and there was in his view little chance of getting more data before a crucial decision needed to be made. What options were left other than a radical strike on the island? Diplomacy? He laughed quietly to himself. How can you be diplomatic with a thirty foot flaming ape intent on destroying you?

"I guess we could isolate the island." he mused. "We did that after all with that other problem island, Gruignard."

Gruignard was another island off the west coast of Scotland. The island's sheep had been exposed to anthrax during the Second World War. But that wouldn't work. It wouldn't stop the beasts from travelling to the mainland. Or would it? Could they travel across the ocean? Damn it, he just didn't have enough information. And then there was the ultimatum that had been delivered by that Adventure Island employee on behalf of the fire beasts. The Prime Minister had read the transcript. What was his name? Justin. Justin Hardwick. Could what he had said be a fabrication? It seemed unlikely, given that they had all witnessed the force that had completely and mercilessly destroyed the scientific research party and the military expedition. Why would he lie? And given that his interrogation had been undertaken by exceptionally well trained personnel using the best methods known to man, the Prime Minister seriously doubted that an untrained civilian would be able to beat the system. Everything he had heard suggested that the threats were real.

His thoughts were interrupted by a loud knocking at his study door.

His secretary, Diana Goldstein, a dowdy, conservatively dressed forty year old spinster with a razor sharp memory and formidable administrative skills, opened the door. She always reminded the Prime Minister of Miss Moneypenny from the James Bond movies, but he had absolutely no romantic interest in her. Indeed, if he even cast an eye outside of his household, Gemma, his wife of over twenty years would have him hung, drawn and quartered. Briefly he had a vision of himself hanging by a noose until he was almost dead, being cut down and eviscerated, with his genitals being removed and stuffed in his mouth, then being tied to four strong horses each pulling in opposing directions until he was literally torn limb from limb. He wondered if that would be his fate in a post nuclear strike era where he had ordered inadvertently the destruction of many thousands of innocents. Diana brought him out of his reverie.

"Sir, your car is ready to take you to the cabinet meeting." she said. "You are on a very tight schedule today, sir."

"I know. Thanks Diana."

The Prime Minister stood up, and wheeled his leather backed chair back under the well of his ancient oak desk. His mind remained extremely troubled.

Unbidden, more thoughts tumbled through his consciousness.

What about another frontal assault? Sending in more troops to combat an alien menace that could manipulate the very ground on which they stood? Not an option. Starting an aerial bombardment with creatures that could turn plain rock into a weapon of enormous power for which they currently had no countermeasure? No, that would be a foolhardy waste of equipment and life. Not only would it rapidly deplete the country's military resources, but waging a futile war would quickly turn public opinion against him, as had happened to many of the supreme commanders of the United States in recent years. He had heard the threat from the creatures to rid the world of what they saw as human pests. Something must be done. Yes indeed, something must be done.

What about the General's thoughts? They could indeed try to eliminate the threat using massive force? They had the weaponry and technologies to obliterate the island. They could reduce it and its monstrous inhabitants to a nuclear wasteland. But so near to the Scottish mainland? The Prime Minister was blessed with a very visual memory. He had seen the disaster movies. Smoking barren wasteland without any vegetation. Nothing living. Humans who survived in shelters huddled in the debris of formerly proud buildings, covered with burns and sores. They didn't know it but they were dead already, slowly succumbing to infections and anemia as their bone marrow failed to produce red and white blood cells after being exposed to cumulative radioactive toxicity. Yes, the nuclear approach had both immediate and longer term consequences. The amount of nuclear fission required to vaporize the island would deliver a large and deadly cloud of radioactive fallout. Carried on the prevailing winds, the radioactivity would travel several hundred miles eastward. The cities of Glasgow, Edinburgh and Dundee would in all probability become uninhabitable. The total population affected could exceed two million people. If they did pursue this drastic option, the Prime Minister knew he would have to order evacuation of central Scotland and relocate terrified and hysterical people to temporary camps well away from the danger. And the reality was, there was so little time to get such an evacuation organized, and despite the best efforts of his military and civilian commanders, some people would refuse to leave and would die in the holocaust.

That way at least, he considered, casualties could be kept to a minimum. Knowing he was on a tight schedule, but with Sandeagh Mhor now his top priority, the Prime Minister of Great Britain opened the door of his office. He looked back into the room that had served him so well for the three years he had been there. What indeed would happen later today, tomorrow and for the rest of his tenure? He sighed once again, and turned to face the world. He descended the broad staircase of the Downing Street townhouse. David Fowler, his portly and good humored butler opened the front door of number ten for him. He strolled rapidly towards the black sedan with tinted windows that was waiting to take him to the cabinet meeting. The car journey gave him additional time to collect his thoughts, but no alternative solutions came to mind. The driver pulled up the car at Checkers. Armed policemen were visible everywhere.

He was guided to the large conference room where his cabinet team had been assembled. It was a room designed to impress visiting statesmen, with ornately carved wooden columns leading up to a delicately painted ceiling, depicting cherubs and roses. Dark paintings of by-gone prime ministers stared down disapprovingly at the men and women gathered in the room. A huge carved teak conference table and accompanying chairs occupied the center of the room. The massive table legs connected with an ornate thick pile Persian carpet stretching almost to the walls of the room. Normally the Prime Minister found this a peaceful room, but when he arrived, the room was in an uproar. His cabinet ministers had all been provided with a synopsis of the horrific attacks, and they clamored him for more information as soon as he entered the room. The Prime Minister strode the length of the room, and moved to a portable lectern that had been placed at the far end. Despite his imposing entrance, he was annoyed to see that several of his cabinet ministers were still holding multiple heated conversations.

"Silence!" he commanded, and picked up a heavy wooden hammer which had been placed for the purpose on a ledge at the top of the podium. He slammed the gavel twice in quick succession on the wooden lectern, and yelled once again:

"Silence!"

Gradually, with some muttering, the ministers ceased their conversations and sat down. The Prime Minister waited in silence until he had their undivided attention.

The Prime Minister stared at the familiar faces of his twenty two member cabinet. John Mortimer, a portly and heavy jowled man sat on his immediate right. He acted as Secretary of State for Foreign and Commonwealth Affairs, and as deputy for the Prime Minister. He had already been in contact with his counterparts across the globe to alert them to the situation. Madeleine Jeffries, an imposing lady in her late forties sat opposite him. She acted as his Secretary of State for the Home Department, and had been one of the first to hear about the growing threat. Jennifer Justice, aptly named for her legal qualifications and for being his Secretary of State for Justice, sat next to her, and looked grim. Sir Nicholas Gregg sat next to her, a grey haired Baronet, and his Lord Chancellor. Lady Tracey Maine, the Prime Ministers favorite, sat next to the Chancellor, her face a picture of concern. She had the responsibility for being the Secretary of State for Defense, and the arrival of a threat on UK shores was clearly within her portfolio. The remainder of the cabinet he knew less intimately, but he nodded in turn at each of them.

He paused, and took a deep breath.

"You've all read the briefing documents. No doubt some of you read through all the information at least twice. I did. It is very hard to believe that a disaster of this nature is happening here in the United Kingdom. But this is no joke. This is no farce. Civilians have died. Our troops have died on the Island of Sandeagh Mhor off the coast of Scotland, trying to deal with a menace that threatens us all. The information you have is what I have, no less no more. Late yesterday, these creatures, some call them devils, some call them fire apes, threatened the peoples of the world with total annihilation. Can they do this? Most of us who witnessed the way in which they dealt with our troops would say yes."

The Prime Minister stopped, reading the faces in front of him. In some, there remained disbelief. Others had quiet acceptance. Grim determination showed on the faces of others. But there was no evidence of fear. Yet.

The Prime Minister had received a call from General Porter as he had travelled to Checkers. The news was grim. The advisory committee had discussed options at length, and had decided unanimously to recommend a nuclear strike.

"Friends, colleagues, I thank you once again for your words of advice. I have listened carefully to you all. I have also taken advice from the military and from civilian intelligence sources. I have come to one conclusion. For the sake of the world we must do something. Our nation and our countrymen are under threat. Our neighbors in India, in the United States, in China and Mexico are all under threat. I'll repeat, we cannot sit back and do nothing.

No doubt, each of you has your opinion as to what we can or cannot do. That's good, but on this occasion, we don't have time for debate. You are all aware that there are a number of options, and the consequences of each option are far reaching. I have no new solutions to offer. You all know of the reputation of General Porter and his military think tank. You are also aware of Professor Mitchell and his scientific advisory committee. We are facing an unprecedented threat in the United Kingdom, and both committees have recommended radical action. Fortunately, as yet, we have no evidence that this vile malignancy we have discovered off the coast of Scotland is spreading.

But we have been threatened. The beasts we have roused have said they will kill us all. They have also demonstrated that they have a means to do so. This decision has been tough, but in time I think you will all see that we really have no option. So this is what we will do. The plan is drastic, and it will involve major hardship for a sizeable portion of our population. We will undertake a surgical strike on the island of Sandeagh Mhor using conventional and nuclear weapons to eliminate the beasts."

There was a collective gasp from the assembled ministers. The Prime Minister continued unfazed.

"The complete destruction of the island will pose enormous logistic difficulties, but it is my belief and the belief of our advisers that such a course of action will in all probability eradicate the threat. It is no small task to vaporize an island. It will require use of high explosive and nuclear weaponry in a way that is unprecedented on this planet. I have been advised by experts in the United Kingdom, the United States and Europe that we must fracture the island's backbone using precision guided bunker bombs, shatter the underlying rock formation with nuclear blasts and proceed to douse it and its hellish inhabitants with a dose of radiation that would be lethal to any life form. Given prevailing wind patterns, and the extent of the nuclear blasting required to do the job, we have no option but to evacuate a great part of central Scotland. I have also been in discussion with key dignitaries in Norway, Sweden and Denmark. It is possible that nuclear fallout will spread to these countries too. I hold enormous admiration for the spirited leadership of those in power in the Nordic countries. I talked with Olaf Bjornssen the Prime Minister of Norway, and he offered us any support we need to eradicate the beasts. Gunnar Hildebrand in Sweden gave us the same support. We are blessed with cooperative and understanding neighbors in Europe. I know we would do everything we could to help them in times of trouble. I am still amazed at how quickly they all understood what we are all facing. The visual images from Sandeagh Mhor are very compelling in a terrible and tragic way. I thank them all immensely for supporting us in the momentous decisions we must make."

Several ministers raised hands aloft to request a turn to speak. The Prime Minister waved them away dismissively.

"Let me finish." he said. "We may have time for debate later. But for now, let me give you the details of the remainder of the plan. We have also to consider the commercial fallout that will inevitably be a consequence of making this decision."

He stopped, breathing heavily.

"The whole damned world runs on commerce and money, and it would take one little trigger to induce panic in the world markets, and a collapse of trade across the world. If it is managed correctly, the damage can be contained."

Secretly he wondered if the nations of the world had that sort of time. As the General had said, who the hell would be left on the world to care about the price of bread if the demons got their way. Feeling the weight of command on his shoulders, he wondered if he could continue.

"I didn't get here by backing off from a challenge." he told himself. Summoning an inner strength, he straightened his back, and continued:

"I have also been in talks with the Chief Executive of British Petroleum, Shell Oil and other prominent leaders in the oil community. The production of North Sea oil will be required to be shut down for a period. We will have to evacuate workers on the rigs until we know if they'll be affected by the fallout cloud. This action will indubitably raise oil prices, and gold prices will rocket. But as you all know, people and markets are resilient and unpredictable. Our business leaders will grumble, but they will comply. We do not want an oil disaster on par with the British Petroleum fiasco in the Gulf of Mexico in 2010.

We would all like to understand in much more detail how bombing the hell out of Sandeagh Mhor will affect the mainland. Thankfully, we have access to the best minds in the world. The advisory groups have consulted on a hypothetical basis of course, with meteorology experts in the National Oceans and Atmospheric Research Agencies, the Massachusetts Institute of Technology and our own Cambridge University. Their computer modeling has indicated that the radioactive cloud at this time of year, with current weather patterns, should not reach as far as Aberdeen on the east coast. Perth, a little further south, has a fifty/fifty chance of receiving fallout. The North Sea oil fields should completely escape contamination by radioactivity, but we have to build a safety buffer. If all is well, North Sea oil production will be able to resume less than a week after the explosion."

The conference room had been set up in the Long Room at Chequers. Normally it housed antiquities, and had the largest collection of Oliver Cromwell memorabilia in the world. Today it was bristling with all the latest communication technologies. A large LED display screen had been set up at one end of the room to display computer generated imagery. The Prime Minister picked up the remote control for the audio visual equipment and pressed a small button shaped like an arrow. On the screen behind him, and image showing Scotland and the North Sea sprang to life. Using a tablet computer in front of him, he took a stylus and drew on the tablet. Mirrored on the projected display, the approximate extent of the area of fallout to be expected from the obliteration of the island of Sandeagh Mhor took shape. The circle he drew encompassed an area from Oban in the southwest of Scotland, and travelled across the Scottish border with England on the east coast. On the north side, Inverness was included, and the circle passed through Arbroath on the east coast and then onwards out into the North Sea. Both Edinburgh and Glasgow, major population centers were included in the area of fallout.

"That is the area we will need to evacuate. Over three million people will be displaced."

Using a different color he circled an area in the highlands north of Inverness near Fortrose, a smaller circle in Lincolnshire near the east coast and another in northern England in the North Yorkshire Moors.

"These areas of land will be requisitioned for us to create holding camps for those people displaced by the evacuation. They are well away from the expected fallout, and relatively uninhabited.

We will have to monitor radiation patterns very carefully though, and handle further evacuations as required."

He paused, and took his time to gauge the reaction of the cabinet ministers.

At length he continued. "I believe we have time to implement this solution without causing panic, if we arrange for those in the direct path of the nuclear fallout to be relocated during the next seven days."

He paused once again to allow the concept and the time frame to sink in with his audience.

"I need input from you all. Come on, give me your thoughts."

The Minister for Health stood up. He was the sole Scottish member of the cabinet, and the bad blood between the Scots and the English was well understood by all present in the room.

"Prime Minister, it's all very well to be talking about this as a theoretical plan. There are real people living in the circle you just drew who will be directly affected by this disastrous idea. Just how long will the radioactive fallout last in the areas you have outlined? How long will we have to keep the fertile lands of the Scottish Lowlands as a nuclear wasteland? Surely there has to be another way to deal with the situation!"

"Angus, let me deal with the first question you asked first. It's a difficult one to answer, given that we don't know what the weather conditions will be on the day. Rainfall in the area might restrict how far the radioactive cloud will travel. We know that half the debris from the bombs will be deposited as radioactive dust on the ground within twenty four hours. The other debris, mostly fine particles, and vaporized water will travel further but will be more diluted. We believe the area contaminated by the blast will be about seventy miles wide and three hundred miles long.

I have brought Professor Gordon Cartwright to the meeting. He is a nuclear physicist and a physician, and I thought he might be able to explain the radiation exposure to you and what it will mean for the land and for the people much better than I can."

The Prime Minister beckoned to a grey haired balding man in a dark pinstripe suit who had been sitting quietly in the rear of the conference room.

"Professor Cartwright?"

The Professor moved towards the lectern, and stood in front of an audience he knew might turn confrontational. He paused, cleared his throat and started to explain.

"Fallout is inevitable when there is a nuclear explosion. Fallout is literally the tiny pieces of soil, water, bomb casing and dust that is exposed to radiation, and then blasted into the atmosphere, descending following the laws of gravity. We have learned much from nuclear explosive tests conducted after the Second World War. You are all aware of Geiger counters. They measure exposure to radiation in Roentgens, the number of ionizations occurring in a unit of air. What is much more important is a unit called the Gray, or Gy for short. The Gray measures energy per unit mass, not air exposure. The lethal dose of radiation in Grays is about two and a half Gy, or in alterative units you might have encountered, two hundred fifty rad. One hour after the bombs explode, the radiation in the crater will be about thirty Gy per hour. The fallout rapidly drops off the further the distance from the explosion crater. One hundred miles from the crater, in the direction of the prevailing wind, the level of radiation will be ten Gy per hour at twenty four hours. Within approximately one month, the levels will be low enough in the affected area for people to enter the area and for decontamination to occur. So ladies and gentlemen, the problem will not be there forever, but we wouldn't want any civilians in the area for at least two months, and certainly no one will be visiting Sandeagh Mhor for the next 6 months."

The Professor finished, looked around for questions, and seeing no one raise a hand, he returned to his chair and sat down again. The Prime Minister once more took the stand.

"Although we have our own warheads, the US President has volunteered to supply us with as many megatons of nuclear explosive capacity as we will require. He and his advisors also see the need to protect the population of the world from this incredible danger.

It is obvious that some people within the circle I drew will choose to remain in their homes. If so, we can do nothing to help them. We have formulated a communication plan that will spell out to everyone concerned exactly what will happen if they remain in their homes. We wrote the document aimed at people with sixth grade education. There is an audio version for the blind, and for people who are unable to read. It is graphic. It shows what happens when a human body is exposed to radiation. Unlike the ridiculous warning on cigarette packs, it states that if you do not evacuate your home, you and your loved ones will die. Period. You are opting for suicide if you stay.

The choice to live or die will be in the people's own hands. Make no mistake, ladies and gentlemen, we are at war, and there will be collateral damage."

While there were a few members of the cabinet who were stunned into silence with what they had heard, the majority stood up and applauded the Prime Minister.

"I am leaving the organization of the evacuations in the capable hands of the military. General Porter, have you got the picture?"

The General had been listening to the Prime Minister's speech through a second secure phone line.

"Yes, sir, I'm here, and I thank you all for your understanding of this terrifying situation."

"General, I will leave it to you to establish military curfews, and for our army to handle the details of the evacuation. Once a clear plan has been put in place, I will broadcast what will be happening to the nation. We must avoid panic at all cost, and so our decision today will remain a secret. Anyone found to be in breach of confidentiality today will be considered a traitor, and the death penalty in the United Kingdom still remains in effect for that offence. Do I make myself clear?

Nods of assent came from the members of the Prime ministers cabinet.

"General, you have your orders. You have a hell of a task ahead of you, and we're running out of time!"

Although it had been with great reluctance that the Prime minister had agreed to this solution, now the decision was made, he would support it to his grave. He sincerely hoped that would not be the final outcome.

"I declare this meeting closed." he said, and marched out of the room. It had been a tough speech for him to make. And he was well aware that tougher ones would follow. His head hurt. He walked down the magnificent hallway of the Chequers residence, and out into the open air. He took several deep breaths of the sweet shire air, and found that his headache had eased somewhat. His car was waiting for him outside.

"Simon, take me back to Downing Street, old chap." he requested his driver, a little more tersely than was usual for him. Simon nodded.

"Yes, sir." he said thoughtfully, knowing that something major was brewing. He could read the man, and it was very unusual for him to display any negative emotion. Something was indeed up, but he knew better than to pry.

Once again, the Prime Minister used the journey time to continue his dialog with world leaders and with the military over a scrambled and secure line. Traffic that evening was thin heading into London, and Simon made good time getting back to number ten. Once he arrived, the Prime Minister headed directly for the communications room, located in the rear of the ten Downing Street complex, in the part known as the mansion. The communications suite always cheered the Prime Minister, and it had a good view over the half acre garden towards St. James Park. Today however, his brows furrowed deep with thought, he hardly glanced through the plate glass window towards the well-tended flowerbeds.

15. Countdown

June 25th, 2012 9:00 am

HE PLANNING STAGE FOR THE NUCLEAR eradication of the island progressed with military precision. General Porter had taken charge of the process, now had updates every two hours from the trusted aides he had hand-picked to cover every aspect of the mission. Now he sat in the large sparsely furnished conference room in the great hall of the Aldershott barracks. In front of him, Mitchell Donnely and Michael Grady, both Lieutenant colonels in the brigade had been ordered to provide him with details of progress they had been making.

"Mitch, what progress have we made with the coordination of the bombing raid?" asked the General.

"Sir, we have enlisted the help of the United States Air Force, and the mission will fly out of the Lakenheath USAF base on Saturday at precisely 0500. The bombs will be dropped in sequence and guided to their targets. The US has also been extremely cooperative, if a little nervous, about supplying us with the nuclear and non-nuclear explosive. It was an act of genius to suggest they fly the mission. No need for them to have to protect the weapons, and there are no concerns about the bombs getting into the wrong hands. Everything will be in place Friday morning. The mission will be computer coordinated, and we have back-up computers in case of any failure. Sir, I believe that we will be in position Saturday morning as planned to nuke the island."

"Splendid, Mitch. I knew I could rely on you. This whole thing gives me the willies though. There will be enough nuclear explosives flying above Scotland next Saturday to wipe out Edinburgh and Glasgow. You can stand down Mitch. Make sure the orders are clear. Mike, how about the civilian evacuation? This is a tough one. We can't afford to let anything go wrong here either."

"Sir, we are also making progress. Damn shame we can't order the public to obey orders yet. I can't wait until we have martial law enforced, and we can speed up the whole thing. Anyhow, we have secured the land for the camps. That caused a bit of a stir. We had to cite the war act, and requisition the parcels of property from some grumbling owners. We had to cart a few of them off to our local detention center to keep their mouths shut. Anyhow, we now have each of the properties in our hands and sealed off from prying eyes. We are furthest advance with the camp in rural Aberdeenshire on the queen's estates. That one was no problem to secure. The camp in the Yorkshire Dales was a little trickier. These damn farmers are a tough breed, and stingy with their money. If they couldn't see a profit in it, they weren't going to budge. The camp land is secure and we are moving the accommodation in tomorrow. We did a little better in Lincolnshire. Work has started there on the roads, and we'll have the tents in place by Tuesday. We estimate the three camps will be ready for occupation by Wednesday at the latest, and we'll have provisions there for three months for starters. Our lads will provide the local policing of the area to prevent trouble."

"Thanks Mike, your boys are doing a great job. I'm surprised nothing has leaked yet. The PM will be broadcasting to the nation soon. Then we'll be able to get away from this cloak and dagger stuff."

The plan was for the vast tracts of land to be equipped with temporary sanitation, tents, emergency rations and a huge amphitheater where updates on the progress of the battle, and the timing until the temporarily displaced Scots could return home would be updated daily. Hundreds of trucks would be involved in the process to enable supplies and temporary accommodation to be taken from the storage reserves, The Construction Brigade was in charge of carting truckloads of rock to create rough gravel roads leading from the nearest highways to the camps.

In Downing Street, the Prime Minister was nervous. Knowing the number of people who would be involved, he knew it would be impossible to keep the whole venture confidential for much longer."

"It's time for me to talk to the nation, Diana." he said. "At least then we can enlist as many civilians as we need to get the process completed on time. Please get me Queen Elizabeth on the line. She has agreed to tag team with me so that we can bring the British spirit to the forefront. That might help. She understands the gravity of the situation, and is very willing to help. I just need to check that she has her speech in order, and that we complement each other. I wish we had more time, but the clock is now ticking."

"Yes, sir." said Diana, and she placed the call.

"Your Majesty."

"Prime Minister."

"Is everything ready at your end Ma'am? I just received a copy of your proposed speech, and you will have received a copy of mine. To me, I think it is the best we can do. Our prime aim is not to alarm the general public and the world, but it won't be easy. We will be broadcasting from the Palace at six o'clock this evening."

They had chosen the state room at Buckingham Palace for the television broadcast. The Prime Minister felt sincerely that having Her Majesty deliver a soothing message after he had to let the world know what was going on might help blunt the absolute enormity of the choice they had taken. He couldn't fault his staff. They had sent out a message to the British people alerting them to the fact that he had very important information for them. The details of the timing of the impromptu broadcast were notified through e-mail, cellular phone message, radio and television broadcasting, and word to mouth. A YouTube video announcing the broadcast went viral in 30 minutes. By the time the six o'clock broadcast was to occur, more than ninety percent of the British population, and over fifty percent of the world population knew that something pretty extreme was happening. In an unprecedented move, the Prime Minister and his equivalents overseas had arranged for the key stock markets to be closed around the world at six pm Greenwich Mean Time to prevent massive panic selling of stocks.

There was a collective hush around the world as the British Prime Minister appeared on screens in a tailor made dark pin stripe suit, with a somber dark blue plain tie. His facial expression was neutral.

"I have some news I wish to convey to you all." he started. He paused, and sipped some water from a glass in his hand. "One week ago, a party of visitors to a remote island in Scotland encountered some strange creatures, the like of which have never before been seen on this earth. It turns out that they had been disturbed in some way by the presence of the people visiting the island. The giant creatures were apparently woken from their prolonged hibernation in a cave beneath the surface of the island. They are aggressive, they are extremely powerful, and they have threatened the security of the entire world. Our initial attempts to communicate with them have failed. Many of our brave troops were killed while trying to eliminate the menace they pose. We attempted to destroy them, but our attempts were unsuccessful. We were met with a counter force so extreme, that we have no way of containing them by traditional military methods. Currently they remain on the island. I'll say it again; our standard weaponry has failed to contain them or to harm them in any way. Our major concern is that they may start moving away from the island sometime in the future, and although it is extremely unlikely, they may pose a hazard to all of us in this world. In conjunction with military and civilian leadership in the key countries round the world, we have decided to act now with a surgical strike. This attack may involve some risk for the local population in Scotland, and we have decided to evacuate certain areas and relocate people to a safe haven until the problem is solved. We ask for your cooperation, as we have asked before, and received in times of War. The British people are up to this challenge. We ask you to cooperate fully with military instructions, and to welcome your fellow British to new townships we are creating on a temporary basis.

Donations of non-perishable food, blankets, tents and bottled water are most welcome and we will place drop-off points for these articles in every major town. As yet, the extent of relocation is unknown, but we will keep you fully informed as we know more. We believe that relocation will be limited initially people living near to where the creatures were found off the west coast of Scotland. We will undertake the relocation in a staged manner as we believe there is no immediate cause for alarm. Thank you. I will not take questions at this time.

Her Majesty the Queen has most kindly agreed to speak with you all today."

On cue, the face of Queen Elizabeth, monarch of Great Britain, grandmother and blue blooded patriot appeared on the television screens of seventy million people in the United Kingdom, and over three billion people worldwide. She appeared unruffled by the Prime Minister's revelation, and she gazed deeply into the camera.

"Loyal subjects and peoples of the world." she began, speaking calmly, with little emotion.

She had dressed for the occasion in a very formal severe blue dress. Her only jewelry was a simple pearl necklace. She clasped her hands in front of her and stared into the camera, directly at the watching eyes of the world. Hers was a face the people of the United Kingdom could trust.

"Loyal subjects, we have been asked to talk to you today about an issue of national importance. We will need all of your support in the coming week. It seems we are at war with an enemy so fierce and determined to do us harm that we need immediately to make a critical strike on them and eliminate them from our land. They have threatened the people of this island, indeed the people of the world with a plague of destruction. We will not allow that to happen. We will destroy these beasts before they can harm any of our people. The British people have pulled together in the past to defeat enemies that seemingly would overwhelm us. We won through two world wars and we will win again. When we defeat this menace, we will celebrate as a country and a people. We will win, if each and every one of us puts our own personal interest aside, and holds our glorious country's best interests at heart. It is not for nothing that our land is called Great Britain. Our military have created a plan to contain and destroy the threat. As you are all aware, we can wield some very powerful weapons. Some of these weapons have far reaching effects. We do not want any of our people to be potentially in harm's way. In order to keep you all safe, some of you may need to move to a temporary new home while we deal with this invasion of our homeland. This home will be safe, Spartan but comfortable, and will be supplied with as much food and drink as you need. Our military are already organizing the places for people to stay. They have already set up temporary towns in the countryside, complete with schools, hospitals and they have stocked them with provisions. There will be entertainment, and you will be able to bring your favorite things with you. Although we need to deal with the enemy very rapidly, we still have more than enough time to move people calmly and safely to these temporary new homes. And I say it again; it will be for a few months at most. For those of you who will need to move to a safe place, it will not be long before you will be able to return to your homes. We know we can trust you all with the task of defending our homeland, while still getting on with your everyday lives. The backbone of Great Britain is unbreakable. Do not doubt we will win in the end. We thank you all for your support and your determination in the face of adversity. Each and every one of us will help defeat the rogue menace in Scotland. We'll do so while the world watches us, and observes the true British spirit.

We thank you all for your loyalty and support in troubling times. May God bless you, and bless us all!"

The picture of the Queen slowly faded from the myriad of video screens, television tubes and computer terminals around the world.

The broadcast had taken only fifteen minutes, but it had seemed like a lifetime to those who had been listening. In homes, in hotels, in hospitals and most especially in government offices where the speeches had been heard, the question was on all lips.

"What does this mean for us?" and more frequently "What does this mean for me?"

PreParation For Evacuation

NDER THE GUISE OF ROUTINE MILITARY training exercises, troop carriers rumbled through the small villages of Scotland. In order to prevent panic, the military leaders had decided to wait until the Prime Minister and the Queen's communiqué to undertake the majority of the preparation required to keep the populace safe for the nuclear strike. Most of the activities to be undertaken by the military required cooperation and support from the general populace. The landowners who had initially been incarcerated were returned to their homes. In order to placate them, they had been offered considerable financial compensation for their troubles. Grumbling mostly, but grateful for government support, the Majority had returned home to count their proceeds. Those that objected disappeared. While there was no military dictatorship in charge, the leadership of the country understood what peril faced them. Nothing and nobody could get in the way of the fixing the dire threat.

Generally, apart from a few folks on the west coast of Scotland who felt that they would not be affected by the exercise, life went on as normal. There was no sense of alarm, although some panic buying of food occurred in the stores, as people stocked up to cover themselves for a period of paucity. Supplies to the stores were uninterrupted, and since there were no shortages, the stockpiling generally slowed to a trickle.

James Duggan and his family had lived in their Glasgow tenement apartment for over twelve years. James was forty three years old, balding and developing a paunch, but he tried to keep fit as often as he could at the local gym. He worked at a local transport firm as a driver. His wife Brenda was several years younger than him, and was still an attractive red head. He delighted in the fact that she still had the good looks to turn heads on the streets of Glasgow. The couple had two twin fourteen year old sons, Ian and David, who had both inherited their mother's red hair. The family sat at the breakfast table and talked together about the news story that Jim had read aloud to them all.

"Don't you think we should be concerned about what is happening on that island, Sandy thingy?" asked Brenda, a cup of tea in her hand.

"It's too far away for us to be worried." replied James, waving his toast in the air as he spoke.

"I mean, just look where Sandeagh Mhor is. It's out there in the Irish Sea. And look how far away we are from the island in our home here in Glasgow."

He picked up the local paper from the top of the breakfast table.

"Brenda, Ian and David. Have a look at this." James pointed to a map of the west coast of Scotland that adorned the front page of the Glasgow Herald newspaper he was carrying in his hands.

The news hounds and the editor had taken great delight in sensationalizing the story. The map they had produced made it seem that Sandeagh Mhor was only a few miles away from Glasgow. Jim looked at the small print and the scale that placed miles onto the map. The Herald may have taken the opportunity to highlight the location of the island, but he could see the reality. Sandeagh Mhor was in close proximity to nothing much in particular. The nearest town to the island was Campbeltown, if a distance of 11 miles could be called close.

"The island is at least a hundred miles away from us." said Jim. He spanned the distance between Glasgow and Sandeagh Mhor with his fingers, the matched that up with the scale at the foot of the map.

"We're in no bother here. I can't see how what is happening there will affect us in any way."

The two twins begged to differ. They were of an age where they could not separate fiction from reality and their keen young minds had been fuelled by reading too many surreal adventure stories. Harry Potter had indeed fired up many imaginations. They were also guilty of watching too many movies depicting a graphic destruction of the world. Adding fuel to the flames, they were both avid fans of video games, especially those featuring alien invaders.

"Dad, what if we are being invaded by aliens from the other side of the galaxy?" asked Ian, his expression more one of excitement than anxiety.

"You and your space monsters!" scoffed his father.

"You both read way too many science fiction books and comics. There are no such things as aliens from outer space. Besides, the Prime Minister said that these trouble makers are creatures from this earth. Apparently we disturbed them while they were sleeping. We woke them up by accident. It is very likely if we leave them alone, they'll go back to sleep and leave us in peace. As far as I know, there is no alien fleet out there waiting to take over the earth."

He scratched his head, and gulped a mouthful of lukewarm tea.

"The only monsters in Scotland are you two!" he decided.

The twins grinned at their father. He was known for his unsubtle humor.

"Dad, you don't know the half of it." said Ian cheekily. "Just because you haven't seen any aliens, you think they don't exist. You know how big the galaxy is?"

"Get on with your breakfast. We don't have any space monsters here in Glasgow."

Hunger overtaking their appetite for the bizarre, the twins picked up their spoons and proceeded to finish off their congealing platefuls of porridge. Brenda looked up the clock over the mantelpiece. It was fast approaching nine. She got up from the table and looked at the twins.

"Get yourselves ready for school, and no more of this space monsters business. You've got a busy day ahead of you both today."

The twins scurried away to pack their schoolbooks into their shoulder bags.

Brenda looked closely at her husband. She could always tell when something was troubling him.

"You're scared aren't you?" she asked quietly. "You think there's something more to this than they're telling us?"

"I didn't want to bother the lads," he confessed, "but yes, why such a fuss about something innocuous, like a tiny rocky island out in the Atlantic? Why take the trouble to tell the whole world? Why not simply evacuate a few folks from the area until it all blows over?" He looked at his wife, with an anxiety he could not conceal.

"Yes Brenda, I'm scared! Give your cousin in Kent a call. Maybe we can stay with them for a few days until this blows over. There's something about Sandeagh Mhor and its inhabitants that they are not telling us, and I'm terrified!"

16. Evacuation

June 28th, 2012 2:45 Pm

COLONEL MICHAEL GRADY STOOD AND SALUTED when General Porter entered his office.

"Give me the latest, Mike."

"We have identified the area we will evacuate and have communicated this information to the law enforcement officers in the affected area. The main thing is to avoid panic. Look what happened when people left New Orleans prior to Hurricane Katrina. The roads were clogged for miles with people trying to escape. There were no rooms available in hotels, and people slept in cars. The poor folks got left behind to die in the storm. It was a total disaster. We are planning this evacuation to succeed. No one will be left behind. For each post code area, we have a list of people, and our volunteer group is compiling a database for each family and residence. We ask some simple questions, and provide instructions to the families and residents. The hospital evacuations have been completed, with just a skeleton staff remaining to look after people who get sick between now and the final person's relocation."

"So what do you ask the families, and what do you tell them?"

"Well, the main thing we need to know sir is whether they have a friend or relative outside the quarantined area that has a bed for them. We have organized a government grant for everyone who takes in a friend or relative to pay for the additional food.

Second thing we need to know is; do they have the ability to get themselves to that friend or relative. If not, we have organized transport to take them there.

Thirdly, if they do not have anyone to stay with, we tell them that we have established temporary towns for them to live in until the all clear is given. We give them a choice of the camps, and then arrange to pick them up and give them advice on a few belongings to take with them.

Fourthly, we provide them reassurance that although this will disrupt their life somewhat for the duration of the emergency, they will be looked after well, with all medical support required. We will provide education for their children, a bed to sleep in, and as much food and drink as they need.

We tell them that there will be stores open in the camp for luxuries.

Generally we try to keep every family or individual reassured that we are looking after their needs, and that they will be safe in their temporary homes.

We also reassure them that their houses will be looked after, and that should any damage be done while the beasts are being eliminated, the government will compensate them to fix it.

You know, keeping the communication simple really works. We have had very few people put the phone down on us, and those we have visited in person to ask the questions and get the message across.

As of Friday evening, we will have set up check points on all the roads leading to the quarantined area, and all vehicles will be off the roads as of then. No public transport will be running as of Friday, and there will be military patrols in every region.

We know the first wave of evacuations has begun, and we have instructed people to call our call center when they get to their safe location. There has been some traffic congestion, but not as much as we expected. Each person's data are reconciled so that we can follow up on stragglers on the Friday. The whole area will be clear by Saturday morning, and heaven help anyone who is stupid enough to remain behind.

Fortunately, most of the hilly areas to the north and south of the Central Lowlands of Scotland are sparsely inhabited. The cities of Edinburgh, Glasgow, Dundee and Perth are a different matter, but the evacuations are proceeding smoothly there too.

Most of the employers in the region have been very cooperative, and have given their staff paid leave of absence at our request. Of course they are expecting the government to cover their costs of lost business. We asked them to guarantee the jobs of all their affected staff, and they have done so. In many ways, we've made it like a giant paid vacation for people. It helps to plan ahead sir."

"Mike, you and your staff of thousands are doing a great job. Simplicity is the key. We will lose some civilians, but we'll have done everything in our power to minimize the losses. Do you have any relatives in the affected area?"

"Yes, sir, and they moved down south yesterday to join us."

"All right, I won't keep you from your business. Let me know if anything changes, Mike."

"Sir."

Construction of the three camps proceeded according to the precise military plan. Long lines of identical military green tents sprouted alongside mess tents, portable toilets and water reservoirs. Large trucks came and disgorged huge piles of gravel onto the grassy plain. Foremen supervised workers recruited from the local labor force as they laid down gravel tracks in precise lines rimming and bisecting the tent city. Although it was technically summer, the commanders of the field engineering corps knew that based on past experience it would most likely rain frequently on the camping sites. The key goal was to avoid too much mud being carried into the tents. The gravel paths would serve for the occupants of the tents to travel safely to mess halls, and to the entertainment center. Cleanliness in the camps was of key importance to prevent the spread of disease.

Military hospital tents, in true MASH tradition, were constructed for each camp. For entertainment, giant screens were erected to provide the bored population with television programs and movies. Local entrepreneurs had been invited to create a temporary shopping mall, to supplement the rations to be provided to the evacuees, and make a few luxury goods available for those that could afford them. Still, it was anticipated that in time, the boredom of living a confined camping life would lead to crime. The key culprits would be teenagers unaccustomed to the rigors of the camp. It was like a giant rock concert encampment, but unlike a Woodstock none of those conducting the operation knew how many days or months it would need to be in existence.

"At least this time we have the luxury of time to get our act together." commented Lieutenant Michael Forester, one of the engineers who had been tasked with the construction of the Highland camp. He had built refugee camps in times of natural disaster, typically without the supply infrastructure he had in place today. His colleagues agreed.

"I always prefer being in the driving seat." said Gordana Smetlana, the chief engineer.

"Most times we've had to put together a relief camp, we didn't have the luxury of time to do the planning. We have always had to react to a disaster that had already happened. This is so much better. We have had the chance to do some precision planning for the logistics of building a camp for 100,000 people. I feel so much better when we are in control."

"We'll be finished in the next twenty four hours, ma'am." Lieutenant Forester predicted.

"Thanks Mike. You helped make it all happen. And it has gone very smoothly, as I expected, under your leadership. I just pity the poor buggers who'll be stuck here for months until radioactive Scotland stops glowing."

17. Out Of Adversity, Opportunity.

June 30th, 2012 3:26 Pm

IKE THE OTHER AFFECTED REGIONS OF Scotland, the evacuation of Campbeltown progressed in an orderly fashion. Most of the citizens of Campbeltown were more than happy to get away from the disaster threatening their town. A few diehards remained behind, grumbling that they had lived there all their lives, and they weren't going to be moving for anybody. The old man in the tattered suit who had provided such a dire prediction to the Island Adventures party was amongst them. Despite reassurances from local officials that their property would be safe, these stalwart Scots remained behind, barricading themselves in their houses, having stocked up with enough provisions to last, as they saw it, through the crisis. Others lined up in the village square, to board one of the endless line of buses making their way up the A4 dual carriageway on the long journey to Ballater, and to the Highland camp. Campbeltown became a ghost town, with the exception of the strong military presence remaining in the area to prevent looting. Most people had taken their key possessions and locked them in basements, or carried them in suitcases for the journey. There was plenty of food for their travels, and the camps were well stocked with provisions and supplies for when the evacuees arrived.

Justin, who had been freed without compensation from his military confinement once the world had been alerted to the beasts by the Prime Minister and the Queen was one of the first to leave.

"I won't miss this boring old town." he said to his neighbor, Kenneth Ramsay.

"I hear you." said Kenneth. "I'm going to visit my sister in Blackpool. There are loads of things to do there. Next to Las Vegas, it's one of the most sinful places on the planet."

"That's not for me, Ken. I need to try something completely different. I'm heading off to the south of France. I've heard there are some very spicy young women there just looking for a stud like me."

"You have a one track mind Justin. After all you've been through, you deserve better than that. Not!"

"Thanks Ken. Good luck to you too!"

Justin had been given strict instructions to reveal nothing of what had happened on the island to anyone, on pain of death. He believed the threat.

"I can't even sell the story and make a few bob." he grumbled to himself. But he had told Ken that he had been through hell on the island and he needed to break free from his boring existence in Campbeltown.

On the spur of the moment he had decided to take a job in Nice in the south of France. He had read about Nice and Cannes and the Cap D'Antibes, and they seemed pretty cool. He could find some warmth for the winter there, and perhaps a girl or two to warm his bed. Being the stingy Scot he was, he had managed to arrange a ride for part of the way with Stewart, who was travelling to meet his aunt and uncle in Neasden in London. Justin wished Stewart well. Island Adventures was no more, having fallen into receivership. Stewart dropped off Justin at the departures level in terminal four at Heathrow airport for his flight to Nice, and gave him a hug.

"If it doesn't work out for you down there, give me a call, Justin. I still have a few ideas up my sleeve. And I won't hold it against you. Not unless you ask me to."

Justin just shook his head, and walked down the walkway into the terminal.

The steady stream of cars and trucks flowing out of the central lowlands steadied to a trickle as the weekend approached. Somehow the thought of nuclear fallout spurred the affected Scots to take up their belongings and move away for a time. Most moved south to the Lincolnshire and Yorkshire camps, if they didn't have anyone else to stay with.

Saturday dawned bright and clear, and with the exception of wild birds and the occasional lost dog, nothing moved in the largest cities of Scotland. It was indeed like a scene from the end of the world.

It was a taste of things to come.

18. Onslaught

July 2nd, 2012 6:15 am

HE SIXTY UNITED STATES AIR FORCE bombers approached the island from the south at a height of forty three thousand feet, flying in close formation. From the ground, any curious observer looking skyward could see the contrails they produced striping the sky. There was no need for subterfuge, stealth or camouflage. The sky that morning was clear. A wreath of cloud capped the peak of Sandeagh Mhor far below. Per the plan that had been crafted and reviewed with meticulous detail, two hundred nuclear bombs were targeted at the island. Each had a fifty megaton combination fission/ fusion thermonuclear warhead. The military commanders were taking no chances. This menace would be destroyed, and then they could all sleep at night. Prior to the nuclear devices being released, bunker buster bombs were to be positioned to crack open the lava capping the mountain. Four hundred of these devices were scheduled for release in the first fifteen minutes of the bombing raid. As a follow on, the nuclear devices were precision aimed to crack open the back of the island, and to inject a lethal radiation blast throughout the rock. The strike had been computer designed to open fracture lines in the underlying rock, then shatter the island like an egg thrown from the Empire State building. All that would be left would be a fused radioactive pile of slag with no ability to support life in any form. The goal was to obliterate the island and its terrifying inhabitants in one fell swoop.

The bombing run proceeded exactly according to plan. The stream of BLU 113 bunker buster bombs, containing over five thousand kilos each of high explosive rained from the sky, shrieking in unison as they fell. They had been laser guided to explode in a defined symmetrical linear pattern along the long axis of the island. Their placement was perfect. As they smashed through layers of rock, and exploded deep under the surface of the island with cataclysmic force, huge fissures opened across the island, as if it was a nut being pounded by a sledgehammer. The surface of the island shattered and was blasted into millions of rock shards, flying skywards in huge clouds, and landing miles away on the surface of the sea. Each successive wave of bombs buried deeper into the infrastructure of the island, exposing cores of rock that had previously seen light of day over sixty million years earlier. The plateau was forced, inch by inch to separate from the volcanic peak. Ribs of basalt broke away from the cliffs and shattered as they fell to the rocky coastline below. The island had been smashed into several distinct pieces and now the nuclear bombs were released. The precision guiding strategy that had been so successful for the bunker busters, also worked for the nuclear warheads. Targeting the gaps that had now appeared between the peak and the plateau, the nuclear bombs were primed to explode as they reached the surface of the island. Again, according to the plan, they did so, one after another, with tumultuous explosions blasting great truck sized boulders sideways and upwards. The peak began to disintegrate, shredding rock in layers, with ancient strata evaporating, or shooting off laterally as huge walls of rock. They flew for a brief time skywards, and then descended into the ocean, causing massive eruptions of salty water as they careened into the sea. The pilots of the bombing wave witnesses the enormous mushroom clouds as they boiled over the shattered island, ascending many miles into the air. But the key energies of the explosions had been expended in causing the fractioning of the rock infrastructure, and casting the pieces to the four winds, and any turbulence experienced by the aircraft was minimal.

Eventually as the cloud from the final explosion cleared, a high level surveillance of the target commenced. As the smoke and steam drifted away on the winds, and a huge cloud of radioactive fragments boiled towards the Scottish coast, what remained of the island could be seen. Sandeagh Mhor had been reduced to three shattered stumps of stone, each a little over one hundred feet high, and isolated from each other by a raging ocean. The raging surf pounded the remaining rock pillars. In a few thousand years, they would disappear into the ocean. Of the plateau, nothing remained. The peak was reduced to smoldering slag. And there was no sign of the beasts.

"We got'em!" roared the General as he viewed the pitiful remnants of Sandeagh Mhor. In the command room, there was loud cheering.

"Send our boys home."

"Yes, sir!"

The bombers returned to their bases in Europe.

The US president and the British Prime Minister appeared together to broadcast the good news to the world. The resultant mood around the globe was cheerful. In the view of the peoples of the world, disaster had been averted, and now it was time to get on with day to day living. The Fire Tribe had been destroyed. The world would once again be able to return to its normal routine. Nobody could have predicted what would happen next.

19. Awakening

July 3rd, 2012

HE NUCLEAR EXPLOSIONS HAD DONE MORE than shake up the Scottish mainland. The use of nuclear weapons to eradicate the threat of the Fire Tribe was roundly condemned as overkill, with strong support surfacing for green politicians who vowed never again to use such force. And worse than that, the elimination a new life form was considered by some as unsavory at best, and to be genocide at worst by others. Now that the threat appeared to have disappeared, the dreadful loss of life that had occurred on Sandeagh Mhor was almost forgotten. Several questions were asked at sessions of the British Parliament and in the US Senate.

"Prime Minister, how did you know that this new species did not want to live in peace with us? Did you speak with any of the creatures in person? Do you have any written communication from them that we can see? Did you negotiate with them in any way? Did you offer them sanctuary?"

The leader of the opposition, Tony Fordyce, was ruthless with his probing.

The Prime Minister was quick to deflect the attack.

"This government acted in the interests of the people and for the people. We planned, and executed against the plan. I think you are forgetting the terrible danger we faced."

The leader of the opposition was delighted to milk this situation for all its political worth. After all it was back to business as usual, wasn't it? And he wanted that Prime Ministerial position.

"You can't trust politicians." said James Duggan to his wife, as he read the paper.

The Duggan family had moved in to a large country house in Kent owned by her sister, whose husband was a merchant banker in London. "You know how they exaggerate the situation to meet their own ends. It wouldn't surprise me if they invented those beast things to get rid of some other more down to earth problem in Scotland. They just wanted everyone out of the way for a while."

"Well we're safe here, dear, and they say it'll be a few months before we can all go back. You're getting paid to be here, and the boys are getting good schooling. Count your blessings."

"Listen to this, Brenda."

He read aloud from the newspaper.

"Fallout from the nuclear attack has, as predicted, blown over southern Scotland, reaching as far as Edinburgh, but drifting very little beyond there. The evacuations in Sweden, Denmark and Norway were all cancelled, and the local population was able to return home with minimum disruption to their lives. Meanwhile, life in the townships is spartan but bearable, with adequate food and water. The children are receiving a quality education they might not have had previously."

Jim made a frown.

"That's a nasty poke at the Scottish education system. We have damn good schooling in Glasgow."

He read on.

"It is estimated based on the half life of the decaying nuclear particles that are scattered across the Lowlands of Scotland that it will be safe for people to return to their homes in Edinburgh and along the east coast within three months, and for the worst affected areas on the West Coast near the site of the explosion, people should get home within a year at worst. They might have to face Christmas in the camps, but our government will no doubt ensure that it will be a jolly festive occasion."

"They were saying that we should be back in our flat in Glasgow early next year." said Brenda.

"So much for the world economy collapsing." said Jim. "Listen to this."

He turned the page of the paper, and smoothed it flat.

"The world economy, far from tanking as some pessimists had predicted, surprisingly has had a boost. Stock markets all over the world, and especially in London, have traded higher as investors see the opportunity associated with government funded rebuilding of Scotland. Gold, the natural investor's haven during troubled time, has tumbled to below one thousand dollars per ounce. Oil, which reached a record one hundred and seventy five dollars per barrel recently as speculators gambled on the loss of North Sea oil production, traded sharply lower as the oil wells resumed full production."

He folded the paper closed, and placed it on the glass top of the coffee table.

"I think we're going to be all right, Brenda my dear, I think we'll be just fine."

20. Tibran's Revenge

August 30th, 2012

AMES DUGGAN WAS WRONG. IN A big way. Bigger than he, or any person on the planet with an opinion could realize. Deep beneath the surface of the earth, trouble was brewing for the entire human race. All seven billion inhabitants of the earth. The Fire Tribe was much more sophisticated that the politicians and military thinkers of the world could ever know. Over countless millennia, Tibran and his kin had developed extremely powerful communication skills. The fiery beasts had the intrinsic ability to communicate with each other that rivaled what could be achieved by the best satellite communication network above the planet. As a race, living deep in the magma of the planet's core, they had evolved a powerful form of non-verbal communication. They could listen to each other's thoughts, and transmit their own as needed to any of the Tribe, or indeed to any creature on the earth. It was that ability to use powerful mental telepathy that had drawn Robert, Julia, Marcia and the scouts to their deaths. It was so easy for Tibran and his family to instill lust, or greed, or any other emotion into the minds of their victims.

When they had realized that the puny humans were trying to launch an attack on them, it took only a few moments to focus in on the thoughts of the military commanders. They could hear the verbal discussions, and they could sense the fear and aggression being directed at them. They tuned in on the conversations related to use of nuclear weaponry to destroy their home. Just as the human population above them had taken time to get as many people as possible out of harm's way, thus did the Fire Tribe as well. Days in advance of the puny attempt to wipe them out, the group of fiery horned gorillas had burrowed through the solid rock to the fluid magma below. They had then retreated to deep and well established Tribal territories, many miles below the earth's surface. The members of the Tribe did not need to breathe, and they absorbed all nutrients they required through their skin from the liquid rock that was their home. Although their number counted only in the thousands, the Tribe was well aware that they had the superiority to eliminate the trash above the surface of the planet. They had the resistance to what this foolish tribe of monkeys called weaponry, and undeniable ability to withstand the monkey attacks. In the safety of his underground caverns and lava pools, Tibran moved to action.

"They think they're so powerful. What a joke. I can kill them all with one blow of my fist. They'll all regret the day they disturbed us!" said Tibran menacingly to Beerum.

"Rouse the entire Fire Tribe!"

Beerum gathered her formidable mental strength, and concentrated all her energies on sending out a message to her kin.

Her thoughts travelled at the speed of light through the magma, radiating to all corners of the sub-earth kingdom in milliseconds.

"Fire Tribe members. The miserable creatures on our planet's surface have dared to challenge us. It will be their undoing. We need you to come to the great caldera under what the humans call Yellowstone Park. We will hold a tribal gathering to discuss the plan of attack. Now is the time to act, to eradicate them all. We will expect you there before the day is out! Make haste, and we'll be rid of the worms on the planet's surface."

Whenever there was a need, the Fire Tribe members tended to congregate in the various hot spots that produced volcanic activity around the world. There the nutrients in the lava were the freshest, and they energies they needed to keep them alive and well were abundant. But the message relayed from Tibran was crystal clear. They were all under the threat of attack, and must rally to the cause. It was embarrassing really to be threatened by such tiny and insignificant creatures, but they would destroy them, and return to a peaceful existence in the deep caverns and molten rock of the mantle of the earth.

From Hawaii, the Horgoth sect set the pace. Then from the

Aleutians, Jarval and his tribe flew down a lava tube to start their journey. Hulvar and his family set forth from Iceland. Soon the entire Fire Tribe were slithering and swimming through the magma pools on the crusted surface of the core of the planet, travelling at unbelievable speed, fuelled by the fires and pressures of molten rock. The rallying cry had come. They had to answer to the threat to their very existence. As never before, the fire tribe was united and now it was on the warpath. In the history of the Fire Tribe, there had never been a threat so great that they would all come together. Tribe members and clans had previously fought relentlessly against each other, a perpetual energy sapping feud. But now they were united against a common enemy, mankind. In their thousands, they travelled from their underground habitats in the myriad of lava baths and pools under volcanoes around the world. They travelled from Tierra del Fuego in the south, from Iceland and the Aleutian Island chain in the North, from Mount Fuji in Japan and Mount St. Helens in the United States.

"We are coming!" they roared. "We are coming!"

Tibran heard the roaring as he sat with Beerum, and he growled with satisfaction. They had joined the Pyrith clan in their home in the enormous volcanic caldera that few knew existed under Yellowstone Park.

Late summer is normally a wonderful time for tourists in Yellowstone. That August, many thousands of visitors walked along the wooden boardwalks that passed attractive bubbling multicolored algae pools. Mainly though, tourists went to witness the steaming eruptions of Old Faithful. But this year, something was amiss. For the first time in the history of the park, Old Faithful lost his fidelity. Normally, the park's main attraction would fire off a glorious steaming cloud every hour, to the delight of his admiring crowd. He even had his own webcam to allow those not fortunate enough to travel to Wyoming to see his splendor. But as of three o'clock on a hot summer's afternoon on August 30th, 2012, the world famous geyser inexplicably increased his frequency of eruption to once every fifteen minutes. The enormous energy generated by the congregation of the Fire Tribe had triggered off a quadrupling of the thermal output of the caldera. Other geysers also increased both their output and their frequency of eruption, and normally quiescent warm springs became bubbling and steaming furnaces.

As they watched the spectacle, initially with astonishment, and later with growing fear, the park rangers and tourists drew back from the superheated steam, nervous about what might happen next. This had never happened before. A geology team was in the area, chipping rocks to determine the pattern of past eruptive events. Martha Hill was the chief of the team, and now they huddled together.

"The geothermal activity in the park has just reached unprecedented levels." said Martha. "We've all been speculating about the next major eruption in Yellowstone. It will be a doozy!"

"Martha, we have to warn the park rangers. We may be approaching a colossal eruption here. Much worse than any nuclear explosion!" said Joel Gershwin, her very able second in command. "It could blow at any moment!"

"I'm not so sure, Joel. We have had no increase in earthquake frequency, and the tilt meters show deflation, not inflation." Martha was of course referring to the global positioning system monitoring for any expansion of the caldera, that might indicate magma was flowing into the caldera, very often a sign that an eruption was about to take place. "But I agree with you, as a precaution, let's alert the authorities."

True to their word, the geologists contacted the park rangers. After a brief discussion, the rangers decided that caution was the best approach, and ordered an evacuation.

Yellowstone Park was quickly emptied under the threat of an eruption, and everyone within a ten mile radius of the entrances to the park was warned to be on the alert. They were informed somewhat alarmingly that they might have to leave the area at very short notice.

Then, just as abruptly as it had started, the geothermal hyperactivity ceased at 8:42 am on September 5th, 2012. The geologists were left scratching their heads. Old Faithful resumed his hourly spurt, and the hot springs settled down to their formal tepid selves.

The Fire Tribe had dispersed to wreak havoc on the world. The geothermal surge beneath Yellowstone had been the only indication of the presence of the Fire Tribe to the human world far above, and no-one on the planet had any idea about what had just happened, or indeed what would happen next!

Tibran was a well respected and fearsome leader, and many centuries before had been elected as global chieftain for the Fire Tribe. It was he who led the strategy discussions, and helped coordinate discussions across the diverse Fire Tribe population. Tibran looked on with satisfaction as the thousands of members of the Tribe gathered before him.

"Fellow Tribe members!" he roared. The members of the Tribe stared with rapt attention as he spoke.

"We will lull these creatures into a false sense of security. They will believe we have been destroyed. Then, like lightning, we will strike massive destructive blows on their fragile world above us."

Tibran continued.

"We of the Fire Tribe have fought each other over the millennia. We have until now had no reason to unite. The battles we fought were petty compared to the one we have to fight now. Looking back, we wasted centuries warring over pieces of land, and mates, when the reality was there was more than enough for us all. Despite all the fighting, always we have each respected the Fire Tribe code, and allowed those we defeated the luxury of sanctuary to heal their wounds. That moral code has allowed us to keep the Fire Tribe overall strong and triumphant. This insult from the vermin that inhabit the surface of our planet will not be tolerated. They are weak, and we are strong. Now we must wipe them out and return us to the world we knew before they evolved. We have the power to do so. Right now! Fire Tribe, are we united?"

The roar of thousands of the Fire Tribe, accompanied by an almost universal beating of chests, answered his question. He smiled. The Tribe was as one.

"We all know what we can do to rid ourselves of this pestilence."

Tibran raised himself to his full and powerful height.

"We will incinerate the human race. Completely. We have the

power to burn these pests in their nests above our lands, and we will do so!"

The crowd of assembled Fire Tribe members responded with another rapturous beating of their chests.

"It's time for action. We must execute our plan immediately! You all have your orders and you know what must be done."

Like a cancer spreading uncontrollably throughout the human body, the Fire Tribe members split up to go to their predetermined locations for battle. They travelled swiftly through the fluid magma to disperse to the all parts of the globe. Satellite groups of the Fire Tribe, each containing twenty members, gathered at the key locations proposed by Tibran. It would not take them long to prepare for their attack. Their two weapons were surprise and fire, and they knew how to use both. The members of the tribe were normally patient, but on this occasion, given the strong feelings that had blossomed, there was a sense of urgency and determination about them. It would soon be time to carry out the task of total eradication of mankind.

21. Genocide

October 15th, 2012

"IT WAS ALL A STORM IN a teacup." said the Prime Minister. "Maybe we did overreact a bit." He was in the library of Ten Downing Street clutching a cup of Earl Gray tea. General Porter sat next to him in a large leather armchair.

The General disagreed. "Sir, I strongly believe we did what needed to be done. I hope we got them all."

"Well, they haven't resurfaced, have they? Our reaction to the beasts stirred up some trouble, but people have short memories. The furor over the nuclear strike on Sandeagh Mhor has settled into a background muttering. Apparently one nuclear event can be tolerated, as long as it does not need to be repeated."

The Prime Minister sipped his tea thoughtfully.

"At least we'll be able to repopulate the evacuation zones in a few months. We'll get the country back to normal in no time. Soon, all this will be a distant memory."

"I hope you are right, sir. But I'm nervous. In some ways it was too easy."

Tibran listened to the conversation many miles beneath their feet. He was well satisfied with the location of the Tribe, and their preparedness for an attack. Those annoying creatures above would not know what hit them until it was far too late to do anything.

The plan that Tibran and his cronies had put together was simple but deadly. The huge advantage they had was that they possessed almost limitless ammunition. Lava. Molten rock. There was nothing above the ground that could withstand their hellish assault. It had been decided that the first strike would be on the Hawaiian Islands. The magma caldera of the Kilauea Volcano on the flanks of Mauna Loa would make a perfect gathering ground for the fire warriors. Since time immemorial, they had mastered the use of molten rock as a weapon, and they intended now to bring it to bear with overwhelming force on the inhabitants of the islands chain. Through physical and mental manipulation of the geothermal super-fluid lava currents, they had mastered a powerful ability to direct the flow of molten rock, much as their chosen enemy channeled water to create dams, lakes and canals. Each fire demon could move thousands of tons of molten rock per minute in any direction they chose purely by the power of thought, and the magnetic forces flowing through their veins.

And now they had the opportunity to do so. Now they would demonstrate their superiority. Buildings would burn. Lakes would boil. Fields would be laid to waste and the footprint man had created on the planet would be obliterated. Humans would die by the billion. The time to strike had come!

22 Destruction!

October 16th, 2012 3:00 am

T THREE A.M. ON A QUIET and breezy, balmy Hawaiian morning the Fire Tribe started their assault. As Tibran had predicted, the populace of Hawaii was caught totally unawares, mainly asleep in their beds. The islands inhabitants dreamed peacefully under a dark and starlit sky.

"It is time." said Tibran. "Summon the magma!"

The first attack commenced quietly, but soon built to a crescendo. Using the enormous mental powers they possessed, Tibran and his demon cronies pulled vast reserves of low viscosity liquid rock in enormous volume from deep beneath the surface of the earth. Huge plumes of fiery magma from the earth's core opened cracks in the crust of the earth, and then proceeded to inflate large caldera pools under the thin rocky skin of the planet. The surface of the earth burst open like the skin of an over ripe apple. Huge gaping fissures opened on the slopes of Kilauea, and on nearby Mauna Kea and Mauna Loa. But the fissures were not limited to the existing volcanic mountains. They also tore open along the slopes on the dormant and extinct volcanic islands of Kauai, Oahu and Maui. Under the sea, a ring of new fissures extended in a circle around the peak of Loi'hi, the undersea mountain. The rocky sea bed was pushed upwards and outwards by the golden flow from deep in the bowels of the planet. The cracks and fissures extended until they formed a great glowing circle around the islands. Even if the populace had been alert and awake, escape from the islands by sea was now impossible. As the seabed was pushed upwards, huge tidal waves raced shoreward, and the inhabitants of the Hawaiian Islands were shaken awake by the constant rumbling of earthquake activity. The inhabitants of Kona, and of Hilo, of Honolulu and Lihue, rose to see huge clouds of boiling steam floating in off the ocean on prevailing winds. Horrified, they looked landward. Impossibly tall and fiery gushers of glowing lava fountained from cracks on the hillside. Long curtains of fire were pouring from peaks that those living on the island had long thought to be forever extinct. As with the attack on Pearl Harbor by the Japanese in 1942, the inhabitants of the islands were taken totally by surprise. But this time it was not only the American fleet that was the target. As Tibran had desired, the destruction was overwhelming and ubiquitous. In minutes, gushing rivers of white hot rock flooded down the ancient volcanic slopes, and fountaining geysers of molten rock created gigantic spatter cones. The undersea eruption was no less catastrophic. Billions of gallons of sea water evaporated in minutes and exploded skyward in a great ring, reminiscent of the Bikini Atoll nuclear explosion, but millions of times more powerful. Huge waves were generated by the seismic activity under the sea and continuously raced towards the sore, slamming into the molten rock rivers, and sending up thunderclouds in seconds high into the stratosphere. The islands were ringed with fire and steam, and for the entire population of Hawaii, there would no escape.

Yoko Mazugumi and her husband Tomo woke to an ominous rumbling shaking their small apartment on the thirtieth floor of their oceanfront condo block on Waikiki beach. Tomo raced to open the curtains. He looked out, and his eyes open wide in horror. Their normally placid view of the ocean was lit by an eerie golden glow far out to sea. As he looked down, he could see wave after wave flooding around the base of the building. Many of the waves were over fifty feet tall. The view from the apartment was quickly obscured by thick fog, and the temperature in the apartment rose as boiling condensate ran down the windows.

"Yoko. Get dressed. I think we're in real trouble."

She raced over to join him. "What's happening, Tomo?" she cried.

"From what I can see, there's a massive volcanic eruption occurring out to sea. I saw tidal waves coming towards us before this fog appeared. I hope the building is tough enough to stand the beating it's about to take. At least we're high enough up to escape the waves.

I don't think our neighbors lower down will stand a chance. But we can't get out of here now. We'll have to ride it out up here."

Yoko tried the light switch. The power was out. She tried the battery powered radio, but failed to tune in a station.

The floor started shaking more violently, and Yoko clung to Tomo as they found it difficult to stand. Trying not to stumble, Tomo moved through the apartment, to the rear bedroom. He opened the curtains there, and realized in an instant that they were doomed. Below him, a deep golden glow diffused through the fog. There was no doubt in his mind what it was. Lava! And it was flowing around the base of the apartment block. He wrapped his arms around his wife and he started to pray. The floor tilted at a crazy angle, and they were slammed into the wall.

With a deep rumbling, the tower block toppled over. The last thing Tomo saw was a huge river of fire rising up to him, as he and his wife were engulfed in a hell of scalding steam and flames.

Over the entirety of the Hawaiian Islands the screams of terror and pain from the few remaining souls finally subsided as the unstoppable surge of molten rock washed over them.

Hawaiian Islands:
October 16th, 2012 4:48 am

APTAIN JONATHAN HARRIS AND HIS BOEING 747 crew complete with two hundred forty five passengers bound for Hawaii were destined to land at five o'clock that morning in Honolulu. But something was wrong. The plane had descended to ten thousand feet on its approach to the Big Island, and they were now only forty miles from landing.

"What the hell is that!" exclaimed the Captain, seeing a massive billowing white cloud rushing towards them from the Hawaiian Islands.

"I don't know sir," shouted Captain Larry Perkins, his co-pilot "but we need to take evasive maneuvers, now!"

He pulled back rapidly on the stick, causing the aircraft to surge skywards at a steep angle.

"Thank God the passengers should all be strapped in their seats for landing." he added. "This is going to be rough!"

At that moment, the thick roiling cloud smashed into the Jumbo Jet, causing it to bounce around crazily in the turbulence. In the cabin, the passengers began to scream, and loose objects were thrown violently around, careening into the unfortunate passengers in their paths. Captains Harris and Perkins fought to keep the plane under control, but it was a losing battle. Both men heard simultaneously the incredulous news from air traffic control. Satellite imagery of the destruction of the Hawaiian Islands had just been picked up military observation satellites and communicated round the world. Air traffic control had broadcast an immediate warning to all pilots flying in the vicinity of the islands to keep clear of the massive eruption and its deadly steam and ash cloud. For Captain Harris and his crew and passengers, the warning came too late. Fine particulate volcanic ash mingled with the boiling cloud of steam. The gritty particulate matter simultaneously entered the intakes of the four engines of the plane. With a vibration and grinding noise that could be felt and heard in the cabin, the jet's engines seized up one by one. Without power, the ferocity of the turbulence had the craft at its mercy. The two Captains had no chance to control the descent of the plane.

"We've lost power, Larry. I can't handle her! We're going down!"

"Brace! Brace!" he broadcast to the main cabin.

Blinded by the ash and steam, out of control, the aircraft spiraled downwards through the hellish cloud and smashed into the raging sea below.

Hawaiian Islands:
October 16th, 2012 12:00 midday

BY TWELVE NOON, AS THE SUN flooded the once lush tropical islands, not a trace of greenery remained. From being a raging maelstrom, the sea had calmed, and the mists were dispersing, blown away on the prevailing easterly trade winds.

Harpreet Singh stared though his satellite based electronic telescope at the islands below. He was in conversation with the President, and what he could see live to the White House. He felt tears in the corner of his eyes, and tried to keep a tremor out of his voice as he relayed the news.

"There were over a million people down there yesterday, and they've been totally wiped out! I can see no sign of life, no evidence that we ever settled the islands. There are over one hundred islands in the chain. They're all still there, but there is nothing on any of them. Lava has covered every hillside, every town. I can't even see one palm tree. Even the high rise buildings have been totally destroyed. Hawaii is gone." He stopped, and choked back a tear.

"All the buildings are covered with lava. I can see one partially submerged ocean liner off the coast, but there's no movement on board. The lava is smooth silvery and featureless, but it is everywhere. There are lava trails criss-crossing every inch of land, and the coast of the island has been extended by at least a mile in every direction. All the beaches have gone. There are waves are breaking on the new coastline, but I repeat, there is absolutely no sign of life."

"Thank you Mr. Singh. Did you have any relatives on the

island." asked the President, his voice soft and strained by what he had heard.

"No sir, but they were all Americans. We've just lost one million Americans. Wait. On the top of Mauna Loa. There's something glowing. Let me increase the resolution. It's one of the fire apes! Just sitting there. We didn't get them all after all."

The president was silent, and then he cursed. "Now we're in for real trouble." he said beneath his breath.

The destruction of humanity, as threatened by Tibran several months before, had only just begun.

Tibran had smiled as he witnessed the obliteration of all the people on the islands. The entire flora and fauna of the former Hawaiian tropical paradise was now buried under hundreds of feet of fresh rock.

Tibran had emerged triumphant from the summit of Mauna Loa, fittingly, prior to his efforts, the largest volcano in the world, and now enhanced by a silvery cap of fresh lava. He had just created the most monstrous mountain on the planet by increasing the volcano's height by several hundred feet. He surveyed the scene from this lofty throne and smiled a deep smile of satisfaction. It was a good beginning for the Fire Tribe and for his plans, but it was just that, only the beginning.

"It is a good start." he growled. "But there is more to come. We will kill them. But we will leave a few to tell the tale of the Fire Tribe. But we will destroy their habitat so that they will never again thrive on this planet. The maggots will fry in the fires of hell. They will be wiped out. We will never again let them destroy our peace. Let the punishment continue!"

Predictably, panic seized hold in the cities and countries of the world. Many innocents were killed in riots as people sought to hoard food, anticipating lean times to come. The world rapidly descended towards anarchy. The press headlines added fuel to the flames.

"The fiery beasts are back!"

"Hell on earth!"

"The day of judgment is here!"

"Humankind is doomed!"

"The Hawaiian Islands are no more. Where will these beasts strike next?"

After the nuclear blasts had eradicated Sandeagh Mhor, world communities had collectively breathed a sigh of relief. No-one had believed that the threats that Tibran had made were real. It was now all too obvious now that he could and would carry out his promises.

From high on Mauna Loa, now his throne, Tibran gave another command. "It is time to cleanse the world of this plague of naked apes. Destroy the cities first."

Hawaii had been but a scratch. The carnage now commenced in earnest.

Tibran and his cronies placed the world under siege. Systematically, the Fire Tribe ringed key population centers with virulent volcanic eruptions. The tactics they used each time were identical. The giant fire apes would open a ring of fissures twenty to fifty miles wide using the extreme pressure generated by molten lava welling up from the earth's core. The coordination of the fluid lava expansion and the creation of an impassable fiery wall were always timed to prevent escape of the population of the city by surface routes. A few fortunate individuals managed to escape by using their personal private planes and helicopters. They were forced to circle around inside the wall of splattering red lava to reach sufficient height to avoid being melted by the inferno, or boiled alive by steam. Escape routes by sea were obliterated by explosive superheated steam jets, directed at any unfortunate craft in their path. Rivers dried up and their beds cracked open. Their dry beds formed a perfect conduit for the supermafic lava streams to course into center of the world's largest cities without encountering any resistance. All round the world, it was the same gruesome story.

The people of London, England, died a horrible, screaming death. Firstly, the ring of fire was opened just outside the M25 motorway that circled the city. The River Thames evaporated quickly as streams of sulfurous flows from Dartmouth and Kingston met near Tower Bridge. In a matter of minutes, the Thames embankment was conquered by the lava and it overflowed down the streets of the city, overwhelming everything in its path. The parliament buildings at

Westminster held out for a short time, but the extreme heat of the flows eventually caused the clock tower of the House of Commons, known after the bell in the tower as Big Ben, to topple over into the maelstrom. The bell itself was forever silenced as it melted into the incandescent sludge. London had been challenged before as a city during the great fire of London in 1666, and by the Nazi Luftwaffe during the Blitz in 1942, but this time the destruction was complete and would not be reversed. Within hours, all that remained of the city was a half dome of cooling silvery rock. Of her people, none in the city remained.

New York suffered a similar fate. Here the ring of fire was even broader. The Hudson River evaporated, pouring huge clouds of steam into the air. The deep channel it left behind funneled white hot rivers of molten rock into the city. The old pier pilings flashed into flame and were buried under millions of tons of molten stone. Where gentle waves had lapped against the Manhattan shores, cruel waves of golden lava streamed encrusted the Hudson Expressway, and were channeled deep into the city. New York had not experienced the ravages that London had, but it had been under attack. Just as in September 11th, 2001, the tallest buildings initially resisted the intense heat from the lava. But their steel frames could only last so long. The Chrysler building was the last to go, long after the Empire State Building dissolved into the ferocious lava bath. As with London, the people of New York stood no chance.

City by city, the Fire Tribe poured billions of tons of freshly minted rock onto the surface of the planet. Tokyo, Delhi, Mumbai, Shanghai and Hong Kong were destroyed early in the diabolic plan. Tens of millions died trapped in the conflagration. Other megacities were next in the list. It took a short two weeks for the Fire Tribe to reduce the population of the world from seven billion to one billion frightened souls, and for Tibran and the Tribe, there was more to do.

23. Survival

November 27th, 2012 10:00 am

UMAN BEINGS ARE RESOURCEFUL. THEY WILL always take on challenges. Sometimes the best comes out in our race during times of greatest adversity. It was very quickly realized by those remaining in power that something drastic would need to be done if the human race was to survive. That was the topic of conversations at a top secret retreat in the Grand Teton Mountains. The human race had been decimated, but there were still prestigious leaders who would now try to shape the future of mankind. The heads of governments of those countries still keeping a rudimentary structure in place had arranged to meet in Jackson Hole, a remote ski resort in the United States Rocky Mountains. There had been some trepidation from the security advisers for the meeting about using this location given its proximity to Yosemite, one of the largest volcanic caldera sites in the world. However, the attendees could use the first class airfield near the town, and there would be some protection offered by high density rock of the Grand Teton Mountains. The sparse population meant that the area would not rank high on the Fire Tribe's list for destruction. At least not yet. The project was code named Noah after the biblical legend of Noah's Ark.

On that cold November day, with snow dusting the tops of the Grand Teton mountain range and late fall sunlight dappling the Snake River, forty of the remaining world leaders descended on the normally sleepy ski resort. The Prime Ministers of Australia, Germany and Norway and the Presidents of the United States and leaders from Chile, Canada and Argentina were gathered together in a large pine beamed room in the Crystal Ski Lodge, perched next to the bare slopes of the ski runs that this year would be almost devoid of skiers.

The agenda was simple, but the topic was complicated. They would have a discussion about how to save the human species from complete destruction.

During their meeting, they were kept in constant touch by satellite with colleagues in the few remaining countries where the destruction had not been complete. At the time the meeting was supposed to commence, the dignitaries were listening to reports that were coming in from Italy. Rome was the latest city to come under attack.

"We have nowhere to go!" shrieked Cardinal Franchetti, as he broadcast the horrors he was witnessing to the assembled leaders in the remote ski lodge.

"May God have mercy on all our souls. Italy is dying, and our people are being massacred. Thank the Lord that the Pope has been airlifted to safety. There are huge fissures circling Rome, spewing forth lateral flows and waves of lava. The city has been completely surrounded overnight by the walls of liquid stone. Now they are coming towards us, flowing towards the Vatican. They say the flow depth is over fifty feet and rising. There is no hope for us. The molten rock just keeps moving inwards. Nothing can stand in its way. We've seen huge trees explode in front of our eyes as their sap is vaporized and ignited by the intense heat. Cars are crushed like tin cans. Their tires explode and their metal melts into puddles in the extreme heat. There is no escape for us!"

The atmosphere in the ski lodge was somber.

"It's upon us! The Day of Judgment is here! It's so hot. It's..." At that point, the Cardinal's voice lapsed into silence. After a few minutes, the live video feed from the Vatican flickered and shimmered as the intense heat from the engulfing lava crumbled the bricks and mortar of the building. Flames flickered closer and closer, with the feed finally ceasing as the camera melted.

The German Prime Minister, Rudy Steinholz, tears in his eyes, voiced the mood of the assembled leaders.

"We have just witnessed the destruction of Rome. May the good Lord have mercy on the souls of the people of Italy. We grieve for the twenty million inhabitants of one of the oldest cities of the planet."

In the remnants of Rome, the Tribe frolicked in the flames. Their delight in the total destruction knew no bounds. Towering above them all, Tibran roared his encouragement, and extolled them to even greater acts of savagery. The extinction of the human race was proceeding according to plan!

After many minutes of silence, the President of the United States spoke. It was a short but powerful speech.

"Gentlemen, now is the time for us to pray as we have never prayed before for the safety of mankind. We are being visited by the fires of hell. Perhaps a wrathful God is punishing us for our sins, or perhaps it is by pure chance that we are under such an awful attack, but either way we have a short time to do something about it before we are all consumed by fire. Today is not about a theological debate. Today is a day for action. I understand how you all must feel about the enormous loss of life, and the complete destruction of entire countries, but there is nothing that we can do about that at this time. As you all have observed, we do not have much time. By our estimates given the rate of destruction of the surface of our planet, we have a matter of weeks before the human race is completely destroyed. We have to find a way to protect as many people as possible from the flaming hell these creatures are creating round the world. Our geologist experts have concluded that no landmass in the world is a safe harbor for humanity. Even the Antarctic ice can be thawed and vaporized into scalding steam. Every day, millions of innocent men, women and children are being sacrificed in our cities, and we are powerless to prevent it. We are being wiped out. We have a duty, gentlemen, to save as many people as is practically possible from all ethnic groups and all walks of life to repopulate our world once the menace is eradicated."

"Sir, we believe we have a workable solution." The Norwegian Prime Minister stood up, and surveyed the room. He was an imposing tall sandy blond man, and he dominated the room.

"Norway has yet to be affected by the fires from hell. We still have an intact expert advisory panel, though how long we'll be spared we have no idea. Here's their plan for consideration. May I speak?"

"You have the floor, Per." said the US President, his deep blue eyes staring at the Swede through his varifocal glasses.

The tall Norwegian picked up a paper from in front of him to reconfirm the elements of the plan. Like all good schemes, the thrust was simple.

"There is nothing complicated about our plan, but its execution will take intense planning and activity. We need to move as many people as we can far out to sea. We can pull together a flotilla of boats, and place the flotilla over an area of deep water, for example the Marianas Trench near the Philippine Islands. No amount of volcanic activity will be able to disturb the buffer created by thirty thousand feet of freezing cold sea water. If the monsters try to create a tidal wave to swamp the boats, it would produce no more than a ripple on the surface of the ocean above the trench. There is an abundant seafood source there to keep people alive, and we can take dried and canned foods on barges for supplementary nutrition. We can equip a hospital ship, and aircraft carriers to allow us to launch helicopters to return to land when we can. If we effectively disappear from the fire creature's radar for a period of time, we believe they will return to hibernation and we can repopulate the world. It does not eliminate our enemy, but we may still be able to have a peaceful coexistence with them."

"But realistically, how many people can we save?" asked the US President.

"We can save our species, sir, and at this point in time, that's seems to be a pretty good objective."

"Are there any other viable solutions?" asked the President, his face furrowed with the tension of the moment. There were no additional suggestions.

"I think we have consensus. Our own advisors offered a similar solution."

The assembled delegates nodded in agreement.

"Then the motion on the table is to cooperate with each other to assemble as many sea going vessels as we can in the next two weeks, and an army of people to sail with them."

"All in favor raise your hands."

In unison, the forty assembled dignitaries raised their hands in swift assent.

"Then the motion is carried. We will create a floating city unprecedented in the history of the world!" The President of the United States bowed his head. "May God have mercy on all our souls."

24. Selection

December 2nd, 2012 9:15 am

OLONEL STEVE MASTERTON PACED ANXIOUSLY UP and down the worn carpeting in his office. The voice of his superior officer, General Marcus Blaney, and been soft but firm as Steve had been delivered his orders by secure landline.

"You have three days, Steve, to put the selection process in place that will provide us the people we need to shape the future of this world, and deliver humanity from this evil subterranean menace. You alone will make the decisions as to who will get a ticket to the Ark, and who will be left to burn in the volcanic hell that our earth has become. It's going to be an impossible job, Steve, but I trust you to do it right. Any questions about your mission? By the way, the project has officially been named Project Ark."

"No, sir."

"Of course you won't be on your own. We are going to make your life a little easier with a few guidelines that we have prepared for you."

"Number one, if anyone offers you any bribe or incentive to be on the list, they are automatically referred to me. I have a permanent solution to that problem, and the US government backs it fully. Number two; no adult over fifty years of age, no matter how vital his or her skill set, will set foot on the decks of our ships. Number three is a tough one. We need able bodied fertile men and women to repopulate the planet. That means we have to look very carefully at any person with physical or mental disabilities. Only the fittest will be allowed to join our expedition. No exceptions. Understood? We cannot jeopardize such a mission with anything less than our best citizens to carry the flag for humanity. It will be tough enough to survive out there, and we can't carry any spare baggage with us."

"I will not write that one down, General. And I don't agree with the concept. But I will carry out my orders."

"Yes indeed, colonel. You will carry out your orders, with no exceptions. Number four; we have set you an ethnicity quota. We will mix the gene pool of the planet as much as we can. I'll tell you this now, finding the people fulfilling all these requirements will be really tough for you in the time remaining to us. At the end of the day, you'll wish you had never been chosen to do this job."

"What is the ethnicity quota, sir?"

"One fourth of the population of the Ark will be Caucasian, one fourth Hispanic, one fourth Asian, and one fourth from all other ethnicities."

"Just how many people are going to be saved by the Ark, General?"

"You will have around three hundred thousand lives in your hands, Steve. Make every one of them count towards the future of our race. I know. You have been given an incredibly difficult burden to bear. Remember though, we are all under orders from the President to help you with your task. And by the way, Steve, right now I don't qualify for the Ark, and as of this instant, neither do you. For the sake of humanity, Steve, do whatever you can to pick the right people in the time we have left. It's up to you now."

Colonel Steve Masterton had put down the phone, breathing heavily, his body covered with sweat. He would not survive. His family would not survive. All he could do was select the genetic pool that would guarantee that the human race as a whole would carry on into the future. It was an unbearable burden. The responsibility was huge, and it was one that he doubted that he would be able to bear.

"The Masterson's are tough." he decided "But am I tough enough to discard myself and my family to make sure that the human race survives? Lord God, what do I do? I love my family, and I love my neighbors. How can I let them all down at this time? Please, give me strength to make this all happen."

He opened the top drawer of his desk. Inside was his service revolver, glinting gunmetal cold in front of him. The eye of the steel circle of the barrel glared accusingly at him.

"Go on." he could hear it calling to him. "Pull my trigger. Blow your brains out. End all of your miseries, and let others do all the hard work."

"No way in hell!" he shouted, and threw the offending weapon into the trash. He sat down again at his desk, and drew some deep breaths.

"I will do what must be done. But I will try to save my family. I owe it to them too. Damn the high command. There will be new orders now, and I'll be making them."

Julie and the twins would survive. It was up to him to work out how and when.

After several minutes of deep thought, he sat down at his desk and pulled out a pencil and some paper. For such a momentous task, he did not trust the security of his computer.

"The brass will be monitoring everything I do." he thought. "But Hell's teeth, I can do this job. I can make it work for the sake of our species, and I can make sure that my family is part of the Ark. Damn their pompous military hides. I'll do it for mankind, and I'll make it work out for my family, too."

Slowly, he picked up a paper and pencil. How on earth could he choose a fraction of mankind to survive, and more importantly despite the direct orders of General Blaney, how could he make his family be part of it?

"All right. Marcus and his cronies have given me the framework, but it's up to me to alter it out for my benefit and the benefit of my family. Screw all the top brass. If they find out about my plans and I'm history, then at least I tried. Julie, Jim and George, I owe this to you."

Taking his pencil in hand, he started to craft the rules for selection of the survivors. A thought entered his head, and he picked up the phone again and called General Blaney.

"Sir, sorry to trouble you again, but to help me with narrowing down the selection pool, I need to know where the boats will be coming from to build the Ark? Are we commandeering vessels in the name of the government, or are we letting the owners think that they will be part of the flotilla of vessels?"

Marcus Blaney carefully considered his response.

"The governments of the world will get you your flotilla, Steve. You don't need to worry about the ships and where they will be sourced. That's not your job. Sure, some other folks will take to the ocean independently in their own vessels. They will almost certainly run out of food and water after a time and they'll most likely die at sea. We will have picked out the population of people that the world needs to survive. Our expert geneticists gave us the final numbers, both the number overall for the flotilla and the genetic variability in ethnicity to allow humanity to regenerate over time. As of today, by the way, you have been allocated a staff of fifty people who will be fully engaged to help you make the selections. Get to work, soldier. You now have two days and twenty three hours until the Ark launches."

Twenty four hours a day for the next two days, Steve remained totally engrossed in his task, confined to his office. Despite the secrecy it had not taken long for the word to get round that he owned the tickets to salvation. At first, his phone rang endlessly off the hook, and he eventually pulled out the plug from the wall. He had been assigned fifty two staffers to scour though the details of myriads of likely candidates for rescue. He diverted all of his calls to Alison Macready, a pretty blond haired sergeant who had been assigned as his administrative assistant for the duration of the selection process. She was very thorough at selecting only those people who could help the cause. When it was clear that he was not available for consultation, other desperate people tried a different tack. A diplomat from India gave Steve's wife a bag full of uncut diamonds. A billionaire from Mexico transferred one hundred million dollars into his bank account. Two of the ruling royal family in Saudi Arabia offered him a share in an oil field. There were others who offered him bribes their way to take part in the Ark initiative. He did as he was ordered. He didn't know what exactly what the General's solution to the problem would be but he could guess. He had made a note of each person's identity, and had passed the contact information to General Blaney's staff. He never heard from any of them again.

"What would I do with money, or diamonds, or an oil field for crying out loud." he muttered. "These people have no common sense!"

He scrolled again through the lists of candidates floating in front of his eyes on the large computer screen on his desk. His staff had been diligent in selecting qualified people to save. There were no radicals, no extremists, indeed no persons holding a political party leadership position. There were no evangelical ministers. No religious bigots. No royalty. No prisoners or criminals with a record. He understood the rationale for the selection process. There would be no people selected who could attempt to subvert the Ark's purpose for their own.

He glanced back at the instructions he had provided. He had just wanted normal people, if such existed. Quietly, he arranged for his wife and children to adopt the identity of a family that had tragically been killed in an automobile accident, after their ticket to freedom had been granted. At least his family would survive.

He had painted a picture in his mind of the new population to seed the planet. The ideal couple would each have two degrees, could speak at least two languages, were aged between eighteen and fifty and were demonstrably fertile. An unmarried Miss Ideal was aged under thirty-five, was fertile, had an advanced college degree and could also speak at least two languages. Unmarried Mister Ideal's would have to be exceptional to be included in the list. In his view they had not demonstrated any long term commitment to the human race, and could very likely turn out to be outcasts or loners. There would be no drug users, alcoholics, or anyone with an active chronic disease. Ruthlessly, Steve and his staff cut through the lists of proposed citizens of the Ark. Eventually, he found the demographics of people selected for him all fitted his criteria for acceptance. After thirty six hours, he had a list in his hands of over two hundred seventy five thousand lucky people who fit the bill.

He called Marcus Blaney and asked for additional help.

Marcus laughed, and said "How many more people do you need? We are all human redundant spare parts right now. I can give you a whole army of volunteers that will do anything you ask, if they think they have a chance of joining the Ark."

"I need you to round up enough of a staff to call up the people you have selected to make sure they all get the information they need and the transport to get them to the embarkation points."

"Done!" said the General, and he hung up the phone.

Within six hours, using every trick in the book he knew, the General had collected a list of over one thousand volunteers to make the calls. The kicker had been a lottery at the end of the call marathon where fifty of the volunteers would win the opportunity to be part of the Ark. A five percent chance of survival, although small, was a huge incentive.

"It's time to put out the press release." said Steve. "I want every able bodied person glued to their phone for the next six hours."

The news of the presence of the Ark circled the globe at viral speed.

Mostly, the individuals who were lucky enough to be contacted reacted with elation, but some reacted with shocked silence. Others responded with tears when they heard that their relatives would not be joining them in the Ark. The instructions were harsh and designed to instill fear and respect.

"If you want to be a part of the future, and you want to save the human race, be at your appointed embarkation station one hour before the ships sailor you will lose your place on the rescue craft and you will most certainly die."

25. The Day Of Launch:

January 12th, 2013 8:42 am

STEVE MASTERTON WAS COMPLETELY EXHAUSTED, BUT he felt a faint triumph. All his plans had been executed like clockwork and had run unfailingly to time. Through extensive video connections, he had watched thousands of boats of all shapes and sizes as they left prearranged ports around the world. Not surprisingly given the security forces teeming around the launch sites, each vessel that left their port of origin suffered no interference. The Captains of the vessels had not been informed of their final destination. That information would be sent later through secure channels in order to discourage individual unauthorized persons from trying to sneak a craft into the sea going city undetected.

Steve called Marcus Blaney as the last of the vessels, the aircraft carrier Ulysses left the naval base at Dartmouth.

"What are my orders, sir?" he asked.

"The President has had a change of heart." said the General. "He would like you to join the Ark as a reward for your efforts. We have a cruiser standing by to take us to the rendezvous point over the Mariana's trench. The President will be joining us on the ship."

Steve felt hope welling up in his breast.

"You'll be able to join your family once we get there. Yes, Steve, we knew you would try to save them, and we turned a blind eye to your subterfuge. Now get your ass over to Norfolk. We have evidence that the Fire Tribe are concentrating right now on destroying the United States. There has been a massive eruption from the Yellowstone Caldera which has destroyed most of the West Coast and the central states."

"Yes, sir!" said Steve and hung up the phone.

He thought once more about the provisions he had ordered for each ship. The boats, no matter what size, had been equipped with sufficient firepower to defend themselves against pirates, or other stray vessels. The intelligence reports coming in from around the planet were consistent. Separate from the vessels of the Ark, many thousands of small and large craft had been launched around the world, desperate to escape the encroaching lava. He knew that within a few years, all but a handful would succumb to the ravages of living off the ocean, being dispatched by storms or through a lack of supplies.

Steve made his way swiftly to the helicopter pad for the short flight to Norfolk.

From the safety of the cruiser, Steve Masterson, Marcus Blaney and the President of the former United States watched as video feeds from the remaining cities of the world slowly winked out one by one. With them went the remainder of the world's population, its plant life and its animals. Over the course of a few tragic weeks, there was nothing left living on the Major landmasses of the world.

Tibran looked on with satisfaction. The Tribe had fulfilled its promise. He could see that there were survivors, living in a few boats in the deep ocean waters. Good. They would tell the story of his people, and the death and destruction that would surely haunt them if they disturbed the fire tribe again.

"Enough!" he shouted to the Tribe. "There is nothing left alive on the continents of the world. We have done our job, and now we can rest."

"We will keep the lava flowing for some years to scare them away from returning to the land. We'll take it in turns to create a random flow of lava across the world."

His wife leaner over, and gave him a fiery kiss. "Consider it done, Tibran. You have had your revenge."

26. The Flotilla City.

February 12th, 2013

HE FLOTILLA OF SEA GOING VESSELS carrying the remnants of humanity and the seeds for the future finally met up in the South Pacific Sea directly above the deepest waters of the Mariana trench. Although the volcanic activity generated by the Fire Tribe could boil water, and create earthquakes which could produce massive tsunami waves, the sheer mass of water above the thirty five thousand foot trench floor created pressures at its base of over fifteen thousand pounds per square inch. At such pressure, even using the massed strengths of its members, the Fire Tribe as a collective had insufficient ability to boil away enough sea water to influence the boats above. The enormous pressure also minimized any eruptive lava flows in the trench. Therefore, although the fire creatures could create massive shock waves in the trench, there would be absolutely no effect of their powers on the floating city on the ocean's surface. It was also be impossible for the beasts to use the power of lava to create tsunami waves with that depth of water. The mass of water above the trench would simply absorb the energy, and send it harmlessly ashore. The trench was not in close proximity to any Major landmass. The closest land was in fact the Mariana Islands, and the Island of Guam. It was a blessing for the flotilla that the ocean in this part of the world teemed with marine life of enormous variety. Whereas the world's oceans had been coming close to being overfished in the past, now the loss of the human predators allowed the stocks of fish to recover. The life giving ocean meant that the position of the floating city offered an abundance of food, and relative safety from the fire creatures. The quality of life in the floating city was generally good, but for those unused to life on the ocean waves, sea sickness was an unwelcome friend for the first few days. Those involved with the planning of the trip had pulled together many essential supplies and equipment. They had installed portable desalination devices on the larger vessels to convert seawater to life supporting fresh water. Huge barrels collected rainwater from the frequent storms, and fresh water was hoarded like gold. To supplement the catch of various sea creatures by fishing, food had been assembled from stores in countries where total destruction had not yet occurred and the provisions were placed in deep water barges and towed behind the aqueous caravanserai. Huge steel booms were assembled in a giant circle around the new city to protect it against the frequent storms in the area. The booms also generated electricity for the city. Each was connected to the next by giant steel poles. As the waves energy pushed the giant tubes up and down, they turned a turbine encased in the hollow containers. And so, as the monstrous beasts converted all the land surfaces on earth to barren lava plains, the human population, depleted to a pitiful remnant of its former self, clung tenaciously to life.

"There is a plus to all this destruction. The earth has been restored to a newly minted state." Tanya Ismelin, the Ark's resident expert on all things to do with geology was talking with her colleague, Jun Bhin.

"You know, as it was in the beginning before the world cooled sufficiently to let the rains form rivers and oceans. We'll be able to start afresh, and this time we can restock the world with our own choice of inhabitants. No mosquitoes or yellow jackets!"

Her colleague Jun Bhin was more pessimistic. "Somehow I don't think we'll be rid of those pests forever. They have a way of coming back. They may be knocked down for a while, but I bet we'll be meeting up with them again soon. And the bad bacteria. And viruses."

"Don't be such a pessimist, Jun." Tanya scolded. "But you're right. No doubt that's what the Fire Tribe is thinking about us." said Tanya." And I hope they're right!"

Admiral Henry Cantor stared through his binoculars at the boats surrounding the aircraft carrier.

"How many people made it here?" he asked Vice Admiral Tony Foster. "Let's take a census Tony. How many mouths do we have to feed?"

"We have a never ending supply of fish, and loaves we can generate by growing corn in the hydroponic farms. I don't think we'll go hungry. I'll get Steve Masterton to organize a survey right away, sir." he replied.

Steve Masterton sighed with satisfaction. His census took three weeks to complete. As a result, he had created a fully updated computerized database of the remaining population of the world. A total of three hundred and twenty seven thousand people had survived the holocaust to keep the human population going. Less than one in twenty thousand people who had inhabited the planet prior to the destruction of Sandeagh Mhor had survived. The survivors ranged in age from a few days old to their late forties, and the sex ratio was evenly split male to female, just as he had planned.

Justin Hardwick had become one of the luckiest humans to be alive. He had twice survived the ravages of Tibran's Tribe His trip to the south of France had been a great success. He did the usual tourist things, and had recovered from his recent traumatic experiences by sipping cocktails by the pool of his hotel. While the life he led was fun for a while, he rapidly became bored, and started to look for any kind of work he could find along the coast. As chance would have it, he met up with Danielle Friedmann in a bar one evening. She was the daughter of the wealthy shipping magnate, Armand Friedmann. She was an also an attractive brunette, with a golden sun tan covering her lithe body, and Justin was immediately attracted to her.

"I need an experienced sailor to help me crew my yacht." she had explained to Justin.

For Danielle, having a hunky Brit to crew with her on her boat was a real plus. He had looked so handsome, even though he was wearing cut off jeans and an off-white T shirt. Danielle was not averse to having attractive crew on her yacht. She had taken one look at Justin, and had decided he was her man. One evening, far out in the Mediterranean, Danielle had sidled up to him, and whispered an offer in his ear that he could not refuse. They had spent the night together, and Justin, who considered himself an expert in all things sexual, was surprised by new things Danielle could teach him. Next morning, he was signed on by Danielle as first mate on her yacht. It was a fitting title.

Over time, their evening trysts became a routine. Justin had fallen in love with Danielle, and he was desperate not to lose her. He made it his primary focus to ensure that she felt wanted and loved, and she in turn was extremely pleased with her catch.

When the Fire Tribe attacks had started in earnest in France, Danielle ordered the yacht to sea, and in the same breath, asked Justin to marry her. Justin had immediately agreed, and they kissed passionately on the dock. With a few well timed conversations and some rather devious connections, Danielle had arranged for her yacht to carry some passengers to the Ark, and now they were all together, sailing towards the rendezvous far away in the South Pacific Ocean. While the sun still shone on Capri Island in the Mediterranean, Capri itself shimmered in a new light with a silvery cap of lava. The Island had been born of fire in the Mediterranean's youth, and it had returned to its past. Danielle's boat, the Capri Sun was named after the island. She was a medium sized ocean going motor boat, fifty five feet long with space for ten occupants. She was powered by twin five hundred horse power diesel engines. They had an uneventful journey to the rendezvous point. Once they had arrived, and been connected with the vessels surrounding them, Danielle and Justin looked on sadly as the Capri Sun was cannibalized for spare parts. She had no further need of her engines, and became welded to the floating city, anchored now to vessels on either side of her. Her diesel engines were recycled for other purposes. Most of the non-structural metal fittings had also been removed for other projects. Justin was no stranger to the sea, but the life he now led on the Ark was very different from the backwater West Highland town of Campbeltown. Six months after they arrived in their new home, Justin married Danielle in the state room on the neighboring vessel, a magnificent three masted schooner named Troubador. Danielle was deeply in love with Justin. Although she loved his hunky body, more than that she was in love with his gentle nature. All the fights he had endured when he was in his youth had turned him against violence. Now the mass destruction of humanity had made him a confirmed pacifist. Danielle and Justin lived harmoniously on their yacht, and in time Danielle bore him twin sons. Danielle outlived Justin by two years. He died peacefully in his sleep at the ripe old age of ninety two.

He was considered a hero in the Ark. He had retold the tale

of his adventure on Sandeagh Mhor so many times. Each time, he embellished the story a little, but the gist remained the same. His sons grew up to be strapping lads, and each was blessed with a beautiful wife, and a single child each, as the Ark laws dictated. His son Derek married Roseanna, and their child was named Richard, known to the family as Rich.

27. Rebirth

February 11th, 2113

NE HUNDRED YEARS PASSED. THE FLOTILLA city was pleasantly comfortable for the survivors of the Fire Tribe's ravages, but it always felt a little claustrophobic despite the vastness of the ocean, and the huge canopy of sky above them. The sea dwellers were plagued by frequent storms, but the thick rubber booms dispersed most of the wave energy, and stopped the smaller vessels from being tossed around. In order to keep minimal but usable living space on the boats, in the early days at sea, the city elders had placed a mandatory very strict population control on the inhabitants of the Flotilla city. There was a finite amount of space for each person in the cramped vessels of the sea city. No-one on the board the sea city was malnourished, given the huge stores of canned goods and multivitamin supplements stored in the barges, but fresh food was certainly at a premium. The population survived on fresh fish, supplemented by hydroponic produce from the greenhouse barges. A chicken dinner was only reserved for special occasions, and then only when the hens scurrying around the decks outgrew their space and usefulness. Unlike the diseases that had been rampant during the voyages of past explorers, such as Vasco da Gama or Amerigo Vespucci, there were no cases of vitamin related diseases. The founding fathers of the Flotilla had been determined to create a self sustaining environment, as it was impossible for them to predict when their occupants would be able to return to farm the land. Most people grumbled from time to time about the lack of variety in their diet, but as time progressed, and a certain routine was established on the boats, the grumbling gradually ceased. The population had been capped in the year 2043 at three hundred and fifty five thousand seafarers. The human race's footprint on earth was now miniscule, compared to the seven billion souls living on the planet prior to the Fire Tribe's ravages.

The key concern voiced by the foresighted experts who had planned for the survival of mankind was that there would be insufficient genetic variability in the remaining pool of human beings. Their primary worry was that in time, certain inherited diseases would become rife in future generations. Their warnings were heeded. With over three hundred thousand unique human beings, unless close relatives interbred, there really was no need for concern.

Steve Masterton had done his job well. He had brought together a diversity of races and creeds that would be more than adequate to keep the common genetic diseases at bay. In the floating city interracial marriage was encouraged as there was much less prejudice about the backgrounds and races of young couples. Equally important for the future, those who had planned the voyage had thought ahead to when humanity would once more be able to return to land. Two vessels had been dedicated to house science laboratories. Both had been equipped with powerful deep freezes, powered by both wave power and solar energy. The flotilla city had been renamed New Beginnings and the ships had been dubbed Ark One and Ark Two. Inside the array of twenty minus seventy degree freezers was a collection of frozen embryo's of many different species of animals. The flotilla already had hordes of chickens running around the decks of the boats, and livestock herds tethered in the barges, but conservationists involved with planning the great escape had demanded that as many species as possible be saved. There was also a seed bank to supplement the hydroponic farm.

Therefore, despite its isolation, the sea city bloomed. Mankind has always been known for its versatility in finding a way through seemingly impossible situations. New Beginnings and those who lived in it epitomized how in adversity mankind would not only survive but thrive.

28. Celebration:

February 12th, 2113

EBRUARY 12TH DAWNED BRIGHT AND CLEAR in the warm seas of the South Pacific. It was to be an important day of celebration in New Beginnings. One hundred years had passed to the day since the creation of the ocean going city. Every year, the population of the city celebrated the liberation of mankind from the death and destruction unleashed on the planet by the Fire Tribe, but the centennial was to be marked by a party to exceed all parties. It was to be a gloriously happy day for almost all those present, and many festivities had been arranged. Everyone, with the exception of a few people required for essential support services to keep the city running, had been given the day off work. In the luxury liner Queen Mary, in cabin F423, a cramped cubicle with one small round porthole facing the ocean, Nadia Korotskova was sitting on her bunk bed. Beside her, holding her hand, sat Rich Hardwick, the twenty four year old grandson of Justin Hardwick. Nadia was a stunning twenty two year old redheaded school teacher of Russian ancestry. Rich was an olive skinned muscular maintenance engineer for the engines generating power for the Queen Mary. He knew that his British grandparents had met shortly after the flotilla city had been launched, and his father was one of the first babes to be born at sea. But to Rich, Great Britain was just a name. He had seen pictures of the green and lush lands of his ancestral home, but now he knew that the old country was no more. He had no recollections of land, let alone an island, and it simply wasn't worth him worrying about it. Besides, here in New Beginnings, nobody discussed anymore where they or their parents came from. It was an unwritten law. Every person on board the ships was regarded equal and equally important, and they were all citizens of the city. Rich remembered his history lessons well. After thirty years at sea, the New Beginnings governing council had outlawed the use of money for any purpose. The old coins were sometimes used as gambling chips in card games, but they had no value. The Flotilla was a true commune, and everyone contributed something to the wellbeing of others. It was the highest honor to be chosen to be a teacher of any variety, and Nadia excelled at her profession. Those fortunate people working to keep the health of the population at its peak were also highly respected. But even sanitary engineers, and those that toiled daily to keep the ships clean and seaworthy fulfilled critical roles in the society.

Both youngsters were in great spirits. For months now they had been planning together to add their own personal ceremony to the official celebration. Today was the day they would get married! The Captain of the Queen Mary had been persuaded to take the time off from officiating at the celebrations to perform the ceremony for them. As their courtship had progressed, they had talked frequently about their future. They had decided together that when the time was right, they would be the ones to return to dry land.

"We have our whole lives ahead of us." Rich had said when they decided to get engaged. They had been sitting together on the deck of the Queen Mary staring at the stars. "I'm damned if I'm going to be doing the same thing with my life every day for the next fifty years."

"I know Rich," said Nadia. "You've got ship's cabin fever in a big way." She giggled at her play on words.

"Besides, my dearest, we're limited to having one child only. You know the NB rules. If we go ashore, maybe we can have a large family."

Rich kissed Nadia tenderly on the lips.

"A boy for you and a girl for me?" he teased.

"No silly, two boys for you and two girls for me."

"You wanna practice now?" she had said suggestively, and had pulled him into an embrace.

But that was six months ago. Today, Nadia pushed Rich away when he smiled suggestively at her.

"You'll have plenty of time for that later young man. Now I have to go to my mother's cabin to get ready for the ceremony."

"Nadia, I love you." said Rich and nibbled her ear.

"Stop that Rich, we haven't got time. Save it for later." She pushed him away again, and stormed out the door, leaving him alone in her cramped but comfortable quarters.

"I'll get even tonight." he told himself. "She's as hungry as I am."

His thoughts shifted gear.

"Today is also the fiftieth anniversary of us finding any evidence of volcanic activity, outside of the usual eruptive hot spots." he reminded himself. "That's also something to celebrate! The tracking satellites are still up there allowing us monitor the world without putting anyone in jeopardy."

He had chatted the previous day with Marco Phillipi, his best friend and one of the technicians who monitored the satellite feeds from the surveillance satellites. The "birdies", as they were affectionately known, were the four remaining observation spy satellites in orbit above the planet. There had been eight to start with, but there was no way for the satellites to be serviced, and gradually four had died. Each had had a wake worthy of the most prominent Irish potentate.

Rich was aware that they had had direct access to the feeds from the birdies since the flotilla had set sail. A procession of technicians had been stuck in that dark cabin tracking any volcanic activity for a hundred years now. It must have been damn depressing for them for many, many years. He had read some of the logs. For the first twenty years, although they searched diligently, they had been unable to find a single green spot on the planet. At least they still had the video record of the planet prior to the overwhelming damage caused by the fiery apes. There were lush tropical rainforests, and vast grass covered plains. It all looked alien now to Rich, who had been brought up with hydroponic farms and an endless horizon of ocean. He dreamed of roaming the savannahs, teeming with millions of animals, and blazing a trail through jungles covered by rich canopies of forest. Then within a few short weeks the beasts had wreaked havoc on the world as it had been known, and left nothing but the silvery grey lava cap. For the first fifty years, too, all the technicians could see were glowing golden hot spots emerging from the lava fields. Such events were totally unpredictable, completely random. The Fire Tribe continued to cover the landscape with a thickening cap of lava. Then, one hot February morning fifty years ago, just like the one today, the volcanic activity suddenly ceased, as something had pulled a plug on the beasts.

"I wish we'd been there to see that. What a day!" he said wistfully.

The crews had watched the video feeds round the clock. They had waited anxiously to see if the lava eruptions would recur. From time to time they could still see occasional lava flows, but they were limited to areas of former volcanic activity where eruption had occurred prior to the Fire Tribe's appearance. Day after day when nothing more threatening was seen, the scientists had become cautiously optimistic.

"So why are we still out at sea?" Rich asked himself, not quite sure of the answer.

He remembered a conversation he had had with Nadia. She had posed the same question to him. His answer then had been simple, and reflected the paranoia instilled in him by his parents and teachers as he was raised in the floating city.

"Nobody wants to tempt fate. The last time we disturbed the beasts they blew us off the face of the earth. Seven billion people died. Seven billion!"

Rich had paused, and looked deep into Nadia's eyes.

"I cannot imagine that. Seven billion people. I think our city is big enough. We have almost four hundred thousand people now, and that feels crowded some times. Just imagine a world with seven billion human beings." he had said quietly. They had sat back, unspeaking, and unsure how to move forward.

"There wasn't much we could do if we had gone back. Barren rock is barren rock. There was nothing buried that we could dig out. We had nowhere to farm. We were better off out here in New Beginnings. I think the most amazing thing is how quickly the planet started to heal itself. It did not take too long before vegetation started appearing on the lava fields once the monsters quit their activities."

"But where did the seeds come from?" Nadia had asked.

"It took two things to happen to start to bring our planet back to life. All that volcanic activity vaporized huge quantities of water, and it rained almost constantly over land for the first fifty years. All that rain flushed nutrient filled rock particles into river beds. The sediment became a fertile breeding ground for seeds transported by birds from off shore islands. Volcanic soils are extremely supportive of vegetation."

"So there must have been some plants that escaped the fires?"

"Thank goodness those monsters left a few remote islands intact. The planet is dotted with tiny enclaves of greenery. There might even be some animals on the islands. To supplement our animal embryos of course. It does no harm to add to the gene pool."

"Thank the Lord for the foresightedness of the scientists one hundred years ago. Otherwise we might have lost everything." Nadia was a true believer that one day, she and her descendants would reinherit the earth.

Rich continued. "Over the last fifty years, we've seen isolated pockets of vegetation bloom and grow, and they are starting to merge together. We'll have a garden planet again soon."

It had been a comforting conversation, and the two lovers had held each other close, dreaming of their future together.

Rich pulled himself back to the present.

"Stop daydreaming, Rich," he advised himself, "or you'll be late for your wedding!" He rushed out of the cabin, having rapidly donned on his best suit.

It was a simple but time honored ceremony, conducted by the Captain of their vessel. Nadia was resplendent in a short white dress. The citizens of New Beginnings had no need for the extravagance of long silk trains. The only luxury allowed for the ceremony was a bouquet of flowers from the hydroponic farm, a dozen red roses.

"I now pronounce you man and wife. You may kiss your bride."

Captain Reginald Harvey smiled at the young couple, and thought how much fun his responsibilities as the chief of the Queen Mary could give him on these occasions.

"Thanks Captain."

"I'll see you both at the council meeting this afternoon. Good luck to you both!"

The happy couple ran off, hand in hand, towards the mess hall where they would have a celebratory chicken dinner with friends and family. After a final toast, Rich stood up and made a short speech.

"Thank you all for coming to our wedding. You've made our day! But we have an even more important engagement this afternoon. We're meeting with the New Beginnings High Council. We are going to ask them for permission to make the trip to Iguajan."

There was a shocked silence in the hall. Iguajan was an uninhabited Mariana island in close proximity to the city, but strictly off limits per the New Beginnings code.

"Somebody has to test the waters." he said. "It's been fifty years now. We'll sail over there. It's the opportunity of a lifetime for us. Personally, I'm hoping that we'll find somewhere there that we can live our future lives together."

Nadia smiled at her new husband. They had both spoken a month ago with Dr. Brigham Felder, the NB chief of science. She remembered the conversation.

"We know from direct observation over the last few years that Iguajan has been unaffected by the lava firestorms. No doubt Tibran and his cronies didn't feel the need to destroy an uninhabited island." Dr. Felder paused for thought, and then continued. "More importantly, Iguajan has fresh water in abundance from the frequent storms that brew up over the peak on an almost daily basis. I think you'll find sea birds, and perhaps even some small mammals there. If you want to subsist on the island for a time, it may be possible. I'll do my best to get you a positive outcome at the council meeting. Good luck to you both!"

Now they would have their chance.

After rounds of handshaking, and hugs, the newlyweds headed over to the Queen Mary stateroom where the council held its monthly meeting. They were escorted into the room, where the eight person leadership of the New Beginnings sat in hushed silence. The room had been opulently fitted with carved oak moldings, and there was a crystal chandelier dominating the center of the ceiling. In a city with few luxuries, this room had been designed to impress people. It had also been constructed to highlight the importance of the council. After all, they were the government of the city and the people. Nadia looked round the table, and caught a slight nod from the Captain and Dr. Felder. Two of the eight were on their side at least.

"Explain your thoughts to us, Rich." asked the Captain.

"Well, the gist of it is, it has been fifty years now since Tibran fired his final lava shot. We are humans. We explore. We put ourselves into danger on occasions, and it has stood us in good stead most times. Sure, we have a comfortable existence in New Beginnings, but there's more. We didn't secrete ourselves away here just to survive. The thought was always that we would once again reclaim our rightful place on the continents of the planet, and restock it from our freezers and farm. Nadia and I want to make the leap. To be the first to return to dry land. We think it is time. We know it may pose the risk of reawakening the Fire Tribe, but we'll tread carefully until we know it's safe. Please. Please give us the opportunity to be the explorers we need to be."

The council members listened to him, with thoughtful expressions clothing their elderly faces. None of them had ever set foot on dry land, and each person around the table was experiencing a mixed feeling of apprehension and jealousy. Rich repeated his request.

"We want to be the first of the city's citizens to go ashore. Will you let us do that?"

Captain Hargreaves rose to his feet.

"Nadia and Rich. Today, irrespective of what we discuss about the future of our world, this is your day. Congratulations on your wedding! You represent the future of our civilization. You are also fine upstanding citizens of New Beginnings. We know you mean well. However, since this is a very serious request, we as a council need to deliberate carefully before providing you with your answer. Now please leave us here while we talk this through. We'll call you back again when we have made our decision."

Captain Hargreaves walked towards them both, winked surreptitiously, and opened the council chamber door for them.

Nadia and Rich sat quietly in the antechamber, nervously waiting for the door to reopen. Thirty minutes later, the Captain emerged, a smile on his weather-beaten face.

"Come on in." he said simply.

The couple entered the room. Rich was relieved to see that each member of the council was smiling.

The Captain placed his hands flat on the table.

"To put you out of your misery, on what should be the happiest day of your lives, we have agreed that you will take the first steps on land that any human being has taken for one hundred years."

Nadia and Rich beamed delightedly. The Captain continued.

"As you said, Rich, humankind has never been known to shy away from adventure. We got to the moon by the unbelievable efforts of many people, and we'll retake the land by doing so as well. It's been over fifty years now since the last unnatural volcanic activity was observed on the earth, and someone has to make the leap for us all. To show us the way. Someone has to make the push for us to return to our homelands. You two have volunteered to test the waters. We thank you for your courage and determination. Go with our collective blessing. Anything you need for your journey, you'll have provided for you. But a caution to you, you may be in severe danger. If in any doubt at all, if any danger threatens, return to New Beginnings."

Nadia was overwhelmed, and burst into tears. Rich handed her a handkerchief. When Nadia finally recovered, she spoke for them both.

"Captain Hargreaves and members of the council. You don't know what it means to us to have your support. I don't see us as brave. We weren't alive when the Fire Tribe invaded our earth. But we did hear all the stories and we have seen the horrendous pictures. I don't think we'll be disturbing Tibran and the Fire Tribe, but if we do, what harm would we do to New Beginnings. The city is safe here in the ocean, and no matter what happens, it always will be. We're the ones at risk. It is a risk worth taking. We'll report back as soon as we can."

Nadia and Rich shook hands with Captain Hargreaves, and then they left the room, filled with excitement. They had much to plan and to do over the next few days, but this evening was reserved for nuptial pleasures.

29. Nadia and Rich:

March 14th, 2113

ON A BRIGHT MARCH MORNING, NADIA and Rich boarded the small sailing vessel that had been meticulously crafted for them. The boat used a combination of a solar powered engine, and two small squat sails, to generate forward momentum. The weather for a sail was perfect, with a stiff breeze, and not much surface chop. Not that they cared much as both the newlyweds were expert sailors, as were almost all of the ship city's inhabitants. Once the sails had been set and a course plotted out for Iguajan, knowing they were well out of sight of the binoculars following their progress, the couple lay back on a blanket draped on the flat bottom of their boat and made passionate love to celebrate what they hoped would be a new beginning for themselves. Still, they became wary as they saw the green topped island approaching in the distance. The Mariana Islands had been formed by massive volcanic uplifting where the pacific tectonic plate was forced under a similar plate in the Izu-Bonin-Mariana arc. As the two tectonic plates collided, an enormous volume of sea water was forced under the Mariana plate. The water had boiled instantly, and created the volcanic eruptions that had formed the Mariana Islands between five and thirty million years before. Who was to know if their presence was being monitored in the molten volcanic lava deep below the surface? Thankfully, their approach to the island was uneventful.

They beached the boat on a sandy shoreline above the high tide mark in a small inlet next to some craggy cliffs. Rich scouted around for some firewood, and they lit a campfire. After eating some grilled fish for lunch, they set off to climb the two thousand foot peak. Although they were both wary about any retribution by the Fire Tribe, the only attack they faced was from the spines of small shrubs and pokes from the branches of small trees. The island's rough vegetation did not measurably impede their progress and it took them both just under two hours to make the climb up the peak. When they reached the top, they were bleeding from minor lacerations and out of breath, but exhilarated. The view over the turquoise ocean was magnificent. Rich removed a pair of binoculars from his pack, and stared out to sea. In the extreme distance, he could make out the dot like shapes of the outer boats of the floating city. He handed the binoculars to Nadia.

"That's our home out there, Nadia. At least it was. We are going to change all that! This will be our new home."

It was a very odd sensation to be on dry land for both of the young lovers. For the first time in their lives, there was no rocking motion from the waves. The vegetation around them seemed alien but very beautiful. It was, on the whole, very exciting!

"Come on Nadia. Let's get back to the yacht. I think we have seen enough to let the council know we may have our future here on this island."

They slowly descended from the mountainous peak. While fighting their way back through the brush, they found a sunlit clearing covered with thick green grass. To their delight, they watched two rabbits hopping away from them in fright. Under the shade of a walnut tree, just beneath the rocky cliffs that rose up to the peak, Nadia pulled Rich aside and kissed him deeply. Once again they made love, tenderly and slowly. Both Nadia and Rich had read the Bible. This green haven reminded them so much of the story of the Garden of Eden.

"I keep thinking about Adam and Eve," said Nadia, as they lay in each other's arms. "and how much they lost through being sinners. This time, we'll have to get it right for the human race, won't we Rich?"

"We'll do it Nadia. Together."

The lengthening shadows around them reminded the two lovers that they needed to get back to their current home. It would not do to risk lives having a search party trying to find them. The two set sail, and charted a course for New Beginnings.